BLOOD PROPHET

BOOKS BY JOHN MICHAEL CURLOVICH
Blood Prophet
Mordred and the King
The Blood of Kings

AS "MICHAEL PAINE"
The Night School
The Mummy: Dark Resurrection
Steel Ghosts
The Colors of Hell
Owl Light
Cities of the Dead

BLOOD PROPHET
John Michael Curlovich

alyson books
NEW YORK

MANUFACTURED IN THE UNITED STATES OF AMERICA.

THIS TRADE PAPERBACK ORIGINAL IS PUBLISHED BY ALYSON BOOKS,
P.O. BOX 1253, OLD CHELSEA STATION, NEW YORK, NEW YORK 10113-1251.
DISTRIBUTION IN THE UNITED KINGDOM BY TURNAROUND PUBLISHER SERVICES LTD.,
UNIT 3, OLYMPIA TRADING ESTATE, COBURG ROAD, WOOD GREEN,
LONDON N22 6TZ ENGLAND.

FIRST EDITION: APRIL 2006

06   07   08   09   a   10   9   8   7   6   5   4   3   2   1

ISBN 1-55583-930-4
ISBN-13 978-1-55583-930-7
LIBRARY OF CONGRESS CATALOGING-IN-PUBLICATION DATA HAS BEEN APPLIED FOR.

COVER PHOTOGRAPHY:
TOP PHOTO: © 2006 JUPITERIMAGES AND ITS LICENSEES. ALL RIGHT RESERVED.
BOTTOM PHOTO: © JAVIER MONTCERDÁ PASCAL / ISTOCKPHOTO
COVER DESIGN BY TAYLOR JOHNSON.

A man's enemies are the men of his own house.
—*Micah* 7:6

PROLOGUE

Death, followed by triumph. Chopin understood that; it is there in the music, in the sonata my fingers brought to life. Danilo understood, too, and he tried to show me. No—show me he did.

I loved Danilo, and Danilo loved me, and his blood was in me, and mine was in him, and in his blood I knew: I saw.

Alexander embraced the world in one arm and his lover Hephaestion in the other. And I was there.

Hadrian made his beloved boy Antinous a god, and the whole world mourned his death and worshipped. And I was there.

Richard Lionheart, lover of men, reigned and rode into legend. I was there.

In one marvelous year James I ruled England, Louis XIII was on the throne of France, and Boris II held the Holy Roman Empire. All of Western Europe was under the direct sway of men who loved men. And I was there.

Then Danilo was gone. Vanished. And I knew the other things he had known.

Edward II saw his lover Gaveston impaled and beheaded. Edward died himself with a red-hot poker forced into his rectum. I saw.

The Knights Templar were tortured, dismembered, burned alive for loving one another. I was there. I witnessed.

In the heart of Rome the popes burned men and boys alive for loving other men. Boys as young as ten. Charred, their lives ended. And I was there. I heard their screams and smelled the stench from their pyres.

Danilo was gone, and even though I could not die, I knew what death was. I searched everywhere and often, anxiously hoping for the least hint of him. In my idle time I studied Egyptology, learned hiero-glyphics, so I could read his papers and his memoir. I wanted to find a clue why he had left me so abruptly and, it seemed, so finally. He had given me life; and he had given me the first and deepest love I'd ever known, or ever will. But he was nowhere.

I had to find him. I knew I'd never be happy again until I did. But how? There were no clues, there was nothing to go on.

Without Danilo, even though I could not die, death was all I wanted.

I was twenty-one.

I was always careful; Danilo had taught me well. The young men, old men, men in the middle, whose sacrificed blood I thrived on were from other places. Weekends, when I was not searching for Danilo, I traveled to other cities and found men whose blood kept me alive and vibrant. Not too far, Johnstown, Altoona, Youngstown, Akron, East Liverpool… Close enough to be accessible, distant enough for there to be no obvious links, small enough for the local authorities to be out of touch.

Not boys; I never took boys. Not that the temptation wasn't there. Young, firm bodies, sweet blood… But they had not had time to discover themselves yet. Some of them would embrace their divine blood and what it meant; some of them would be my brothers. Others…well, they would be men soon enough, and then I could…

When I came home from my little excursions, my cat Bubastis always made it clear how happy she was to see me. And I felt the same way, not only because she was such a sweet companion. Danilo had worked his magic on her. She was the one living link I still had to him, and I loved her.

Sometimes I went to New York, to see Danilo's face in the ancient stones in the museums there. Sometimes I fed there, too…

One young man, an assistant curator at the Metropolitan Museum, noticed me from time to time, always looking at the same relief, the one of Danilo and his father. He smiled, a bit timidly I thought; making conversation with the visitors was not quite the proper thing. Déclassé, I imagine. I smiled back.

"You really like that one, don't you?"

"Yes. It means a lot to me."

"There's something even better in the storeroom back here. It's not in the best shape, so it's not on display, but…"

Again I smiled. Was there another image of my lover, one I hadn't seen? "I'd like to see it, please."

He led me behind a large canvas drop cloth and into a side room. Fragments of statues and reliefs were scattered on a large work table, a foot, a muscular arm, a head; more were propped against the walls. He moved a few and found the one he wanted, a slab of basalt. "Here."

On the smooth black stone was still another image of the Kissing Kings, one I hadn't seen before. Danilo, the young pharaoh, and his father Akhenaten, embracing, their lips touching, their passion showing more clearly and more intensely than in anything I had seen before. They were naked. This piece had been carved for them privately; it was nothing like their public images.

I looked at my companion, and I knew he understood what I was feeling, or part of it. "It's not the kind of thing we can put on public display."

Then without even thinking, I pressed my fingers against it, as if touching Danilo's face in stone might be a substitute for touching him.

The assistant curator laughed at me. "With me it's one of the guys in a Rembrandt upstairs. Dead ringer for my ex-boyfriend. I can never look at it without feeling all kinds of things."

"Do you know where he is?"

"Choreographing an off-Broadway musical Can you believe it?"

"Why not?"

"Nobody does off-Broadway musicals anymore. Nobody with any sense. They all close in the red."

"Oh."

"I'm Rick, by the way."

He noticed Danilo's wedding ring, which I always wore. "That's good. It's a reproduction, from our museum shop, right?"

"No, it's real."

He smirked at me. I was liking him less and less. He would do.

I told him my name, and we shook. He was blond, thin, athletic; his clothes were a bit too trendy to be quite in good taste, but this was New York.

I met him at dinnertime, when the museum closed. We had a quick, light meal. Then he took me to his apartment in Brooklyn. As we were going in, I happened to notice his name on the apartment doorbell. Lawrence Miller. Rick, indeed.

I asked if he wouldn't rather live in Manhattan. He shrugged. "I like being across the river. Keeps some distance between me and…well, between me and all that." He made a vague gesture.

"You like being apart?"

"Yeah, I guess I do. From everything."

"It must be nice to have the choice."

He didn't know what I meant. I wasn't quite sure I knew, either. But he was one of our bloodline; of that I was certain.

His apartment was larger than most I'd seen in New York. There was room for a king-size bed. Almost before I knew what was happening he stripped himself naked, locked his arms around me and pushed his tongue into my mouth.

He was good. The sex was fantastic. We came together, first time that had happened since Danilo. When all I want is sex, there's nothing more exciting than an aggressive bottom. But I wanted more than sex.

When we were finished with our coupling he lit a cigarette.

I smirked. "Isn't that a bit of a cliché?"

"What of it?"

"Nothing, I guess." I smiled and stretched on the bed.

"If you don't mind, I'd like you to leave now."

"Oh. I thought we might talk for a bit." I smiled. "Get to know each other. Are you—?"

"Look, we fucked, we got off. I'm going to the gym now."

"But—"

"I really don't want to 'get to know' a damn dumb tourist faggot, okay?"

"Okay. You won't, then."

I jumped on top of him, pinned him to the bed. There was nothing sharp at hand. I used my teeth. Tore his throat open. Drank. It always interests me that men's blood can taste so different. Some is so sweet.

Some is deliciously salty. Some has a pleasantly bitter edge. His tasted like shit.

Then I crossed the room to where I'd left my backpack and got Danilo's ritual knife. The golden blade gleamed as I did my work. I cut out the organs I needed, eyes, heart. His genitals were still hot from our coupling.

I looked down at his body, drained of blood, wizened and pale. Not for the first time, I found myself thinking that that was what I wanted. To be dead. To feel nothing. Since Danilo vanished, that was all I wanted.

But how? I didn't know, and I was afraid to find out. If I stopped living on the blood of the sacrificed, would I simply revert to my normal age? Or would I…? Danilo said I would age and die if I stopped. I had seen too many old horror movies to want to contemplate that possibility. To die old…no.

I didn't always have sex with them. Sometimes I just…performed the sacrifice and moved on. Over the months, I had come to prefer that, actually. Quick, over with, satisfied. No time for lies, not theirs, not mine.

There were times, looking in the mirror, I thought I could see their faces in my own eyes. There were times when I wondered if they wanted to taste me in the way I tasted them. They denied their blood; but can anyone ever deny himself so completely? Did they feel the same thirst, ever? At all?

Death is the beginning, in the same way that fatherhood is the beginning. I am only beginning to understand, even now. Poor creatures like assistant curator Rick, or Lawrence, would never know.

No one had ever looked for Danilo but me, myself. When he disappeared, everyone—the university and the police—assumed he was simply one more victim in Gregory Wilton's killing spree, one more of the dead and vanished. With no family to make trouble—with no one in the world except me, or so I thought—the police and the university could safely forget him. But of course I could not forget. Every time I took another victim, Danilo was there with me.

And yet I had hardly begun to understand all the things he tried to teach me, or the enormous gift he gave me. I had to find him; I had to be with him again.

There is another world, and it is in this one. I know. I live there.

CHAPTER 1

There he was again. He had been at my previous recital, at the impromptu "Welcome Back" student recital at the end of September, and there he was again a week later. He was impossible to miss.

My music had attracted a number of young men before, but this one was special, one of the most striking boys I'd ever seen. And boy was the word; he was fifteen, maybe sixteen at the most. He had the largest dark eyes, pale skin, and a shock of thick black hair. Just simply beautiful. Across forty feet of concert hall he stood out.

The hall was crowded, not quite full but there was a very good audience. Men, women, there to hear me; I never stopped being pleased and astonished that they found my music so moving. To be quite honest, I always felt a bit of a fraud. It was not, strictly speaking, my power they were experiencing. What would they have thought if they'd known what I did by night to fuel my art?

But this boy… Twice, now. There was something about him…

The first half of the program hadn't gone over well. It was a new composition by Lazar Perske, the composer-in-residence that term. He was one of the "neo-medievalists," and his music was easy to the point where it tended to force daydreams. It wasn't much more than watered-down, jazzed-up church music. Musically watered-down, lyrically souped-up hymns to Jesus, that kind of thing. This piece was for string quartet, harmonium and four voices, including, oddly, a countertenor—a male soprano. How medieval can you get? The applause had been polite, nothing more.

I had seen Perske around the music department, passed him in the halls once or twice, but we had never really met. A tall, thin, nervous man with a terrible complexion and unruly gray hair, he looked like a conductor as played by a character actor in a 40s B movie. He had burst onto the international music scene ten years ago, along with Gorecki, Pärt and the rest of that then-fashionable movement. Once I found out he wasn't related to Lauren Bacall, nee Betty Jean Perske, I more or less lost interest in him. Certainly there was nothing in his music for me. It sounded dead to me, as if some vital spark was missing.

When his composition ended, he stepped grandly onto the stage, obviously expecting an ovation, plainly thinking it was his due. The subdued, respectful applause seemed to annoy him.

Then it was my turn. I opened with a few of the Grieg *Lyric Pieces,* then played a few excerpts from *Pictures at an Exhibition.* The strange, grotesque ones, the musical portrait of the deformed dwarf, and the enchanted hut on hen's legs. My teacher Roland had always noticed that I was drawn to music that was sad or strange; I don't think he ever quite understood why, though. And, really, there was no way he could. But other people were beginning to comment on it too. Roland was the only one who understood, though, why I performed some composers at the expense of others. No Brahms; no Bach; no Beethoven—or at least not until I read about his manic romantic fixation on his nephew.

But it was my Chopin that audiences really loved. They came especially to hear it; I knew that, and I always gave them my best, and my playing moved them. That night I played the second sonata, the one with the Funeral March. It had become something of a signature piece for me; audiences expected it. And when I played that mournful slow movement, everyone became still. They could not quite fathom the sadness I poured into it, a thousand generations of lost kings, of sacrificed artists and philosophers without hope, their noble blood often unknown even to themselves, their lives lost and purposeless. And no one but Roland knew that when I played the Funeral March it was for my missing love, the man who had given me my life and then disappeared.

I was still young, a college senior. The phrase "broken heart" had been just a phrase to me, something screenwriters and songwriters used, not anything real. Then Danilo left, and I was suddenly alone in the world. It was as corny as anything in those old songs and movies. My heart ached. Two years earlier I would have laughed at those words.

A thousand generations of hidden loves, of lives made empty...I knew it all through Danilo, I felt it all, and I played it all... I put it all into Frederic Chopin's Funeral March, and every time I played it I felt more deeply my own loss and loneliness.

And by night, when I needed to…by night I fed on the blood of their heirs, the ones who denied their long, rich heritage; who denied their blood…

Danilo. I wanted him back. At the very least, I need to learn why he had abandoned me. I'd have done anything, given anything, to have him beside me again. I had searched so long and so often. I had even contacted the Egyptian consulate in New York, to see if they could help me find him. But there was simply nothing to go on. I knew, or rather I prayed, that sooner or later some clue would come to me, some hint that would lead to me him. But so far, none had.

The Funeral March seemed to move the audience more deeply than usual that night. I could see it and even feel it; they gave that emotion back to me. Then when I played the final triumphant presto, a thrill moved through them. Roland had told me time and again I had the technique but not the feeling to understand that final exuberant passage. And I knew he was right. How could such exuberant triumph follow such profound loss and grief?

But Chopin had understood. No one could explain it, least of all me. But my playing moved them all, sometimes oddly even to tears.

Knowing it, knowing I could move people I had never met, made me feel so odd. I suppose it even increased my sense of loss, in a way. Jamie Dunn: fraud. He plays this rich moving music, but his own life is empty. The man who loved him deserted him.

What to do with the power that pulsed in my veins? What good would it ever do me, except in a professional sense? I had wondered a hundred times, is it worth it? Is the blood I spill by the dark of the moon worth this music?

Word had spread about me. The piano-playing jock. The musical swimmer boy. The kid who plays Chopin wearing leather.

First the campus radio station and then the local NPR outlet had broadcast some of my recitals live, and the programs were picked up for rebroadcast in all kinds of places. I got mail from people all across the English-speaking world, and there was even some professional buzz.

Sony and EMI had contacted me about recording contracts. Nothing definite; they were businessmen, they were cautious. But they were keeping an eye on me and my career. And I was still only a senior at the University of Western Pennsylvania.

Roland was the chair of the music department now. He had less time for me than before, but we remained close. He was both thrilled for me and a bit puzzled by it all, I think. He advised me not to let my career peak too soon. "You're still young, Jamie. Fireworks can only be set off once."

I understood what he meant, and I knew he was right. But I couldn't resist teasing him, as always. "But a .44 Magnum can be fired again and again."

He was used to my inborn brattiness by then. "From what I hear, you're not that big." He slapped me playfully on my backside. "You're still young. You need to develop. You can't do everything."

"Yet."

He grunted at me, then laughed.

Roland had become like a father to me, and I loved him. At least, he was like what I had always assumed fathers must be like. My own…my own father…no, not yet.

A hundred times I had been tempted to tell Roland about myself, about Danilo and the mystic, dark life he had given me. But how could I? How do you tell a father, even a substitute one, about the kind of thing that kept me alive and fed my talent? How to tell him about the gift of unending life Danilo had given me that night in a cool Egyptian tomb? I loved Roland, but I knew there was a part of myself I'd always have to hide from him. He was not one of us, not part of the bloodline. Danilo had told me so, and now I knew it for myself.

I think he knew there was a part of myself I could never share with him, or that he could never understand. Certainly he knew I had my dark inner places; he said so once or twice. But like a good father he respected my right to live my own life, even a lonely one. And since he was the music department chair now, he had a lot besides me on his mind. But he was always there, helping keep me steady in the face of my growing reputation.

There were ever-larger audiences. Incredibly there was even that fan mail.

And there were boys. And men. I was becoming a bit of a celebrity, after all, if only on campus. And so I slept with them. None of them expected more. I still loved Danilo.

And then there was this particular boy, the first one of them who had ever really caught my attention as more than an evening's sex toy.

I watched him, watching me at the keyboard. I played the presto, and his eyes were wide with anticipation. A teenage boy, thrilled to hear Chopin. To hear *me*.

There was applause when I finished, and people cheered "Bravo!" and even "Jamie!" The boy was not cheering. He was watching me, staring at me; and there were tears flowing down his face.

Backstage everyone congratulated me. Lazar Perske was still there, complaining about the cold audience; I had warmed them up, and he resented it.

Then Paul Koerner, the countertenor who had soloed in Perske's piece, came over to me and told me he had really been moved my playing. I had seen Paul around the department now and then. I'd even had an occasional inkling that he might have the blood, but it was nothing definite. He seemed like a nice enough guy, but he wasn't much to look at—the kind of guy no one ever pays much attention to. And he was a goddamned countertenor.

"Is there any chance we might get together for lunch sometime, Jamie?"

"Uh, sure." I left it vague, quite deliberately. What on earth could I find to talk about with a male soprano?

A few minutes later I left the hall by the stage door. And the kid was waiting there for me. It was an awkward moment. I was twenty-one, he was a boy. A beautiful boy. He was taller than I expected, tall and lanky, a runner's build. Huge black eyes, pale skin, thick black hair. His clothes were disheveled and filthy. I wasn't at all certain how to react.

It was a dark cool early autumn night. There was a moon and there was a breeze. The door hung open behind me and I could hear crowd sounds from inside. He wasn't wearing a jacket. He stood huddled under that utility light by the exit, his arms wrapped around himself. Neither one of us seemed to know what to say.

Finally he made himself smile, a bit shyly I thought. "Mister Dunn." He had a deeper voice than I expected, and there was a faint Southern accent.

"Jamie." I smiled back. "Everyone calls me that."

"I wanted to meet you."

"So I see."

"I—" Suddenly, unexpectedly, he blushed and looked away. "I'm sorry for bothering you, Mr. Dunn." He turned and started to walk away.

"Wait!"

He looked back. I could see half a dozen emotions cross his face.

I made my smile even wider. "I told you. I like people to call me Jamie."

He stared. I could tell he was groping for something to say.

"And your name is…?"

"Adam." He stammered it, quite softly. "Adam Pilarski."

"Adam. Thank you for coming to hear me."

"I…I had to."

"It's only classical music. There's nothing urgent about it."

"There is for me."

Smalltalk was so awkward. What to say, what to ask? "How old are you?"

"Sixteen. Nearly seventeen."

He looked a bit younger. "You are sixteen, going on seventeen."

My little joke was lost on him. "Everyone says I'm a lot more mature than I look."

"Everyone says I am, too. I don't believe it."

"If my parents knew I was here…" He looked away; I had the impression he was a bit embarrassed. Mooning over a strange musician. Uncool.

"What would they do?"

"They say your kind of music—our kind of music—" He smiled again, this time to cover embarrassment. "My father say it's for fags."

Oh. So it was that. There was no doubt about him in my mind. My senses had sharpened in the time since Danilo left; I knew who was a brother of mine. And with this boy there was no mistaking it. The blood jumped in his veins.

I took a few steps toward him and said softly, so no one else might be able to hear, "Just between us, Adam, it is."

Shyly, unexpectedly he reached out and took my hand. And there was electricity in it. It was like the first time I touched Danilo; I felt that kind of power between us. But this was different. Adam was a boy. I had to be very careful.

Suddenly a small group of people came out of the stage door, two of the stagehands and their girlfriends. I stepped quickly away from him. They were busy talking and laughing among themselves. One of the guys waved and said, "Good night, Jamie," as they passed. I made myself cordial and said good night, too.

Adam had stepped back into a corner. I could almost feel how painful his shyness was for him. He was sixteen. There was nothing else to do. "Well, it was nice meting you, Adam. Thanks again for coming."

"Can I come again?"

Odd question. I wasn't at all certain he was only asking about my recitals. "Campus music programs are open to everyone."

"I don't know if I can."

He seemed more and more strange to me. "Well, I hope you're able to. It's been nice talking to you." I smiled as warmly as I could, shook his hand, and left. When I glanced over my shoulder he was still in that same corner, looking lost and…and I wasn't sure what.

It was ten o'clock. I was hungry. I went to the Z and got a quick burger. Then, feeling restless, I headed to the sports complex to do a few laps. Technically it was open to all students. In practice it was reserved for the sports teams. Ever since I had quit the swim team, just after Danilo left, my reception there had been on the chilly side. Not exactly unfriendly, but not really friendly either.

That late in the evening there was usually no one else there. But that night there were a couple of divers from the guys' team practicing, a lean blond and a rather muscular brunette. Diving in sync, and doing it quite well. Beautiful bodies. Graceful leaps. They looked even better after they climbed out of the pool, dripping wet.

I got into my Speedo and dove in. They had their end of the pool; I was careful not to get in their way. I saw them watching me and whispering now and then, between dives. After fifteen minutes of swimming hard, I was ready for a shower.

They followed me into the locker room. At first I wasn't at all certain why. Then it became obvious. They began soaping each other up, doing it quite playfully and for my benefit. My sexual tastes weren't exactly a secret on campus.

I watched them and smiled. Then I moved to a shower head closer to them. "Hi. I'm Jamie."

They introduced themselves. Blond Todd and dark Bryan. They kissed, again so I could see. They were very well-equipped athletes.

Todd looked me up and down. "You're that piano player, aren't you? I heard you once."

Bryan said he hadn't. "I don't know anything about that classical stuff." Todd nudged him with an elbow and he quickly added, "But I'd like to."

Half an hour later they were at my house. Or rather, Danilo's house, the one he had left me. Most visitors found it strange—all the portraits of dead kings and artists, all the stained glass… These two had other things on their minds.

My cat Bubastis—the sweet little creature Danilo had brought back from the dead, and the one living reminder I had of him—sniffed at them, then scampered off someplace.

The sex was hot. Bloody fantastic. Bryan was particularly sensitive. When I ran my tongue along the side of his throat, he shuddered with intense pleasure. Todd, amused at the intensity of his friend's reaction, smiled and said, "You play guys like you play the piano."

I laughed. "Imagine what Chopin must have been like in bed."

Bryan stared at me. "Who?"

"Never mind."

Restraint was never easy for me, not in bed. I could happily have chewed my way through Bryan's throat to taste his blood. He would have loved it, he would have felt an even more intense thrill.

But Danilo's lesson was not lost on me: not close to home, not where it might be noticed, not where you might be found out. And certainly not where a horny diver named Todd was in bed next to you, watching.

They were beautiful, their bodies were smooth and responsive. They had the blood. I could have sensed it even without such close, intimate contact with them. They told me they were living together, more or less openly. And that was an even bigger reason for me not to sacrifice them. In time, when I found a way to explain what we all were, they might have changed the lonely existence I'd been leading since Danilo left.

Outside there was brilliant moonlight. The street was even brighter than it usually was under the sodium streetlights. Something, some movement, drew my eye to the window. And there he was, watching us. Adam.

His hands were pressed to the glass; he looked like a starving man seeing a hot dinner through a restaurant window. He wanted to be with us, or to be with me. Seeing him, knowing he was watching, excited me more than the divers' bodies alone could have. Christ, how we fucked, me in the middle. It was the best sex in months.

When we finished I looked to the window. And Adam was still there, still watching, as if he'd never imagined such wonderful behavior might exist. I could feel him through the glass, his blood pumping, his heart racing. I realized he was jerking off. When he came, it was obvious.

The three of us nodded off for a while, bits of us still intertwined in various ways. When we finally started to shake off our happy exhaustion and they got up to get dressed, I found myself looking to the window. There was no sign of the boy.

I saw them to the door. We all kissed each other good night and promised to do it again, soon. Under other circumstances, none of us would have meant a word of it. But with these two… Part of me knew it was foolish to hope. I watched them walk away, not too close to one another, trying to look butch, and I had a little laugh. Even being open about themselves, they had to compensate. Jocks.

And then I realized he was there, behind a telephone pole on the sidewalk, watching the house. I waited till my two divers had walked off down the street, then called to him. "Adam?"

He didn't move or say anything. He looked terrified.

"Adam?"

He shifted his weight. I walked out to him. Made myself smile. "Hello, again."

He looked away from me. "You're not going to call the cops, are you?"

"Of course not." I put a hand on his shoulder and turned him so he'd face me. "Are you all right?"

"I don't have anyplace to sleep."

"How far is your house?"

"I'm from South Carolina."

It caught me a bit by surprise, even though I had noticed his accent. "From—?"

"I had to come and hear you."

It was late. There was no one else on the street. "I thought I heard a touch of the South in your voice. Where have you been sleeping, Adam?"

"Alleys. Dumpsters. It stays pretty warm inside. You'd be surprised."

"And how have you been eating?"

"In dumpsters."

Oh. I looked up and down the street. "Are you hungry?"

He nodded.

"Come in, and I'll fix you something."

"I don't know if I can. It's wrong."

"Eating?" I tried to make my voice gentle.

"No…you know."

I stayed silent to see if he'd go on.

"My mother beats me. My dad watches. I think he gets off on it." He hesitated. "We're Christians."

"'We'? Do you mean 'they'?"

This seemed to be a new thought to him. "I…I guess."

"Come inside. Let me make you something to eat."

I put an arm around him and ushered him into the house. It was four in the morning. The moon was blazing. On the eastern horizon I could see that Mars was just rising.

I whipped up some hotcakes and fried some bacon and hash browns. After the sex with the diver boys I found I was famished too. Adam ate as if he hadn't had anything for a week. I felt sorry for him, I think.

"Is it okay if I feed your cat?"

I nodded. "Not too much though."

He fed Bubastis a few morsels and she rubbed against his leg, purring happily. I took it as a good sign; she had always been a smart judge of character.

I tried to make conversation. "So you're from…where in South Carolina, exactly?"

"A little town outside Spartanburg. A hole in the wall. Ever been there?" He seemed to know the question was absurd even as he asked it.

"No."

"You're lucky." He forked a mouthful of pancake. "It's really shitty."

"Most everyplace is, Adam. You should see the town where I grew up."

His mouth full, he shook his head. "No, I mean it. You could live your whole life there and never hear any music like you played tonight. Not for real, I mean. Just on the radio and CDs and stuff."

"Sounds like where I grew up. Ever hear of Ebensburg, Pennsylvania?"

He shook his head.

"How did you get here?"

He held out a thumb.

"I started playing when I was a kid. You want coffee?"

He nodded and I put on the kettle.

He was watching me, watching everything I did. "When I heard you on the radio…I don't know, I just had to come and hear you for real."

"Well, I'm flattered."

"I'm crazy. I feel crazy. Maybe I am. I've never done anything like this before."

"I doubt you're crazy. More likely your parents are." He had cleaned his plate and was obviously ready for more. I piled another heap of food on his plate. "That was the last of the potatoes. Should I make more?"

"No, thanks." He tucked in. I wondered how long it had been since he'd really eaten.

"So, how long did it take you to get up here?"

"Five days. I hated it. They say you can always get a ride if you're young and cute. But I didn't have all that much luck." He blushed. "I mean…not that I'm saying I'm cute or anything.. I just meant…"

"I know what you meant." I put on a big smile. "And you are."

"Some of the guys who picked me up were…they were looking for…"

"I'll just bet they were." He didn't seem to want to talk about it, and I didn't blame him. "Why don't you get a shower now? And then some sleep. We can talk more in the morning."

"You're letting me stay?" He seemed genuinely astonished.

"For the night. Then we'll have to find a way to get you back home. I can't just…keep you, like a stray cat. There are laws."

He grinned conspiratorially. "Let's break them."

"I already break too many laws. You don't know."

"Please, Mr. Dunn, let me stay and live with you."

Odd boy, able to survive on the street but so completely naïve. I found myself wondering if I had been like that at his age. A memory of my relatives reading the Bible at me came into my head. Not pleasant. "We're not going to get anywhere if you keep calling me that. It's Jamie, okay?"

"Jamie." He seemed to like the sound of it. "Will you…will you get in the shower with me?"

"No." I was emphatic.

"Can I sleep with you?"

"Get your shower, Adam. It's late."

While he was showering I got my old bedroom ready for him. The bed hadn't been used in ages, and the linens smelled a bit musty. I changed them. Just as I was finishing I realized he was watching me. I turned and faced him. He was wearing nothing but a towel. He dropped it and, self-consciously, pulled on a pair of shorts and a T-shirt. Even in dim light he was beautiful, just beautiful. I made myself smile. "All ready for you."

"You know I saw you with those two guys."

"Yes, I know."

"I wanted to…I wanted…" Suddenly his shyness was back. He looked away from me. I found it sweet. "I don't know what I wanted."

I crossed the room and planted myself in front of him. "Yes you do. We both know."

He looked up at me, then looked around the room. The wallpaper was Victorian, a lush pattern with hundreds of violets. Adam smiled. "This is a great room. I've always loved violets." Then, almost instantaneously, he turned self-conscious and looked away from me. "Is…is that too faggy?"

"There's nothing wrong with loving beautiful things, Adam."

So quickly I hardly had time to realize what was happening, he threw his arms around me. And hugged me so tightly I could hardly breathe. I didn't know whether it was erotic or slightly desperate. He was an inch taller than me; I hadn't realized. "Jamie," he whispered. "Thank you."

He let go of me and crawled into bed. It was awkward; I wasn't really certain what would be the right thing to do. After a moment of standing and watching him, I leaned down, kissed him lightly on the cheek and told him good night. "We'll talk more tomorrow."

CHAPTER 2

I dreamed that night, as I often did, of Danilo. Or to be exact, of Danilo and me in each other's arms. But at the same time, in that weirdly simultaneous way that sometimes happens in dreams, I was still searching for him. Searching, knowing that sooner or later I'd find some clue that would lead me to him. In the waking world, there had been nothing, and my efforts to find him had come to nothing. But in my dreams, I had not stopped looking. And I wouldn't, now till I had Danilo again.

I woke in the morning to find Adam lying on the bed next to me, still in his underwear. He hadn't even crawled under the covers; and the room was cold. Bubastis was at the foot of the bed, watching him.

Asleep, Adam looked even sweeter than he did awake, but then all men do. It's the helplessness, I imagine, or the guilelessness. Not that I thought he had much guile.

I took him by the shoulder and shook him to wake him up. He opened his eyes, gaped at me and blushed. "Mr. Dunn, I'm sorry. I thought I'd wake up before you and go back to my own room. I mean, to the room you gave me. I never thought I'd—"

"It's all right. I guess I should be flattered." He was undressed; I tossed him my robe, and he climbed into it quickly.

"You were so nice, letting me stay here and all. I didn't want to—" Half asleep, his Southern accent was stronger. I liked it.

"Don't worry about it. I'd appreciate it if you wouldn't make a habit of it, though."

His face lit up. "Am I going to be here long enough for that?"

"No." I hated saying it. "No, I guess not. Why don't you go and wash up? I'll start breakfast."

He stood and yawned. "I'm sorry."

"For being sleepy at eight in the morning?"

"For everything."

It was hard to know what to say. It seemed more and more that his upbringing had been rougher than my own, and my own was pretty unpleasant. I sent him off to clean up and shave—he thanked me about twenty times for letting him use a little plastic disposable razor—and crawled out of bed myself. It was going to be a long day.

While the breakfast sausages cooked and Adam caught a short nap, I washed and dressed. As he had the night before, he tucked into a meal like a man who hadn't eaten in years. Teenagers.

It wasn't a conversation I wanted to have, but… "Adam, you have to call your parents and let them know where you are."

He froze. He turned, quite literally, pale. "I—I don't think I can do that."

"You can. And you have to."

"You've been so nice to me. I feel awful."

"Listen, Adam, I'm not much older than you. I can't very well just… take you in. Not eve if it was legal."

"I wouldn't be much trouble. Honest."

"It's not that." I had overcooked the links. "Well, yes it is that, at least partially. But…Adam, my life is more complicated than you think. More complicated than you *can* think. I can't see how you'd fit in. When you're eighteen, maybe—"

"I'll be dead before that."

He said it so vehemently it startled me. My eyes widened, and I literally gaped at him. "You can't mean that."

"It's true."

He stood up slowly and lifted his shirt. His chest and back were covered with scars. Even more slowly he lowered the shirt again. "They beat me. They say I'm possessed by a devil and he makes me want men not girls. Mr. Dunn, please. You don't know. They beat me. They'll kill me."

"I'm—I'm sorry. I didn't know it was that bad."

"Even when I was little, somehow they knew about me. The earliest thing I remember is my mother burning me with cigarettes."

"Oh God, Adam."

"God? If he's around, I haven't noticed him."

There was nothing I could say.

"They've always told me God was there, they always say he loves me. But I've never seen any evidence of it."

Softly I told him, "You're looking for the wrong gods."

We fell silent. There was hardly much room for more conversation. I knew he'd have to leave, and I felt terrible about it. But what could I do?

He insisted on doing the dishes. While he was at it I sat in the living room with a second cup of tea and switched on the news. Bubastis curled up beside me. The national stuff was the usual, politicians on the make, corrupt corporations; I got lost in my thoughts. I'd have to call my lawyer; he'd know what to do with Adam, if anyone would.

Then the local news segment came on, and it immediately caught my attention. There had been a murder on the West Penn campus. The body of a young athlete, found in a back alley behind the sports center. All his blood had been drained, and his body was mutilated, organs missing. The victim's name wasn't being released till his family had been notified..

All I could think was: Danilo. Back.

It had to be him.

It couldn't be him.

He'd have come home to me, or at least called.

Was it possible he didn't love me much after all? Not as deeply as I loved him?

The police were quick to point out the similarity between this killing and the ones that had rocked the campus two years earlier. Greg Wilton had been arrested, tried and convicted, but only for the murder of his boyfriend, my roommate Justin. He was safely on death row, awaiting execution. So now the police were conceding that Wilton's denials he had done the other killings might have been the truth, that maybe they had been wrong. Maybe someone else had done the other killings.

Of course I knew who.

Danilo, my Danilo.

Back.

I felt the strangest combination of numbness and excitement.

A few moments later Adam joined me on the couch. And he sensed my mood at once. "I'm really sorry to cause you so much trouble, Mr. Dunn."

I shook off my mood and looked at him. "It's not that, Adam. It's not you. Something else has happened."

"Something you want to talk about?"

"No. I can't. You wouldn't understand."

"I'm not dumb, Mr. Dunn. Really."

I reached over and tousled his hair, much the way Danilo used to do with me. "If you don't start calling me Jamie, so help me, I'll—I'll—I don't know what I'll do." I swatted at him playfully, and he ducked. Bubastis jumped down from the sofa and ran off.

But his mood went from playful to somber in a flash. "I guess I should be leaving, then."

"No."

"But you said—"

"I know what I said. I want to talk to my lawyer. He'll know what to do."

He didn't seem to know how to respond. After a moment he said weakly, "I didn't know this was serious enough for a lawyer. I guess I didn't think."

"Look, I want you to stay here today. I have to get back to the campus. Music is a harsh lover."

""I'll bet you're not, though." He smiled. "Jamie."

"It isn't really very helpful for you to talk like that. Stay here today. Promise me."

"Okay." He didn't like it. I could tell.

"There's plenty of food in the fridge, and you can catch up on your sleep. And there are plenty of books in the library. But I don't want you out and about. For all we know, the police are looking for you."

"How could they know I'm in Pittsburgh? Do people run away from home and come *here?*"

"Not usually. But you never know." They probably had a hundred bulletins about runaway kids. More. How many could they actually look for? But still… "Just promise me, okay? I'll feel safer."

He looked away from me shyly. "Sure."

I kissed him on the forehead. "Remember, you promised."

It was a cloudy day, cooler than it should have been that time of year. School was a twenty minute walk from my place. So much had happened; my thoughts kept jumping from Danilo to Adam to the law… I could feel the sacred blood pumping through Adam's veins, hot and alive. Having him in the house was almost like being with Danilo again. But he was a boy. And Danilo was back in town, it seemed…

My playing was off that day. Even some fairly simple Schubert seemed beyond me. Roland commented on it. "Something's wrong, isn't it?"

"I don't know, Roland." I told him a bit about Adam, not getting too specific.

"So you have a groupie." Being department chairman had brought out his sardonic side.

"If you want to be cute about it, yes."

"You can't keep him, Jamie. It's not like finding an abandoned puppy in a vacant lot."

"I know. But Roland…" I wasn't sure he was the one to be talking to about this. "I don't see how I can send him back, either. Could you tell a sweet boy like him that he has to go back to the parents who beat him?"

"They're his parents."

"Exactly my point. How can I send him back there?"

"Surely the state youth authorities…" He tried to sound hopeful.

"He's from rural South Carolina, for God's sake."

He lowered his eyes. "I see the problem. Still…Jamie, he's a boy."

"I know it. Believe me, I know it."

"You mean you…?"

"I don't know what I mean." I got up from the keyboard. "Shit. I have to talk to my lawyer about this. About *him,* I mean."

"Good idea."

"Thanks for listening." I gave him a quick hug and headed for the door.

"Hey!" He called after me. "You can use the phone in my office, if you like."

"Thanks, Roland."

With a rare stroke of luck I actually got hold of my lawyer without having to leave a message. I explained the situation to him.

"Jamie, send him home. You could get in all kinds of trouble."

"Did you hear me, Stan? They beat him."

"Under the law, he's theirs to beat, at least until the state decides to do something about it. They're his parents, Jamie, however unfortunate that might be."

"But…but…" I knew he was right, of course. But Adam was not just any boy. I found myself wanting to teach him about himself, about his true nature and the power it gave him.

"Jamie, will you for Christ's sake be sensible? He's a minor. You're a gay man. He ran away to meet you and be with you. You have to realize how that would look to the police."

"Yes, Stan."

"Good."

"Can I at least arrange to stay in touch with him? By email or whatever? I need to know he's all right."

"Jamie, you're not listening to me. He's a minor, you're a gay man. If you start sending him emails—"

"Okay, fine, Stan."

That was that. I felt like hell, wondering how I could tell all this to Adam in a way that would make sense to him. As usual when I was frustrated or needed to think, I decided to head to the sports complex and swim some laps.

As I was leaving the music department I ran, literally, into a young violinist I had seen around. Knocked his books and a stack of sheet music out of his hands. He was a sophomore; I'd heard him play at a few recitals, but I couldn't remember his name. We had one of those awkward moments where we each kept apologizing to the other. Finally we broke out laughing and shook hands.

"I'm Jamie Dunn."

"I know." He had a good, strong grip. Violinist. And a sweet smile. "Kurt Sivers."

"Good to meet you, Kurt. I've heard you play."

"Likewise. I'm not in your league, though, Jamie. No one around here is."

"I'm not that good. I just know what I can play."

"Don't be modest. If I thought there was ever a chance I could move people the way you do…" He stopped self-consciously and smiled. "I mean, the way you move audiences, the way they stand and cheer for you. It's almost like a rock star." A cute smile, I thought. And he was of legal age. "Sorry, I don't mean to gush."

"It happens a lot, Kurt. I wish it didn't. I mean, I wish I could get used to it."

"You really are that good. I heard you play the Barber sonata last spring. I had never even liked Barber's music before, but you made me want all I could get."

"Well…thanks."

Kurt was, like his name, Germanic or maybe Nordic. Tall, blond, peaches-and-cream complexion. He smiled again and looked even more adorable. And my instincts, that familiar itch, told me he was my brother in blood.

He put his hands in his pockets. "Listen, I know your reputation, Jamie."

"Should I be embarrassed?"

"I mean your reputation for only playing alone."

I had been invited to join a few chamber ensembles, but I had always declined. What happened to me when I played…the way my blood coursed and raced, the way I felt one with my blood forebears…there was no way I could share that with anyone else. I think people took it as snobbery. But it wasn't that, it was only… "I'm too much a loner to do anything else."

"I know. I've heard." He wanted to ask. I hoped he would.

But after an awkward moment of silence I decided I ought to go. "Listen, I've got to get moving. It was nice meeting you, Kurt."

He got up the nerve and blurted out, "I want to play with you."

I froze. Looked him up and down. Felt the blood. Or thought I did. All of a sudden I wasn't at all certain. It would have been so strange for me, playing with someone else. But then, I had never tried making music with another man who was part of the divine bloodline. "Let's…uh, let's get together and talk about it, okay?"

"Sure." He pushed his hands deeper in his pockets. "Maybe lunch tomorrow?"

Why not? "I'd love to."

He smiled. I could have fallen in love with him then and there if there hadn't been so much else on my mind. He was handsome and I liked him, but he was no Danilo… I actually found myself thinking, no, and he's no Adam, either. That boy… I pulled myself out of it. "Why don't we meet in the department around noon? Will that work for you?"

"I have a class till one. How about then?"

"It's a date."

His face lit up. We shook hands again and he headed inside.

Then I noticed Lazar Perske. He had been watching us from a dozen yards away. Normally when an older man watched me I knew what it meant. But this was harder to interpret. He didn't look at all happy. Was he still brooding over the fact I got more applause than he did? Poor old fool. One thing was certain: he didn't have the blood. I didn't feel the least tinge of it when I was around him.

I swam for nearly an hour. Coach Zielinski chatted me up about rejoining the team, but I told him I was far too busy with my budding music career. We had had the same discussion half a dozen times. I guess I couldn't blame him for trying.

It rained pretty heavily while I was there. Then it passed, the way late summer storms sometimes do. The sky cleared and there was a breeze.

It was nearly dinnertime when I got home. I put my sheet music on the piano and listened for Adam. The house was perfectly quiet.

He was in his bedroom. At first I thought he was asleep. The I realized he was simply lying on the bed with his eyes closed. And he was holding my leather, the stuff I wore when I performed. Pressing it to his cheek. Bubastis was lying at the foot of his bed, purring.

"Adam." I spoke his name softly.

He jumped up and tried to hide the suit behind him. "Mr. Dunn! Jamie."

It was such a clumsy moment. "How…how was your day, Adam? Did you find everything you need?"

"Every time you find me, I'm doing something embarrassing. I'm sorry."

"Stop apologizing for yourself."

"I'm sorry. I mean—"

We both laughed.

"This house of yours… I love it here. I played around a bit on your piano. I hope you don't mind."

"Not at all."

"I saw all those big old books and scrolls downstairs. With all those Egyptian symbols all over them."

"Hieroglyphics."

"Hieroglyphics." He repeated the word. "Can you read that stuff?"

"Some. Not as much as I'd like."

"And all those pictures on the wall. All those men. I've never seen so many pictures. I mean, we have a little art museum in Spartanburg, but this…in a house…" He smiled. "Who are they all?"

"Our forebears, Adam. Our ancestors."

"I don't get it."

"No." I shouldn't have said anything about them. "There's no way you could. But I want to teach you about them someday. When you come back. When you're older. You, of all the men I've met, will understand."

He smiled a smile that was obviously meant to win me over. "Try me now."

"I can't. There's no way. Come on, Adam. I'm buying dinner. Then we have to talk."

He knew what was coming. "You're throwing me out."

"Don't put it like that."

"But it's what you're doing, isn't it?"

"Adam, listen to me. There are laws. I can't just…just…adopt you and keep you here."

Dinner could wait. We sat in the den and had a long talk. I tried to convince him that he was all right, that the things his parents told him about himself were nonsense.

"Sometimes I wonder, Jamie. I try to be good. I think I am. But—"

"You are good. I can sense it, I can tell. And you're more than that. The world has more in store for you than you can realize right now, Adam."

"That's bullcrap. I'm a dumb upcountry queer who deserves what he gets. The only time I feel really good is when I hear you play your music."

This was harder than I had expected. We talked for a long time. I didn't know if he was feeling any better about himself when we were through; all I could do was hope. I took him to dinner at a little neighborhood Italian place; we were both pretty much talked out. When we left the restaurant it was nearly dark.

I shouldn't have done it. I knew I shouldn't. But being with him was so…he was so much like… Like who? Like Danilo? Like myself when I was his age?

We sat and talked awhile more when we got home. I was waiting for the moon to rise. Then I led Adam outside again. Behind the house, to a little garden where I grew some herbs. The soil was still slightly damp from the rain. In the moon's light the garden looked ghostly. Our feet made squishing sounds in the damp soil.

"What are we doing here? Jamie, this is crazy. Can we go inside and talk some more?"

"I want you to see something. Maybe it will help."

He laughed. "You're kicking me out but showing me your garden first."

"Please, Adam, don't talk like that. I'm only doing what I have to."

He fell silent and stared at me.

Slowly I got down on my knees and took a handful of moist soil, as I had once taken some rich mud from the bank of the Nile. I compacted it and fashioned it into a little animal.

Curious despite himself, Adam moved near to me. "Its ears are too long."

"This is no animal known to anyone, Adam. It's called the Set animal, and it was sacred in ancient Egypt."

This caught him off guard. "So what?"

"It is sacred to us."

"'Us'? What are you talking about?"

"Yes. *Us.* Watch."

Carefully I held the little animal in my hand, whispered the spell, and breathed on it. And it began to move. It took a step or two across my palm, looked up at me, and made a plaintive little cry.

Adam's eyes went wide with astonishment. His voice was hushed. "Jamie!"

"This is part of who we are, Adam. We share the blood of kings, you and I. And I want to teach you."

"But—but this isn't possible."

"Hold out your hand."

He did, and I let the little animal step into it. It looked up into Adam's face and made a tiny purring sound, almost like a cat.

He looked from the animal to me. "This isn't possible."

"Have you eaten any drugs today?"

"No."

"Then what you're seeing must be real." I smiled at him. "Right?"

"I…I guess."

"Good. Now release it."

He bent down and let it run into the bushes. I put an arm around him and led him inside.

We had coffee and talked some more. The bond that had grown between us was so unexpected, for both of us…

I told him I'd give him some money and get him to the bus station in the morning.

"Can we stay in touch?"

I shook my head. "It could get me in trouble. If your parents were to—"

"I know. Sorry."

"Good God, Adam, what are you sorry for now?"

"For asking."

Oh.

How sad his life must have been. How bad he must have felt about himself. But in time I could show him more than he ever imagined. And then and there I promised myself that I would.

We slept in separate beds again that night. After he went to bed in my old room, I went to the den and played for a while. The Chopin nocturnes, the saddest, most beautiful music I know. Bubastis stayed with him. Before I went to sleep myself, I looked in on him. She was curled up beside him on the pillow, purring happily. When she realized I was there, she looked up at me, a vision of contentment, as if she couldn't imagine a sweeter domestic scene.

In the morning when I put him on the bus, he hugged me impulsively, and very tightly. I gave him two hundred dollars, enough for him to get home and to have a bit of independence when he got there.

Watching him ride away was more difficult than anything I had done in a long time. There was so much I wanted to say to him.

I wanted to tell him—explain to him—Adam, we are kings, we have the blood of kings flowing in our veins.

We are the heirs of a thousand generations of rulers, artists, poets, philosophers.

There is power in our blood. I'm still discovering it myself. But when you come back to me, I'll teach you what it means.

There is a price, Adam, a terrible price. You will live on the blood and the flesh of others, of men who deny their birthright. But you will live forever. And you will see things and learn things and feel things like you never dreamed. Like *no one* ever dreamed.

All that I would tell him, in time. I would teach him, as Danilo taught me.

If I ever saw him again. Meantime, all I could do was pray. As his bus pulled away, I raised my hands in a gesture of blessing and whispered a prayer to the god Set, Danilo's god, to take care of him.

I headed home and decided to try and take my mind off it all with the news.

A second body had been found on the West Penn campus.

They had both been identified. Their names were Bryan Williamson and Todd Marquis. They had been members of the campus diving team.

I went a bit numb. Could Danilo have been so jealous that he…?

They weren't hiding who they were; they weren't denying their blood. It made no sense that he would have killed them; there would have been no point.

I realized I was late for my lunch date with Kurt.

Maybe we could try playing together. Maybe it would make me feel better.

CHAPTER 3

When I got home from that first lunch date with Kurt—when we first decided we wanted to play together—I found a note from Adam, pinned to my pillow. Somehow I had missed it earlier in the day.

Jamie,

Thank you again, so very much, for putting me up. And for putting up with me.

Going home isn't easy for me. I have to confess I've thought about taking your money and heading…I don't know where, anyplace my parents and their Christian friends can't find me.

But you seem so certain it's the right thing for me to do, going home. I'm afraid. But I trust you. And you're the only one I've ever known I could trust. The only one who ever seemed to think I was worth anything at all.

I'll be back. The day I turn eighteen I'll have my thumb out. Or I'll kill my parents and rob them and use the money to get back to you. Joke. I hope you know that's a joke. But I will come back.

I don't really understand what I saw last night in the garden, but if you did it, I know it's good. Better than the things my parents want me to believe.

I'll come back, Jamie. I have to. I've never had my own life anyplace else.

So thanks again. If I can find a way to stay in touch with you without anyone getting suspicious, I'll do it. Otherwise you'll see me on my birthday. January 18, the year after next. In the meantime, I'll be listening for you on the radio. Play some Chopin for me, okay?

Love,

Adam

Part love letter, part apology, part…what? Cry for help?

Not even the knowledge that Adam *had* to leave, that there was no choice, made that glum fact easier for me. I hoped he'd be okay.

Word about the murders of the two divers Todd and Bryan spread though the campus more quickly than I would have thought possible. When I left the house that morning to meet Kurt for our lunch date, the atmosphere was already different. Half the student body was new and had no memory of what had happened before. But there were still more than enough people who did remember.

A special edition of the campus paper was out, big headlines, 48-point type, detailing what was known about the dead athletes; there were quotes from coaches and teammates. And a sidebar outlined the facts about the previous murders. There was the whole terrible story of how Greg Wilton had killed Justin and tried to kill me; how the police had arrested him; how he'd been convicted. The killings stopped at the same time he was arrested; everyone including the police assumed he must have done them. Case closed.

But now… Either the original killer had never been caught, or there was a copycat, or… The paper strongly advised that young men not move about the campus alone after dark, especially athletes and arts majors. Since that covered a majority of the male students, I wondered how much good it would do, if any.

I checked in at the department just before meeting Kurt, to take care a bit of business. People made a point of expressing their concern. It must be awful to have all those memories dredged up; one after another, they told me so. And of course it wasn't much help having one after another of them dredge the memories up *for me*. Then they went off to their lessons, rehearsals and what-not. Outside it was dark and overcast; fit weather for the day, and getting darker every minute.

Roland was especially concerned. Of all of them, he knew just how much I had been through back then. And I think he always suspected that Danilo and I knew more about the killings than anyone else ever guessed. When I stopped in his office to say hi, he looked at me over the top of his glasses and asked, point-blank, "Is he back?"

"Who, Roland?"

"Your professor. Your…lover?" He had never approved of Danilo and me, and he had never tried to hide it. The murders were only part of it.

I played dumb. "Which one do you mean? There've been dozens."

"You know exactly who I mean, and you know why I'm asking. Is he back? Have you seen him?"

There was no point pretending. "No, Roland, I haven't."

This half-answer seemed to satisfy him. "Good. I know how you felt about him, Jamie, but there was always something…strange about him."

"I'm strange myself, Roland. Everyone says so. *You* say so."

He leaned back and put his feet up on the desk. "And so you are. But…"

"Yes?"

He backed off. "Nothing, I guess."

The silence between us then was so uncomfortable. Part of me wanted to tell him everything. But the more cautious part of me…

I had never stopped missing Danilo. But at least I had managed to keep up some semblance of a normal life without him. Now… I had missed a semester back when Greg Wilton tried to kill me. Normally I'd have graduated that coming spring. As it was, I'd be on campus till the following winter; and I wasn't sure I wanted to be.

Just after I left his office I ran smack into Kurt. He smiled as if he was actually glad to see me, which I guess he was. He hadn't been on campus two years before. And he hadn't read the paper. I needed company with someone like that.

Smiling, he shook my hand. "I just have to drop this music off in the library. I'll be right back, okay?"

"Sure." I didn't mind waiting.

He was back more quickly than I expected. We stood looking at each other awkwardly for a moment, then he said, "How about the Z? I hate it, but it's nearby."

"Everybody hates it." I laughed and put an arm around his shoulder. "Why do we all keep going there?"

"We're creatures of habit, I guess. Or sheep."

"Or lemmings."

As we were heading there, the sun came out unexpectedly. Kurt's hair seemed almost to glow in it.

Someone in the library had shown him the paper. He asked about it. "I had no idea anything like that had happened to you, Jamie. It must have been awful."

"Awful is the word, all right."

"Are you over it? I mean, are you all right?"

"No."

He sensed that it wasn't a comfortable topic for me, and he backed away from it quickly. But he put an arm around my waist and we walked close together. It was such a simple, protective gesture. I needed it.

And I think I needed to be in love.

Kurt and I seemed to be on the same wavelength in so many ways. We got into the habit of meeting for lunch at the Z, pretty much by default, like everyone else on campus; and we managed to have a great time even though there was a group of half-drunk fratboys at the next table.

Even his sense of humor, which was a lot more sunny and a lot less bratty than my own, seemed to appeal to me. Not that he didn't have sex on his mind. But when he made jokes about me plucking his G-string, or about him pounding my middle C, they didn't sound smutty the way they would have if I'd made them.

And I have to admit he was awfully attractive. Blond, blue-eyed, squeaky-clean complexion. I have always felt a certain attraction to the blond Nordic type, or as Roland called them, the Hitler Youth type. Kurt could have been the archetype. And he was three inches taller than me; that was always a bit of a turn-on.

Kurt's family was well-to-do—upper middle-class—and money didn't seem to mean a lot to him. He quickly got into the habit of buying me things, bringing me treats. That first date, as we walked back to the department from the Z, he stopped at a sidewalk vendor and bought me a red rose. At first it embarrassed me, I have to admit; but after a while I realized it was simply his way of showing affection. And I wanted his affection. Or needed it. No one had ever bought me flowers before, not even one, not even Danilo.

Being with him was easy. There were even moments when I forgot about Danilo.

And Adam.

But there was Kurt, and that wasn't bad.

After that first date, it was a few days before we managed our schedules so we had time to play together. All the rehearsal rooms were reserved, but I played on Roland's sympathies and he let us use one that was normally only for faculty.

He looked at me over the top of his glasses. "I shouldn't let you manipulate me the way I do."

"Everybody loves somebody sometime." I put on my brattiest smile.

"The only reason I'm doing it is because I think it would be good for you to make music with someone else. You know I've always told you so."

"But you never told me where to find a yummy blond violinist before."

"Do I have to do everything for you?" Harrumph.

So we played. I expected to feel awkward the first time, like a nervous virgin, but almost from the start we made beautiful music together, like Charles Boyer and Hedy Lamarr. A bit of the Beethoven C-minor sonata, a snatch or two of Mozart, we even tried that very difficult sonata by Shostakovich. Of course we needed work, lots of rehearsal, but our musical souls seemed to blend. It wasn't quite like anything I had ever experienced. Growing together with someone artistically…

When finding rehearsal rooms proved to be an ongoing problem, I suggested practicing at my house. I always made sure the grand was in tune, anyway, and we could rehearse there for as long as we wanted, as often as we chose.

"You're inviting me home to see your etchings?" He grinned.

"Yes. And they're all pornographic."

"You're a man after my own heart, Jamie Dunn." Suddenly his smile disappeared. "And I'm after yours."

First time he came, I showed him around. I still didn't think of it as my house, even though Danilo had deeded it to me. It was his place, and it reflected his personality. The fact that I hadn't really changed very much must have said more about me than I realized.

Like nearly everyone, Kurt found the place odd. "It's so dark, Jamie. Not what I would have expected. He commented on the diffuse light coming through the Egyptian-themed stained-glass windows. "And there are all these portraits." He studied them for a while, walking up and down the rows, going from room to room.

Finally he looked at me. "Queers. These are all queers. Allegedly." He leaned on that final word as if it was important. "Why do you have them?"

I tried to sound nonchalant. "That isn't the most important thing they have in common."

His eyes narrowed. "What, then?"

"Blood. They all had the blood of kings."

He looked from me to a row of portraits and back again. "They were kings. So what?"

"Nothing. Come on, let's play."

I felt a bit of a fool. It was such an awkward subject. How long had it taken me to understand? Danilo had been so patient with me. There was no way I could explain it all to Kurt, not without seeming a bit mad. And I was no longer certain he had the blood, after all…

Bubastis was usually friendly with visitors. But with Kurt, she was indifferent. She sniffed at him briefly, looked at me as if to ask what he was doing there, then scampered of to sleep or play somewhere. I had the impression she didn't quite know what to make of him, any more than I did.

It was a few weeks before we became lovers, but when it happened it seemed inevitable. We jokingly tried to play each other's instruments, one afternoon. He managed to pick out a simple melody on the keyboard, but I was hopeless at the violin. He stepped behind me, put his arms around me and showed me how to hold the bow properly.

The next thing I knew, I felt his lips touch the side of my throat.

Somehow he knew just the spot that was especially sensitive.

I turned and kissed him back. And it was a wonderful kiss. But…
but…what I wanted to be feeling most wasn't there.

In a matter of moments we undressed each other. Kissed more and
more, licked this and that, made love like crazed rabbits. And the sex was
good. Boy, was it ever. Blonds.

During one of our lovemaking sessions, I accidentally scratched him
with my ring.

"Ow! Be careful." He took my hand to inspect the ring. "That's Egyptian?"

I told him yes.

"Real gold?"

"Mm-hmm. Gift from an old boyfriend."

"Is it real? Really Egyptian, I mean?"

"Yes."

"Where could he have gotten such a thing?"

I dodged the question. I very much wanted to trust Kurt, but…I
couldn't tell. I tried. I tuned every one of my senses to Kurt. But if we
were part of the same bloodline, I couldn't tell. I had been quite certain,
when we first met. Now…

Normally a strong instinct told me about a man, almost as soon
as I set eyes on him; there was a kind of warm radiance I could feel,
stronger in some than in others but always definite. That was what
made it possible for me to sacrifice them so quickly and keep myself
alive. The blood of kings: my sustenance. Or else there was nothing,
almost a kind of positive absence of anything, and I'd know he wasn't
one of us. With Kurt there was nothing either way. Not a hint, not the
least itch.

Had I been fooling myself, that first day? I wanted him to be like
me. I wanted to be able to share myself with him fully and completely.
And I couldn't.

Every time I thought about it, I found myself remembering how
good it felt to be with Danilo.

That semester I had to take a conducting seminar. Not that I had much interest in conducting, but it was required. And, as Roland pointed out, sooner or later I'd probably want to try my hand at a few concertos for piano and orchestra, so I'd need to have some idea what the conductors were up to—how and why they led the way they did. "Concertos—orchestral gigs," he told me, "that's where the money is, that's where a musical career is, not in solo recitals. If there's just the one instrument on stage, people don't think they're getting their money's worth."

Roland was the instructor. And quite honestly, there was less to it than there should have been. There were six of us in the class, and we all pretty much developed our own techniques pretty quickly.

Our final exam for the seminar was a requirement to conduct the campus orchestra at one of the school concert programs. We were to choose a piece we especially loved, and Roland told us our job was to make the audience love it as much as we did ourselves. As luck would have it, I drew the Thanksgiving concert, to be held the weekend before the holiday break. I was the first of the group to have to conduct before an audience.

But what to conduct? The other students had pretty much chosen over-familiar warhorses, the *William Tell Overture,* the *Hungarian Rhapsodies*…flashy stuff that would impress an audience even if the orchestra was off-form. But me…precocious kid that I was—hell, prima donna that I was—I wanted to do something unfamiliar and exciting. Roland wasn't much help. He kept telling me to dust off something simple and recognizable, a Mozart overture or *The Moldau* or some such.

Not me.

I spent some time in the library, looking for the right piece, something by one of the composers whose portraits hung in my house, among all the other artists who had the blood. But after three sessions there I hadn't found anything I much wanted to do. Copland's symphonies struck me as over-familiar. Likewise Bernstein's music. Tchaikovsky was way overdone. I found myself thinking I might just fall back on some Vivaldi after all, part of the *Four Seasons* maybe, just to get the damned assignment over with.

By accident I mis-searched by one shelf. And there it was: a thick folder labeled "Claude Vivier."

I had never heard of him. But there was a biographical note attached. He was French-Canadian. He loved other men, a bit notoriously but quite openly. And he had died in Paris in 1983, the victim of a vicious stabbing. Speculation was that he had been killed by a young man he'd picked up for sex.

Why had I never heard of him? But almost as soon as I posed the question to myself, I thought I could hear Danilo's voice reminding me: they keep our history hidden. And so they did. Do.

I played through some of the scores. There was a *Prologue for Marco Polo;* a piece called *Zipangu,* an ancient name for Japan. I played the scores on my piano at home. And I felt...it isn't easy to describe, but I felt something akin to what I'd felt the first time I played Chopin. This man had been my brother. He died a few years before I was born, but we were brothers, the same blood united us across time.

And then it almost literally jumped out at me. A composition called *Lonely Child,* for soprano (a footnote indicated preferably a boy soprano) and small orchestra—strings and percussion. A synopsis described it; it was the plaintive cry of a gay boy who has been abandoned by his parents, conjuring up a dream lover to comfort and protect him.

I had found what I wanted to conduct.

And so the next month passed. Evenings practicing with Kurt and making love to him. Days practicing at the keyboard and then rehearsing the school orchestra in a composition they'd never played before. There was a bit of resentment among the players; they were used to student conductors choosing familiar stuff, things they'd played a dozen times before. *Lonely Child* threw them. But as they got into it, they began to love it.

An acquaintance of mine from the department, Paul Koerner, agreed to sing the solo. He was a voice major, a countertenor, the one Perske had used in the first recital of the semester. A male soprano. So naturally everyone made jokes about him being queer. Which he was. He said he didn't mind. But when I offered him the chance to sing this startling piece of music, he leapt at it.

At first I thought he only agreed to do it because he seemed to have a thing for me. He had made a few overtures in the past, but I was never really interested in him. But he quickly developed a real enthusiasm for the piece. "Jamie, this is the music I've been waiting to sing all my life."

He struggled with it, but as rehearsals proceeded, he found the emotion. And he sang beautifully for me.

In all that time there were no more murders. After a few weeks the campus forgot, and things returned to usual. It must have been a fluke; the resemblance to what had happened before must only have been incidental to some other motive.

But I hadn't forgotten. Danilo. Nearby. Hiding from me. He had the whole world, and yet he chose to come back to the city where I lived. Where was he?

Mid-October. Saturday afternoon. Dark day; heavy clouds.

Kurt called. "Jamie, let's have dinner."

"Not tonight, Kurt. I have something to do."

He laughed. "You sound so mysterious."

"I don't mean to. I'll see you at the department on Monday, okay?"

Puzzled, he hung up.

No, I could not have dinner with him. I was aging. I was hungry.

Johnstown was two hours east of the city. I had been there once or twice before. But usually when I left Pittsburgh, I headed in other directions. Johnstown was too close to Ebensburg, where I had lived as a boy. There were too many ugly memories.

I could feel autumn in the twilight air. That smell—I've always wondered what it is, decaying leaves or what?—that tells you yes, the world is dying.

I walked around the War Memorial, which, as I had learned on earlier visits, wasn't a proper memorial but a hockey arena. The Johnstown Jets played there. There was no game that night. But in the streets behind the arena, young men hung out, waiting for…well, for someone to pass the time with, so to speak.

I walked through the dark streets; streetlights were spaced far apart in that depressed town. Young men tried to get my attention. None had what I wanted, none had the blood.

Until one. He was beefy, a jock. Football, most likely, maybe wrestling. Why did the blood surface so strongly in athletes, I wondered. Buzz cut, dark hair; I couldn't see his eyes in the dim light. He assumed a nonchalant posture and said softly, "Hey."

"Hey." I stopped walking.

"You lookin' for someone?"

"You could say that."

He stared at me. "What's up?"

There was a strong gust of wind. Some dead leaves blew past us, rustling more loudly than seemed right. "Nothing much."

I decided to let him make the move.

And he did, more quickly than I expected. The game was usually played more circumspectly. "Want some action?"

I nodded. He tossed his head in the direction of an alleyway and then walked off. I followed. There were little foundries up and down, metalworkers, machine shops, body shops. All shuttered, all dark.

He stood in a particularly shadowy doorway, almost black. "Fifty."

I decided to toy with him. "Fifty what?"

"Don't waste my time."

"I won't." I got out my wallet. Smiling I told him, "I'm from Ebensburg. Up here on business."

"What kind of business? There's nothing there."

"Never mind that. Tell me about yourself. What's your name?"

"Don." He was lying. I could tell.

"You a student?"

He nodded.

"Jock?"

Again.

"You play…what? football?"

And a third time. "Look, are you gonna keep wasting my time, or what?"

I acted nervous. "I just want to get to know you, Don. Do the other guys on the team know you're queer?"

"Yes." He said it firmly, emphatically.

And it caught me completely off guard. "They do?"

"What of it?"

"Nothing, I just…I just didn't expect that."

I handed him the fifty. "I've changed my mind. I'll see you around, okay?"

He looked at me as if I was the biggest fool he'd ever met. But he was being true to himself and his nature. I couldn't hurt him. Someday he might… "Uh…sure…thanks." He looked at the bill as if he thought it might explode.

"No problem." I started to walk away.

"You're a cute guy. Young, too. You shouldn't have to…do this."

"I don't, usually. Like I said, I'm from out of town."

"Even so." He hesitated. "You want to… I just live a couple blocks from here. You want to…?"

It was tempting. But I was already feeling a bit of a commitment to Kurt. "No." I smiled. "No thanks."

"Want this back?" He held out the bill.

"Don't worry about it." And I left. At the next corner I looked back and he was still watching me.

Three alleys away I found another one, a little creep who said his name was Dustin. Had the blood. Called me a faggot and tried to kick me. I left pieces of him scattered across twenty yards of back street. He tasted foul, but he satisfied me.

CHAPTER 4

Mid-November. Concert getting close. *Lonely Child.* Why did I feel like one myself, so often?

Kurt began to put a bit of distance between us. The flowers and other little gifts stopped. He said there was too much of myself I kept hidden. I couldn't blame him, I guess. If only I could know his blood, his nature, I could have made things right between us. As it was…what could I do?

But we continued to rehearse. Our collaboration was too good to abandon, for either of us. It turned out we both loved Schubert, so his music was a natural for us. Kurt wanted to tackle the A major sonata, but I thought we should try something a bit briefer and, frankly, simpler for our first outing together, just to see how things went. We decided on the B-minor rondo, a lovely, fairly straightforward piece.

Schubert really suited Kurt, I thought. If his music has one characteristic, it's sweetness. Sweetness mixed with melancholy sometimes, but that was Kurt, too.

One afternoon as I was leaving the rehearsal hall I saw a group of people loitering outside Roland's office. I noticed that one of them was carrying a thick black book. A Bible? The door was closed. Even from a few yards down the hall, I could hear voices raised inside.

Several string players pushed past me in the hall. One of them told me how much they all loved playing the Vivier composition. "See you tomorrow, Jamie."

Whatever had been going on in Roland's office broke up. The door opened and a man came out, a clergyman in dog collar and dark gray suit. Like one of his friends he was carrying a Bible. He collected the ones who'd been waiting outside and they all left rather briskly.

I couldn't resist putting my head in the door. "Have you found religion, Roland?"

"I'm afraid it's found me. Or rather, us."

I asked what one earth he meant, and he told me to close the door and sit down.

"That was Pastor Eldon Heinrich of the Alliance for Christian Morality."

The purity police. They had a record of picketing porn shops and such. "What do they want here, Roland? Have you been doing something really interesting with the trombone slides?"

He ignored this. "It wasn't me they were here about. It was you."

"Me?" I couldn't believe it.

"They have, as Heinrich put it, grave concerns."

I had a thought. "They've noticed the kind of composers I favor."

"Nothing that subtle."

He sat back, obviously trying to find a way to say it. I prodded him, told him that I could take whatever it was.

"Jamie, they say—I can't believe I'm saying this—they say you're possessed by the devil."

"What?!?"

"I don't even know if they've ever heard you play. Heinrich got evasive when I asked if he had, so I took it for granted he hadn't. But someone in their national organization saw some of the media coverage about you. About the way your playing affects audiences. So naturally—" he shrugged—"they've concluded you must have sold your soul."

We stared at one another for a moment. Then, simultaneously, we broke out laughing.

"They're demanding that we kick you out of the program and prevent you from playing in public again. When I asked how we could do that, he muttered something vague about God finding a way."

I had never heard anything so foolish. And I had no idea what to say.

That seemed to please Roland. "I'll have to drop him a note of thanks. I've never seen you speechless before."

"But—but—"

"I can't imagine what's really behind it, except that they don't seem to know much about our kind of music. The preacher's ignorance was fairly obvious. And they seem to hate everything beyond their under-standing." He grinned. "Like a pack of dogs, barking at everything they don't know."

"But—but Roland, I—"

"Don't let it worry you. This kind of thing is nothing new. Did you know the Christers used to claim Paganini had sold his soul, back in the 19th century? His playing moved audiences to enormous, overpower-ing passion. People quite literally lost control, or so the historians say. So naturally he must be evil." He yawned, very widely. "You too. Satan never sleeps."

So I was in company with one of the greatest musicians of all time, a legendary figure. 'I guess I should be honored."

"You should. It's a sign your reputation's growing. If even these crack-pots have heard of you, then…" He laughed and left the sentence unfin-ished. But he had a point.

"Roland, they're nuts. Who knows what they might do?"

"There's nothing they can do. I told Heinrich if he showed up here again I'd have campus security escort him out. He didn't seem to think Jesus would approve of that, but I told him I answer to the dean, not the Lord."

I laughed again. "Well thanks for sticking up for me."

"Don't take it personally. Having a rising celebrity in the department gets attention, which gets funding."

"You think we can get a chunk of what they give the football team?"

"Don't be a smartass. Get out of here."

Sold my soul to the devil. I saw Kurt in the lobby and told him about it. I thought he'd be as amused as I was, but he took it seriously. "They can make trouble."

"Nonsense, Kurt. They're not that big or that powerful. Or that well-funded."

This didn't reassure him. "Jamie, they're Christians. Then have only the finest intentions."

It caught me off guard. "I doubt that."

"You mustn't lock horns with them."

I laughed. "And according to them, I have horns."

"Don't take them on, Jamie." He refused to see anything funny about the situation. "You'd lose."

"I doubt that even more, Kurt."

"At least they know one thing, Jamie."

I waited for him to go on.

"They know there's a part of you that's dark, that's hidden."

"Believe me, Kurt, you've seen every part I've got."

He was still not amused. I wondered if there was something else wrong, or if he really was that impressed by the ACM. I was a bit in love with him, and it wasn't working out. Maybe I should reconsider playing with him.

He was so beautiful, though.

Just as I got home the phone was ringing. I hoped it was Kurt, wanting to talk more. But it was someone—something—quite unexpected.

"Mr. Dunn?" Foreign accent.

"Speaking."

"This is Colonel Sayeed Mahawi at the Egyptian consulate in New York."

"Colonel Mahawi. Hello." I had never heard of him.

"It has come to my attention that you have made inquiries about the possible presence in Egypt of one Danilo Semenkaru."

"Yes!" I almost shouted it. Was there finally word?

"I have information."

"Yes! What is it, please?"

"Not over the telephone. Might it be possible for you to visit New York in the near future?" Despite the cautionary tone, his voice was warm.

"Yes. Anytime." I thought quickly. "Next weekend is Thanksgiving. I could come then. If your office will be open over the holiday, I mean."

"We may not meet in my office. I am telling you what I know as, shall we say, a personal favor?"

"Where is Danilo? Is he in Egypt?"

"When we meet, Mr. Dunn. I stay at the Chelsea Inn, on West Twenty-third Street."

It was where Danilo and I had stayed in New York. "I know it. I've stayed there myself."

"Good. Ask for me at the desk."

"I'll be sure to. Thank you again, Colonel…?"

"Mahawi." He paused for what seemed an awfully long time. Then he seemed to find his resolve. But he lowered his voice and told me anxiously, "Mr. Dunn, we are brothers in the blood. And you—you are the Blood Prophet. You must understand that I will give you any assistance I can, but unofficially."

There were others like me. I knew that. Others with the blood, others who embraced it and everything it meant. But to have one of them declare himself so openly and so quickly… I hardly expected it. And despite what Danilo told me, back before he vanished, I did not believe I was this prophet. I had never felt like a prophet, not down in my gut; I had never known that inner light that prophets are guided by. It must have been someone else Adam, or maybe Danilo himself, or…or I didn't know who. But not me.

But… Danilo. There was news. "Then I understand your caution perfectly, Colonel Mahawi."

He lowered his voice even more. I had the impression someone had walked in on him. "Next weekend, then, Mr. Dunn, at the Chelsea Inn." Before I could say anything else, he hung up.

And I found myself wondering what information he might have. If Danilo was back in Pittsburgh, as I thought, why and how would the Egyptian consulate know about it? And if he was in Egypt, then who had committed those killings?

As for Colonel Mahawi… An Egyptian officer. One of my brothers in blood. Did he know Danilo? Had Danilo given him the same gift of immortality he had given me? Blessed, or cursed him with it? I would know soon enough.

The Dunn-Sivers Duo made its premiere at the Thanksgiving concert, the same one where I conducted *Lonely Child*.

It was the weekend before the holiday. The sky was dark and heavy with clouds, gray as soot, and there was occasional snow. And the recital hall was crowded. Backstage, I joked to Roland that they must have come in to warm up. He snorted at me and walked away.

The program opened with another piece by Lazar Perske, a chamber symphony this time. It was for a string ensemble, oboe and clarinet. It was more of his usual stuff, *faux* chant. The musicians seemed bored, and so did the audience; I certainly was. Applause was polite, no more.

Then came Kurt and I, playing our Schubert rondo. I wore my leather; he had on jeans, sneakers and a sweatshirt. We had talked about it, and he shared my distaste for the rigid formality of the classical world.

The audience was with us almost from the moment we started. But it was hard for me to think about them. The concert was being taped for broadcast on public radio stations across the country. I found myself thinking of Adam, wondering if he'd be listening. No, hoping he would. For an irrational moment I found myself scanning the audience, wondering if he might be there. No; of course not. I should have trusted him to keep his word.

The crowd loved us. We got an ovation, and Kurt seemed unable to stop smiling. Then, quite impulsively, he put his arms around me and kissed me. The applause lessened; some people were obviously put off by it, but others kept clapping. I had the impression a few people were applauding even more loudly, to make up for the ones who'd stopped. I was more than a bit startled by it myself. Except musically, Kurt had been keeping his distance from me more and more.

In the wings afterward he threw his arms around me again, quite impulsively. "Jamie, I never thought I'd get a reaction like that from an audience! And it's all because I'm playing with you."

"Don't sell yourself short, Kurt. You were terrific."

"It's just your magic, rubbing off on me."

"Nonsense. There's nothing magical about it. You're good, that's all."

"I'm better with you than I've ever been alone."

It was kind of embarrassing, like an unexpected declaration of love. "Well, thanks, I guess."

Roland came up and congratulated us. "Splendid performance. I only wish I could persuade you to dress properly."

"Maybe next time we can just wear jockstraps." I grinned at him, and he stalked away, muttering. Annoying people—knowing just how far to push them—is a gift.

After intermission a string quartet played the Shostakovich eighth; it was the one he wrote after hearing how the Nazis at the Treblinka death camp forced their victims to dig their own graves, then dance on them. He wrote music for that. It was one of the few pieces by non-blood composers that always moved me. Dance of Death. I seemed to hear my own life in it.

Then the stage was set for *Lonely Child*. The players took their seats, and Paul and I walked onstage. He was as determined as I was to be open and honest, a rare enough thing in the classical world. And he bristled against its closetedness. It was the first indication I'd had that there might be more to him than I had suspected. So we entered hand in hand, which caused a bit of a stir. Then I took my place at the podium, raised my baton and began.

The deep, rich, haunting music moved the audience. I could feel it, in the same way I could always tell they were responding to my pianism. The rhythms of the music, the stark sadness, the swell and the fall of it, caught them up. The strange, intense harmonies got under their skin. Vivier hypnotized them through me.

And through Paul. He seemed caught up in it too, as if he was feeling or maybe hearing something beyond simply the notes on the page. Lonely child; abandoned boy; searching for love in a phantom world— Paul was all of it. Listening to him, I found myself almost crying.

When we finished, the audience roared with applause. It began at once, before I even had time to turn and face them. And some of them were crying. They couldn't hold back. Tears flowed. I found myself thinking about Adam again. Paul rushed to the podium and kissed me, and I kissed him back, friendly kisses, not erotic.

The audience didn't seem to mind, this time. The classical world was changing, all right. Or at least beginning to.

Backstage there was a sheet cake and punch. And there was a considerable stir. Roland was beaming, exactly as he had done after my duo with Kurt. People were elated, congratulating Paul and me. I didn't quite know what to say. "It was the orchestra. All I did was wave a stick."

Kurt was being lionized. Deservedly—he'd played beautifully. But the attention seemed to be making him uncomfortable. I imagined we'd be playing together more; he'd have to get used to it. A few of the guys were paying him special attention. When he saw me watching, he blushed.

A man I'd never seen before approached me out of the crowd. Twenty feet away, I knew him, knew his blood, it was that strong. And weirdly, the crowd seemed to part for him—involuntarily, without realizing they were doing it. He was tall, blond, obviously athletic. And dignified, terribly dignified. The moment I saw him, I knew I wouldn't be able to play my usual bratty self with him. He approached me, hand extended, and we shook.

"You were marvelous, Jamie."

"It was the orchestra and Paul, not me."

"No. You led. You inspired them to do what they did." He leaned close to me and whispered, "You are the Blood Prophet."

I froze. People kept telling me that, Danilo, Mahawi, and now this man. "Who are you?"

He ignored the question. "As you led these people, you will lead us all."

Everyone else seemed to be busy with the snacks or simply engaged in conversation. Paul was getting a great deal of attention; suddenly the department had three "rising stars," it seemed. For the moment, at least, no one was paying any attention to me. I pulled the man aside, looked around, and lowered my voice. "Who are you? What do you know?"

"You may call me Edward."

"Edward." I repeated it and stared at him blankly. "And who are you?"

"One of your brothers. Or more accurately, fathers."

Again I looked around. My first thought was: is this the man who killed Todd and Bryan? "Why haven't I seen you before?"

"I have seen you." He smiled a benign, rather smug little smile.

"That doesn't answer the question."

"No, it does not." He glanced over his shoulder. "Have you had any cake? It is quite delicious."

Smalltalk. After what he had announced to me, he was trying to make smalltalk. "Never mind the cake." Without wanting to, I let a touch of urgency creep into my voice. "Where is Danilo?"

He shrugged. "He could be anywhere. Or nowhere at all. You should really perform solo, you know. Your Schubert duo was fine, but when you play alone it is even better."

"Danilo is immortal." I moved closer to him and whispered. "Where is he?"

"Believe me, Jamie, I do not know, no more than you do." He smiled that same benign smile. "He asked me once to look after you. From afar."

This was more suspicious than anything else he'd said. "Then why haven't I seen you before?"

He shrugged slightly. "I really must have another piece of that cake. The buttercream icing is quite—"

"Will you stop it? I want to know."

Lazar Perske pushed through the crowd and headed for us. There were cake crumbs on his lips and suit. As usual—and as with Kurt—I got nothing from him, no sign whether he was blood or not. It was so frustrating. How was I supposed to know where I stood with him? He hooked his arm in mine and pulled me aside. "You were marvelous, Mr. Dunn, just simply marvelous."

"Thank you." He was the last person I wanted to be talking to.

"Vivier's music always moves me so. I've never heard *Lonely Child* performed so feelingly."

It quite surprised me. "You know his music?"

"Of course. One of the great unsung masters. Such a pity he died the way he did. And so young."

This hit me out of nowhere. Of all people to appreciate what I had done—or more precisely, what Vivier had done through me... "Thank you very much."

"And of course your pianism always moves me, as it does everyone."

I'd had the reverse impression. He had never done anything but scowl at me. I looked around for "Edward," if that was really his name, and he was gone. No sign. A bit foolishly I looked to where the cake was, thinking he might be there. But he was gone.

Perske went on. "I'm working on a piano concerto." He leaned close to me and told me, in confidential tones, "I'd like you to premiere it."

Audiences had been largely indifferent to his work. It seemed pretty obvious he thought having me play it would get a better reaction.

"I prefer to play alone, I'm afraid. I've played through a few concertos, but never seriously." I put on a big smile. "I'm a loner."

"I knew Vivier, you know." Again he whispered. "We were close."

This was quite unexpected. Perske, unmade bed of a man. Who could have guessed? For the first time he began to interest me.

"Are you planning to conduct more of his music? Perhaps I might be able to give you some insights..." He made a vague gesture; I wasn't sure whether he meant insights into the music or the man.

But I was interested, of course. "Yes, I'd like that very much. I don't really want to be a conductor, but I'd like to know for myself."

"We must plan on getting together, then."

A pair of students pulled him away. The day had turned unexpected in so many ways. I looked again for "Edward," but there was no sign of him.

A few people seemed to be reading little pamphlets or booklets. And to find them quite amusing. A violist from my orchestra must have seen the puzzled look on my face and came to show me the brochure. "They've been handing these out to people as they leave the concert hall." She didn't seem to be able to stop laughing.

But when I realized what it was, I didn't find it very funny. It was from the Alliance for Christian Morals. A crude illustration showed a young man playing the piano; there was a vague resemblance to me. Except that he had horns. The pamphlet was titled The Devil's Music. The text was a rant about me, a fairly vicious attack. It didn't name names—they had sense enough to know the libel laws. But it was unmistakably about me.

This young, beautiful athlete/musician is doing Satan's work, it said. Bewitching the young. Leading them to an unholy, perverted lifestyle. Flaunting his sodomy. There was nothing about the fact that I devoted myself to the music of composers who loved other men; that kind of knowledge, I think, was beyond them. I found myself wondering how many composers of any kind they could even name, if it came down to it. But the final page was a political rant: tax dollars—public money—being spent to promote this evil young man and his evil music. Take action! Speak out!

As if my life wasn't complicated enough. I took it across the room to where Roland was schmoozing a pair of trustees. He beamed when he saw me and made a big show of introducing me to them. They made the usual comments, told me how wonderful I am. I didn't believe it, not just then. All I was doing was making music. Expressing my deepest feelings in my playing. How could I deserve an attack like this one? One of them told me he missed hearing my Chopin and hoped I'd play it at the next recital. I smiled, thanked him, said I would, and took Roland aside.

"Have you seen this?"

He took it. All he had to do was read the title to know what it was. "Jesus."

"No, Roland, just some of his flunkies."

He pushed it into a pocket. "How many of these are there?"

"I don't know. Someone said they were giving them to people as they leave the hall. What are we going to do?"

"We're going to call campus security and have them removed. No one's allowed to distribute literature that doesn't have administration approval. You know that."

"That'll take care of the problem today. But they'll be back."

"Then they'll be arrested."

"Roland, will you think? If they make an issue of this, the publicity will only help them, And it could hurt the department. And you and me personally."

He paused. "You're right. They're idiots, but they know how to generate PR. Let me think about this. Are you on campus over the holiday?"

"No, I'm heading to Manhattan."

"Ah, the New Babylon. Maybe they're right about you."

"That isn't funny, Roland."

"You're letting this get to you, Jamie. That's what they want. I'm not sure they can make as much trouble as you seem to think."

Suddenly through the crowd I caught a glimpse of the man who called himself Edward. He was tall enough, and his hair was bright enough blond, for him to stand out across the room. "I'll catch up with you later, Roland. There's someone I have to talk to."

He tried to follow my glance across the room. "I hope he's cute."

I pushed through the crowd, but when I reached the place where he had been, he was gone.

I waited. The crowd thinned. There was no sign of him.

I decided to drive to New York. No sense dealing with airport crowds on a holiday weekend.

The weather continued dark and wet. Worse, temperatures fell. Bubastis slept more than usual. I made arrangements with a neighbor to look in on her a few times a day, to make sure she was okay.

When I left the house on Tuesday morning, there was snow in the air. Not sticking yet, but the sky looked ominous. The Pennsylvania Turnpike, never a pleasant road under the best of conditions, was busy and slow. Why do so many drivers react to the first snow of the season as if they've never seen the stuff before?

Halfway across the state, there was a major accident ahead of me. Everything came to a standstill. We sat without moving for hours. I made an impulsive decision. Got off the turnpike and headed for the Poconos. Danilo's summer house was there. Well, mine, now; but I never stopped thinking of it as his. I had planned on getting to New York that evening, but it would have to wait. At a rest stop, I called the hotel; they assured me that holding my room would be no problem.

As I headed north across the center of the state, the snow became heavier. There were moments when it was almost a white-out, and I had to slow; once, the weather actually forced me to stop. After a few hours, though, I was there.

Our house. The place where we had first made love. And the place where I had first tasted blood.

The trees all around were barren, naked for the winter; it felt appropriate. But the snow on them was quite beautiful. When I was a boy, it would never have occurred to me that death could bring with it such beauty. Another thing I had learned from Danilo.

Danilo. Colonel Mahawi knew where he was, and would tell me. I would see him again.

But…would he want to see me? Awful thought, that he might not… Why had he stayed away from me? I wanted him more than anything in the world, wanted his touch, his kiss, wanted him to make love to me.

The house was cold. I got some firewood and built a roaring blaze in the main fireplace, then a smaller one in the bedroom. Hungry, I went to the kitchen to make myself some dinner. But someone had broken in; the rooms at the rear of the house and been ransacked, the back door was battered open, and there was practically no food in the pantry. Damn. I was starving. I pushed the door shut, then got some plywood and nailed it over the places where it had been bashed through. The only thing I could find worth eating was a bag of potato chips. I took them to the living room, sat in front of the fire, and ate them. Then, without wanting to, I fell asleep.

There were dreams. I don't remember much about them, but they were vivid and bloody and filled with love. Danilo was there, and Kurt, and even Lazar Perske for some reason. Why are dreams so dumb so much of the time? People think they tell you things, but mostly they're nonsense. Lurking somewhere in the edges of it, a presence I could feel but not see, was the man who called himself Edward. He had the blood. He wanted me, I think. I wanted Danilo.

I woke in the middle of the night. Something, some instinct, told me someone had been watching me. It was mildly alarming. I remembered only too well how our handyman had threatened us...and what Danilo did to him.

There was no one at any of the windows. I went outside and looked around. The snow was coming down even more heavily. No one, nothing. No footprints in the snow but my own. Feeling a bit foolish, I went back inside.

There were fireplaces in all the rooms. Some odd compulsion made me build fires in all of them. It was a waste of firewood; but I thought it might make the place seem less barren. Somehow it had the reverse effect, though, emphasizing how empty the place was and how alone I felt there. I had visited the house a few times before. But without Danilo, it was never the same place at all.

That night the storm ended. There were six inches of snow on the ground. When the clouds parted and the moon came out, the mountains turned into a magical place, a wonderland. Trees glistened; the world was a beautiful ghost of itself. And I was alone. I let all the fires die down except the one on the bedroom.

Just as I was nodding off, I saw him. A man's face at my window. My room was on the second floor. It wasn't possible for him to be there, but there he was. And after a moment I recognized him: Edward.

I got out of bed and got dressed as quickly as I could. Ran outside. There was no sign of him. No footprints, nothing. Gone. A phantom. I had been dreaming again. I must have been. I told myself that over and over again.

And finally I slept again. There were more dreams. Danilo. Edward. Blood. Blood everywhere. Was it mine, or...? I woke a few times during the night. And immediately I glanced at the bedroom window. He had been watching me, much the way Adam had. Finally I fell into a deep sleep, undisturbed by dreams or memories.

Next morning I got out of bed and went to the kitchen naked. It was early, barely sunrise. The house was cold, but I didn't mind. There was no proper food in the pantry. Rather than eat more chips, I decided to wait till I was back on the road.

I locked up the house, made a mental note to call someone to repair the damage to the kitchen, and started warming the car. On impulse I walked around the house one more time, looking for prints. There were none. It had been a dream, that's all.

It was early enough for the highways to be relatively free of traffic. It was also a bit too early for them to have been plowed properly. Progress was slow but steady. At least the storm hadn't brought any ice. Now and then I passed snowplows, busily clearing the road.

I was in Manhattan at noon.

The city was crowded too, but then it always is. Holiday shopping, tourists, Macy's parade… The Chelsea Inn was nearly full, but the manager knew my name and had held a room for me.

"And I'm supposed to meet Colonel Mahawi here. Is he in?"

He checked. "I'm afraid not. But I think…yes, here it is—he left a message for you."

I read it. It was a simple enough note, just a welcome, let's get together as soon as we can, that kind of thing.

"Would you like to leave a message for the colonel?"

"Please."

I wrote a quick note, sealed it in an envelope and handed it to him. And I watched to see which box he put it in. Room 456.

Then I got my bags up to my room. Cute bellhop. As soon as he was gone, I opened Mahawi's envelope. In it was a fragment of a map of Egypt, centered on Amarna, the ancient capital founded by Danilo's father Akhenaten. It was circled in thick red marker. Amarna.

There were a few other scribbles, mostly jottings in Arabic; and he had sketched three little cartoon dogs. Amarna; I had searched there, twice, and there was nothing. And if Mahawi had known Danilo, then he would have known the place. It couldn't mean, much, could it?

Outside there were flurries. But I was in New York again. What first?

The museums? A good restaurant? As I watched at the window, a pair of beautiful young men strolled past, hand in hand. And I knew what I would do first. Kurt had been pulling away from me more and more, except musically. There was no way around it.

By the time I showered and changed, the afternoon light was dying. Even though it was nighttime the weather seemed to be warming up a bit; the flurries had changed to a steady drizzle. I checked to see if Mahawi had come back; he hadn't.

Down Eighth Avenue into the Village. Turn right, head into the warehouse district or, as it was always called, the meat-packing district. The businesses were closing down; workers were leaving in groups, talking sports and city politics. They ignored me. There were other men, I knew, who would be leaving work but not heading home.

At the far west end of the street, just before it reached the Hudson, was the bathhouse I wanted, a club called The Bait. There were a few others going in just ahead of me. Young men, some muscular, some not, some beautiful, some not especially good-looking. I found myself wondering wryly if they were meat-packers, then had to force myself not to make the obvious joke.

The place was a wonderland, more sex club than bathhouse. It was dark, and the air was filled with a musky aroma. There was a bar, a video room, a maze… The maze was made of plywood with pegholes—anyone could watch anyone else; privacy was an illusion there, and it was a turn-on. In the farther reaches of the place there were specialty areas. An Indian wigwam, which I didn't bother with; a dentist chair, which I did. A dungeon, of course. The inevitable sling, happily occupied, young red-haired guy. A pair of bathtubs. A row of cubicles with glory holes. A row of booths with lockable doors.

The men were young and not-quite-young; fair and dark; buff and not-quite-buff; dressed and naked. One young blond boy walked around in a pair of tight white briefs and a pair of new white sneakers, and nothing else; he was too much the jock for my taste. There were dozens of them and there were, by actual count, three I did not want to have sex with.

In the last room of all was the bar. I walked through room after room till I reached it, all of them filled with feverish activity. I fortified myself with a glass of bourbon, Danilo's drink. Even in that supercharged place, I could never quite forget him.

Like everyone else, except the men in the video room who were happily involved in some filmmaker's fantasies instead of their own, I kept in motion. We all moved from one place to the next, circulating like the protoplasm in a cell. Music pulsed. Everywhere I looked, men were making love by twos, by threes, by more than that. Touching, kissing, penetrating. The mixture of styles, some dressed, some nude, some in-between, excited me. I joined one group after another for a while, then moved on.

A young man approached me, short, dark, beginning to lose his hair. Cute, though; tight body; wearing only jeans; his feet were bare. He smiled, and I did too. He nodded in the direction of a booth. I followed.

We made love feverishly; I don't think I realized how much I needed it, and it was clear he did too. He was Irish, in the country on business; named Andrew. Afterward, we talked. And kissed. And fucked some more.

"You haven't told me your name." He smiled; my name didn't really seem to be an issue.

"I'm Jamie." Absurdly, I held out my hand, as if we were just meeting.

Andrew laughed. "There's music in your move-making, Jamie." His accent was sexy as hell.

"I'm a musician." I laughed too, for some reason.

"I can always tell. And you have a swimmer's build."

"I'm a swimmer, too."

He grinned. "Like Esther Williams."

I didn't bother to object to this slight on my butchness; the movie reference hit home. "You're really sexy, Andrew. Where I come from, foreskins are few and far between."

"And where is that?"

"Ebensburg, Pennsylvania. It's not much more than a pit mine."

"It sounds ghastly. Where I come from, everyone has them." He reached out and touched me. "But variety is the spice of life."

Sweet Andrew. Hot Andrew. He wanted me to go back to his hotel and spend the night. But it was late, and I was in the city for a purpose. Being with him had been the perfect climax to my night. He had the royal blood, that much I knew. I wondered if he was aware of it. I gave him one last kiss, got my clothes and left.

It was well after midnight. The rain was cold, hard and steady. Within minutes I was soaked. It didn't seem to matter.

That stretch of the street was paved with cobblestone. In what faint light there was, mostly work lights from the warehouses and packing plants, the stones glistened. The noise of traffic was faint and distant, almost drowned out by the beat of the rain. Even my own footsteps seemed near-silent. I walked, thought about Andrew, thought about Danilo, about Kurt, about my life and my love and my lust... There were shadows; there was the occasional glint of light; there were faint distant echoes. And there I was, alone. The city seemed to stretch on forever.

Eighth Avenue. Lights, traffic. I shook off my mood and flagged down a cab. The driver didn't ask what I was doing out in that weather without an umbrella. This was New York; he knew, or could guess. Despite the late hour, traffic was slow.

Then I saw what was causing it. There were emergency vehicles in front of the Chelsea, half a dozen of them, red lights spinning. Police cars, ambulances. My gut told me what they were there for.

I paid the driver and rushed inside. Then, trying to act nonchalant, I sauntered up to the desk to get my key. Two policemen were there, chatting in hushed voices with the night manager.

"Could I get my key, please? Room 219."

He got the key and checked the registration. "Mister...?"

"Dunn. Jamie Dunn."

He handed me my key. Trying to sound casual, I asked what was wrong.

"Just a slight bit of trouble with one of our guests." Professional smile. "Nothing for you to be concerned about."

"Which guest? I'm supposed to meet someone…"

The cop got between us. "I'm detective Pulaski." He flashed a badge too quickly for me to see it. "May I ask where you've been tonight, Mr. Dunn?"

I could have lied easily enough, told him I'd been to the theater and hoped he wouldn't ask to see my ticket stub. But why bother? "At a sex club. The Bait. Down in the West Village. Do you know it?"

I think he was a bit surprised at my forthrightness. Most tourists must be a bit more circumspect. "Is that why you're in town?"

"No. As I just said, I'm here to meet someone."

"Who?"

"Colonel Mahawi."

He exchanged glances with the manager. "Like the man said, there's nothing for you to be concerned about. I'd suggest you go up to your own room and get to sleep." He smiled, just like a hotel employee. "Good night, Mr. Dunn."

Of course I had to know, had to see. I walked up the stairs to the fourth floor. 456 was at the end of the hall. The door was open, and there were two detectives inside, apparently going over everything. Just as I got there some medics were rolling out a gurney with a body on it. One arm hung out from under the sheet, which was smudged here and there with dark red blood. The arm was in a military uniform.

I walked up to them. "What happened?"

A hand grabbed my shoulder. I spun around; it was the cop from downstairs. "Mr. Dunn, I told you to go to your room."

"But you didn't tell me why. What happened here?"

The medics wheeled the gurney past us and into an elevator. Pulaski watched them go, then turned back to me. "You knew him?"

But I did not want to be questioned. I concentrated, fixed my gaze on him, and exerted my will. "You will tell me what happened here."

His own will was gone, no match for mine. "Someone killed him. Mutilated the body. Drained all the blood. Eyes, heart, genitals torn off, no sign of them. There are teeth marks."

I walked away, leaving him standing there. He wouldn't remember me.

Mahawi, my link to Danilo, was dead. And all I could think was that Danilo must have killed him.

Why?

Why was he avoiding me?

What had I done to make him stop loving me?

I went back to my own room, showered and crawled into bed. The rain outside was even heavier now; I could hear it pounding on the street outside. For the first time in months, I did not dream of Danilo that night. I couldn't let myself.

CHAPTER 5

Thanksgiving morning in New York City. Gray, cold, rainy. I looked out my hotel window, and the streets were nearly deserted. I remembered the parade; that must be where they all were. For the briefest instant I thought about going to watch it myself, but no; giant turkeys and cartoon heroes were hardly what I needed just then.

I showered, shaved, dressed and went back up to Mahawi's room, not expecting to find anything. The door was locked of course. Police tape crossed in an a large yellow X. There were a few stains and scuff marks on the carpet; one of them might have been a trace of his blood, but I couldn't be sure.

A maid saw me at the door and asked what I was doing. I smiled. "Let me into this room."

She registered shock. "I can't do that, sir."

I offered her a ten.

But she wouldn't budge.

Twenty.

Nada.

"You'll have to leave, sir, or I'll call security."

I pulled down the police tape. Then I focused, I concentrated. "You will unlock this door. Then you will forget you saw me."

She obeyed. It worked on maids, on the police, on boys I wanted to have sex with; it worked every time I needed it, another of Danilo's gifts to me. She opened the door and held it for me, quite compliantly, then went on about her business.

The room had been ransacked. I wondered whether it was by the killer or the police. A chaos, clothes tossed, personal articles scattered. I poked around a bit, not expecting to find anything.

Then I went downstairs for breakfast in the coffee shop. I was hungry, ravenous; with some abruptness I realized I hadn't eaten since I left the Poconos the previous day.

If only I hadn't gone to The Bait. If only I'd stayed at the hotel and waited for Mahawi. He might still be alive. And I might know what he wanted to tell me about Danilo.

I tried to tell myself it wasn't my fault, that there was nothing I could have done, realistically, to prevent his death. But the Christian upbringing my relatives had subjected me to had gotten the better of me, and I felt nothing but guilt and remorse. To be honest, I felt like bloody shit.

Andrew had wanted me to go back to his hotel and spend the night with him; if I'd gone…the police would have done their work and gone, and I'd never know what had happened to by Egyptian brother. Roland was always telling me I was oversexed, and that I was taking advantage of my fame—fame on campus at least—in the wrong way. Maybe he was right.

Then with the clarity that sometimes comes with that first cup of morning tea, some perspective one what had been happening hit me.

Bryan and Todd. The divers, dead now. I knew it; it was obvious to me when we met and even more so when we made love that night. They did not have the blood. Danilo would never have sacrificed them. There would have been no point; like me, he needed the true blood to keep alive, the blood of kings. Bryan and Todd… It couldn't have been him who killed them. It couldn't have been. There was someone else…

The thought came as a relief; Danilo was not in Pittsburgh, it seemed, not dogging me from a distance. But then where was he? Who had killed them, and why? And why had they been sacrificed in the blood ritual I knew so well?

Poor Todd and Bryan, they could hardly have known what was happening to them. No more than my own victims ever did. Mahawi, on the other hand…Mahawi must have known and understood. I wondered if that made it easier for him, or the reverse.

Through the coffee shop window I saw a pair of men at the front desk: cops. The clerk pointed to me and they approached, came in, flashed their badges, and gestured me to a booth at the rear of the shop. "Mr. Dunn?"

They wanted to know why Mahawi had had my name. I told them a story about meeting him through a friend of a friend. I was a student of

Egyptology, worked in the department at West Penn, etc., etc.

"The desk clerk said he left a message for you. What was in it?"

"Just a note saying he looked forward to meeting me and telling me he wa sin 456."

They scowled; it was pretty obvious they thought I was hiding something. They were New York cops—heavy accents, rumpled clothes. I had the impression they didn't really care much who had killed Mahawi. The senior detective was named O'Hara, like the cop in *Arsenic and Old Lace*. But his next question caught me a bit off guard. "Are you a homosexual, Mr. Dunn?"

I blinked. "If you want to be clinical about it, yes."

My irony was lost on them. "And was Colonel Mahawi a homosexual?"

"I told you, I never met him. We never had the chance to meet."

"But you know whether he was a homosexual."

"How could I?"

"Homosexuals know each other. Isn't that what you call 'gaydar'?"

"But it only works with people you meet, detective. I told you, I never set eyes on Colonel Mahawi."

O'Hara's tone suggested he was brushing aside a gnat. "The Egyptian consulate says he wasn't one. We think he was. We found homosexual pornography in his room."

"No!" Clever cops.

As if to prove he wasn't kidding me, he held out a photograph. Dingy, battered, taken in dim light. Amateur porn if there ever was such a thing. A naked man was tied to a chair. Someone just outside the frame was whipping him; only an arm showed, lash in hand. The bottom's face was blurred. Even if I had a taste for that kind of kink, it would take better photography than this to turn me on.

I decided I'd had enough of O'Hara and his friend. They couldn't begin to understand what had happened, and I didn't want to try explaining it. I focused all my mental energy on them. "I do not know a thing about this. Mahawi and I never met. You will not question me again, and you will not consider me involved in your case in any way.

Do you understand?"

They understood. They thanked me for my help, smiled and left.

It occurred to me that when I did that, when I used the force of the divine blood to control people, my tone of voice took on more than a bit of Danilo's.

I spent the long weekend in New York. O'Hara and his pal showed up at the hotel another time, but it wasn't me they were looking for. When I saw them in the lobby they smiled and waved, then went back to whatever they were discussing with the manager.

Me, I was in New York, and I plunged into it. Once the parade ended, crowds were everywhere, it seemed, shopping, fighting over merchandise, eating, drinking. This Ebensburg boy, often as I had been there, found it all a bit overwhelming, wonderfully so.

The museums were crowded too. But there were wonderful things to see. I went back to the Metropolitan to visit the reliefs of Danilo and his family. My family too, I told myself. And there were a few paintings by the Renaissance Italian who signed himself proudly "Il Sodoma," the Sodomite. Then I went to MOMA to find paintings by Jackson Pollack, Jasper Johns, Robert Rauschenberg, Andy Warhol, the men who had dominated modern American art, had shaped the way so many of us see things. All of them my brothers.

The restaurants were good. The theater was indifferent at best. Danilo had told me once about the glorious place Broadway had been. We had ruled there, if nowhere else, in the days of our decline. Not anymore. There were queers there, in abundance, but none of them seemed inspired by the blood, or by much of anything else. More to the point, there was not much left to rule. The two musicals I saw were as flat and synthetic as bad TV. Oh well.

Sunday morning I drove back to Pittsburgh. Enough of the big city. It had not stopped raining all the time I was there.

Once again I left early enough to avoid the worst of the holiday traffic. I took I-80 instead of the Pennsylvania Turnpike. It was a much better road; the scenery was prettier; it would be less jammed with traffic; and it didn't take me anywhere near Ebensburg. The thought of ever going back there… My cousin Millie and her family had never made the slightest effort to contact me, not even when I lay near death in the hospital after Greg Wilton attacked me. I'd sent them a few notes, holiday cards and what-not; they never answered. It was as if I had never existed there. Which was just as well, I guess.

Still, driving that route—driving at all, actually—had been a mistake. The long, monotonous hours on the road gave me time to think. Death everywhere. Death has always been with me, all my life.

Two years had gone by, and I still loved Danilo so desperately. I could close my eyes and see him, hear his voice, smell his wonderful musky scent. He was taller than I was, and more muscular; when he held me, I felt loved and protected in a way I never had before or since.

I had asked myself a hundred times why my love persisted so strongly. Others, I forgot quickly, sometimes almost at once. Not Danilo. I still loved him as much as I did the first time we kissed, the first time we fucked, the first time I tasted his blood. Why? Why couldn't I just…let go?

The worst thing was the realization that he had manipulated me. I had a faint suspicion at the time, but now, in retrospect, I knew it. Like a magician forcing a card on a mark, he had maneuvered me into making the choices I made. It didn't seem to matter. I kept telling myself, I would have made them anyway. He had waited more than three thousand years for me. How could I not love him in return?

In the mountains the rain turned to sleet, then snow. At a rest stop along the interstate I stopped for lunch. Grilled Reuben, fries, a Coke. Outside, the most bitter wind was blowing.

There was something odd. I realized that there were more cars and trucks in the parking lot than people in the restaurant. I saw pairs of men meeting, talking briefly, then heading wordlessly into the woods behind the building. Old men, young men, lean men and fat. Truck drivers, students, state cops… I didn't want to know if any of them carried the blood. Kings, philosophers, poets, reduced to this. Reduced, for that matter, to places like The Bait. Royal parks had been ours, palaces, cathedrals. Now… No, the thought was too sad. I forced myself not to think about it.

I couldn't shake that mood. The roads were icy and treacherous, and progress was much slower than I'd have liked. When I finally got back to Pittsburgh, just around dinnertime, Bubastis sensed it. She jumped into my lap, licked my nose, did everything she could to make me feel warm and loved. Sweet cat.

I switched on the TV to catch up with the news. There was Rev. Heinrich and his ACM crowd; they were holding a news conference about the pernicious influence of "certain artists and musicians" on what they called "the family." I thought about my own family and laughed rather bitterly, I'm afraid.

It was the last thing I needed to see. I switched off the TV and curled up on the couch; a nap would be good. Bubastis snuggled up beside me and purred happily till we both fell asleep.

About an hour later, I was wakened by someone at the door. To my surprise it was Paul Koerner. He was grinning like a schoolboy with a star on his forehead. We shook hands and I invited him in out of the weather.

"Jamie, the coolest thing just happened. An agent offered to represent me."

I was still a bit groggy but I managed a smile. "That's great. You're good, Paul, you deserve it."

"He was at our concert last week. He loved me. Us. He says he wants to talk to you too."

An agent. I remembered my manners and showed him to the parlor. "Make yourself comfortable. Can I get you some tea?"

"No thanks. I don't need any caffeine right now."

"Hot cocoa then?"

"Sure." I hadn't noticed his smile before; it was really sweet. He followed me to the kitchen and I put on some water.

"So, who is this guy?"

"Rogers, Martin Rogers. I did some research on the Web. His agency's young but growing."

We sat at the table, facing each other. "He's the only agent, then?" Paul was on the nondescript side, brown hair, average height, not what you'd call especially sexy. We had known each other slightly around the department, but I can't say I ever really noticed him till we worked together. But he did have that great smile.

"No, he has an associate."

"Did he say whether he's heard me play? That's my real career. Conducting—that was just a course requirement."

"You might want to think about doing more, Jamie. You're good." Again that smile. Killer smile. His eyes were deeper brown than I realized, like fine chocolate. Roland was right—I was oversexed.

"Thanks, but it's the piano for me."

"Other instrumentalists have started conducting too, you know. Ashkenazy, Rostropovich… You can do both."

"Yeah, but—"

"You're really, really good. I mean, you brought out more depth in my singing than I ever knew I had."

"That was Vivier doing that, not me."

"You were the conductor."

"Even so." For a moment we looked at each other across the table, awkwardly wondering what to say next. Paul had the blood; I knew it as surely as I had known about Adam. It was a bit embarrassing to realize it—I had never paid much attention to him. He wasn't all that good-looking. Shallow Jamie. Not for the first time, I felt that corrosive guilt my Christian relatives had implanted in me when I was a boy.

Finally Paul shrugged and said, "It's too bad it's not going to work out."

I was a bit lost. "What?"

"The agent thing. We had a long talk, and he told me I'd pretty much have to go back into the closet before he'd agree to represent me. I told him to fuck off." Again that smile. "In pretty much those words." Then he laughed. "He couldn't have looked more surprised if I'd told him I want to perform in a red rubber nose and slap shoes."

It all caught me quite off guard. I'd been pursuing Kurt, odd Kurt, when all the time there was this sweet, open guy right under my nose.

He seemed not to sense what I was feeling. "I wonder, though. Jamie, do you think I did the right thing? I mean, it's hard enough earning a living as a singer." He laughed. "And a countertenor at that. Should I have blown off the first agent who was interested in me?

"It sounds like he was only interested in you as product."

He thought for a moment. "Yeah, I see what you mean. You're right. But then, isn't that what I'd be to any agent?"

"The world's changing, Paul. Slowly but surely. Attitudes like his are dying."

"They won't be dead in my lifetime."

"You never know how long you're going to live." I gave it a bit of emphasis.

I could tell the comment surprised him. The kettle whistled on the stove and I went to get it. I poured the water for the cocoa, leaned against the counter, and we stood watching each other a bit self-consciously.

"Anyway, I wanted to thank you again for asking me to do *Lonely Child*. I mean, you know the repertoire I sing, baroque stuff, early music stuff…" He shrugged. "That's what countertenors do. But singing the Vivier seemed to open my eyes to all kinds of new possibilities."

I shrugged. "You were the right singer for it, that's all. Somehow, I knew it right away." I shifted my weight. "Let me show you the house."

Unlike most of my visitors, Paul took to the place at once. The heavy Victorian architecture, the rooms full of portraits. It didn't take him long to realize they had all loved their own sex; and I think he made a few more connections that that, too. When he saw all the popes, he laughed. "I knew there had to be an explanation for all those silk dresses."

"I've always wondered how anyone can take the clergy seriously when they wear those preposterous costumes. Talk about performing while you're dressed as a clown."

He laughed. "They always look like really bad plus-size fashions to me."

And so we found our mutual bond, laughing at Christian apparatchiks.

When I showed him the guest room—my old bedroom—he noticed something I hadn't. A pair of white briefs was partially hidden under the bed. They were Adam's; they must have been. I actually blushed a bit.

"It's okay, Jamie. I'm a bit of a whore myself."

"I am not a whore." I said it dryly and with emphasis. "I am a *slut*."

We both laughed and went to the kitchen for our cocoa. Every time I saw his smile I liked him more.

He was a Pittsburgher, born and bred. Just after he graduated high school his family had moved to Indianapolis, leaving him on his own at West Penn. His hair wasn't quite brown, more sandy-red-blondish-brown, and his eyes were grayish-blue. He was three inches shorter than me. It turned out he lived about four blocks from me, but somehow we had never seen each other around the neighborhood.

His body was better than I expected, almost as good as the guys on the swim team. When we made love, it was good; not spectacular but definitely good. I'm afraid I nodded off for a moment or two when we finished—it had been a long weekend. When I opened my eyes he was watching me and smiling that smile. That made everything okay.

I wanted him to stay, but he had a paper to work on. It was still raining, and the rain was beginning to freeze; I tried playing on that, but Paul was a conscientious scholar, it seemed. Just as I was seeing him out the door, I saw Kurt coming down the sidewalk. Paul and I kissed lightly, the way men do who've just made love for the first time.

They passed each other. Paul smiled; Kurt didn't. He came up to me, looking unhappy. "I thought you were in New York for the weekend."

I didn't much like the implicit accusation. Or the implicit possessiveness. "If you thought that, why are you here?"

"I wanted to check, that's all."

"I'm not aware that I require checking, Kurt."

He looked after Paul, who had reached the street corner. "I wouldn't have thought he's your type."

I made myself sound lecherous. "He's a guy."

"Can I come in out of the rain?"

"If you promise no more jealousy."

"I'm not jealous."

"No. Silly me. Where did I ever get such an idea?"

In the parlor he looked around at the walls of portraits as if he'd never seen them before. "I don't think I'll ever get used to this place."

I smiled. "You invited yourself, remember? Would you like some tea?"

"No thanks. Listen, I…I wanted to tell you. I'm not sure we'll be able to play together much more."

"Oh." It was a mild disappointment, no more. "Why not?"

"I think I'm going to be signing with an agent." Suddenly he was all smiles, and all business.

"Don't tell me. His name's Martin Rogers."

"How did you know?"

"And he offered to represent you as long as you stay closeted, right?"

He looked to the front door as if he might see Paul still standing there. "You mean I'm not the only one he's…" He frowned. Suddenly his news wasn't quite so new. "I thought—"

"You're not going with him, are you, Kurt? I mean, everybody in the department knows about you. About us."

"'Us' is over, Jamie."

"Oh." It stung, I have to admit. "But even so…"

"No one ever saw us do more than be affectionate with each other. Nothing queer happened."

"Kurt, we kissed. In front of an audience."

"That was only a friendly kiss."

"You're deluded, Kurt, but it's okay with me."

"I just wanted to tell you, that's all." He got up to leave. "He's interested in you, too. He told me so. You should think about it. Maybe then, we could—"

"Unlikely."

"Oh."

I walked him to the door. But he was suddenly reluctant to leave. "Look, Jamie, we have a lot of potential together. All we'd have to do is—"

"Lie." I put on a tight smile. "Right?"

"Well, if you want to look at it like that. But, Jamie—"

"Can serious art be based on a lie?"

"That's what fiction is, isn't it? An elaborate lie?"

"You ever hear of Dr. Leonard Kubie, Kurt?" I leaned against the wall.

"Who? No."

"He was a psychoanalyst. Back in the 50s. You know who Vladimir Horowitz was, don't you?"

"Sure. He was one of the great pianists, maybe the greatest." He was a bit baffled by this, I could tell.

"Well, Horowitz was queer. And tortured by it, like a lot of men back then. He went to Leonard Kubie to be 'cured.'"

Suddenly he seemed to know where I was going with this. He reached for the doorknob. But I put my hand on top of his and stopped him. "Kurt, Kubie cured him all right. He was cured of being queer so thoroughly, he lost his ability to play the piano, too." There was a pause; he was having trouble grasping this. But I put on my best smartass smile. "Happily for the world, he got both back, his queerness and his talent."

Kurt pulled free of me and opened the door. "That can't be true."

"It is. Check any of the biographies."

He scowled at me. "This is bullshit, Jamie. I have this chance, and I'm going to take it. You should too."

"Denying your nature is a kind of voluntary death, Kurt. Any death you suffer after that is…I don't know, it's just a footnote. Remember that."

"Earning a good salary as a musician is a kind of life, Jamie. And it's a life I want."

He walked away without saying another word. I stood in the door and watched him go. Odd man. I still didn't know if he had the royal blood in his veins. Just at that moment, I didn't want to. A few yards down the street he slipped on a patch of ice and caught hold of a phone pole to steady himself. He looked back, saw that I was watching, and blushed.

Behind me I heard the furnace come on. Time to go inside and close the door behind me.

We had a really bad ice storm that night. The house was old, and there were drafts. I put an extra blanket on my bed and slept snugly, dreaming of Paul, then of Kurt.

The next night I found myself hungry. After I showered I saw myself in the bathroom mirror. I looked thirty at least.

Evans City, an hour north of Pittsburgh. It looked like every small town in Western Pennsylvania, only smaller and hillier. A stream, not much more than a creek, really, ran along one side of it. Half the buildings in town seemed to be closed, boarded up. Atop the tallest hill sat a church. The sign in front read Christ Is Coming. I wondered when he'd get there.

There was always a place, in every town, however tiny, however repressed. After two years, I knew instinctively where to look.

An alley ran behind the church, down the hill and into the poorest part of the town. There was a bit of a wind, terribly icy, and it made the bell in the steeple sway and ring softly. For a moment I thought there must be a service, and that people would be coming—the last thing I wanted. Then I realized it was a whisper of wind, nothing more.

In the beam of a streetlight a teenage boy leaned against a post. He wasn't wearing nearly enough for such a cold night. But his blood pulsed, hot and vibrant; I could feel it; I could almost taste it. Too young for me; too young to have a clear idea of his nature or what it meant.

In the next block, at a spot where the pavement was badly cracked, stood a middle-aged man, obviously drunk. We chatted. He had the blood I needed. He was dark, maybe Italian, some variety of Mediterranean. He told me time and again he "wasn't no fag." Then he got his cock out and asked me—told me, in the voice of a man used to being obeyed—to suck it. I sacrificed him. Ate. Drank. As I was taking the last of his organs his wallet fell out of a pocket and fell open. I saw the ID. He was a minister.

A wave of complete revulsion overcame me, and I vomited.

It was late. I needed blood.

The teenage boy had seen. I should have been more careful. He walked toward me; I was still bending over the clerical corpse. Wide-eyes, he asked me, "What did you do?"

I looked up at him; I couldn't think of anything to say. How could I explain?

Then his eyes went even wider. He turned and started to run.

"Stop!" I bellowed it; and he obeyed. "Come back."

He did. He was trembling.

"I'm not going to hurt you."

"You killed Reverend Mastranglis."

"He was a hypocrite. But the blood of men like him will keep me alive."

I compelled him to forget. But not too completely. I wanted him to *know*. "We need to feed on them," I told him, "instead of letting them feed on us."

The boy stared at me. "They don't kill us."

"Not literally, no. But they thrive on our bodies, our lives, our loves."

It seemed to be a new thought to him. "Are you going to kill me?"

I leaned forward and kissed him. "No. Go home."

"My parents—"

"Will believe what they want to, until you are ready to tell them the truth about yourself." I gestured at the remains of the preacher. "He never did. He lived on lies and on us."

"He was a reverend."

"Exactly." I watched him. He seemed unable to take his eyes off the dead hypocrite.

"Reverend Mastranglis was…I used to be his altar boy."

"And did you know about his back-alley life?"

"No." He was shaking again. "Yes."

I moved a step closer to him. "A hundred and fifty years ago Nathaniel Hawthorne, a great writer and one of our brothers, left this country, saying that the dominant trait in America's national character is hypocrisy. We, of all people, must be able to see what he meant."

He looked from me to the minister and back.

I touched my lips to his cheek and kissed him again, lightly. "Remember this night. Not consciously. Not the details. Not my face. But remember what you have learned. They cannibalize us. I sacrifice them."

He walked slowly to the corpse. "The police will investigate."

I shrugged. When I left, the boy was still there. I saw him kneel beside the body, touch his fingers to the dead man's blood, what was left of it, then taste it.

Seeing him do it, I realized the minister hadn't satisfied me. I had thrown too much of him up again. The next town was Butler, larger than Evans City. More men. It wasn't hard to find more of what I needed. When I got home I looked in the mirror again and was young.

CHAPTER 6

"Jamie Dunn?"

I was at the Z getting a quick, greasy lunch and trying not to let myself feel too glum about it. The young woman who'd called my name was coming through the crowd purposefully. I thought I recognized her. She was one of the leaders of the campus gay/lesbian group. They had approached me several times about joining, but I never really had the time, or the inclination. I made myself smile.

"Aren't you Jamie Dunn? The composer?"

"I'm Jamie Dunn, but I'm not really a composer. I play piano."

"We thought you were a composer." She was a bit plump, with hair dyed shockingly red and a bit too much makeup, like a half-hearted Goth.

"I'm a pianist, that's all."

"I'm Joe Maggio. We've met once or twice, kind of in passing." She said this as if she thought it would come as welcome news. It didn't.

"Joe Maggio? Like the baseball player?"

"That was *Di* Maggio." She grinned. "But I play it up for all it's worth. It impresses a lot of women."

"Nice to meet you, Joe." I held out a hand. I suppose I was a minor celebrity on campus; nothing like a football star, but some people recognized me.

"I'm co-chair of the Lesbian and Gay Rights Alliance."

"Oh?" I wasn't sure how to react. They probably wanted me to perform at a fund-raiser, which I would have been more than happy to do. "So your name doesn't impress the guys in the group, then?"

"Most of them don't know a thing about baseball." She laughed. "Listen, I need to ask a favor. We need a composer. A queer one. Do you know any? Students, I mean?"

Odd request. "If you could tell me what you need one for, maybe I can—"

"We're doing a play. For Christmas. A fund-raiser kind of thing, but a chance to raise some consciousness on campus, too."

"A play." I kept my voice neutral; this could be going almost anywhere.

"We're doing a gay take on *A Christmas Carol.*"

"I see." Just what the world needed was still another retread of that corny old thing.

"This closeted actor decides to come out after he's visited by the ghosts of Rock Hudson, Barbara Stanwyck and James Dean."

I hoped they were playing it for laughs. Done seriously, something like that would be ghastly. "You're doing it as camp, right?" I tried not to sound too hopeful.

"Yeah." She seemed not to get my meaning. "We argued a lot about who the main character should be. It had to be someone everybody knows is queer, but who isn't out. We finally settled on—" She named a well-known action star.

"I'd be careful. He likes to sue people. Usually for a million dollars."

"Don't worry, we're dropping lots of hints but not naming names." She scowled slightly. "Not that we're afraid of him. But we have to get this approved by the administration, and you know how they are. Did you know two of the trustees belong to that Alliance for Christian Morals?"

I hadn't known. I wondered if Roland did. "Listen, I know a couple of people in the department. Maybe I can connect you with one who—"

"Would you do it yourself?"

"I told you, Joe, I'm not a composer."

"You know a lot about music. You must. And having your name on the posters would sell some extra tickets. Besides…" She lowered her eyes a bit. "Half the guys in the group have crushes on you. Some of then actually skip student night at that disco downtown when they have a chance to hear you play."

"You're kidding."

"Nope. Even one or two of the women."

"If I'm going to have groupies, I want them to be guys."

She laughed. The ice was breaking.

"Do you think you need something original, Joe? I mean, maybe I could sit in on a rehearsal and then just improvise some things from the classical repertoire."

She thought for a moment. "Yeah, I think that would be great. You'll do it, then?"

"What are the dates for this thing?"

She told me. It was to run three times during the last week before the holiday break. And then she had an idea. "Maybe you could use music by gay composers." After an awkwardly silent moment, she added, "There are some, aren't there?"

"One or two, yes. I guess it's never occurred to the guys in your group, but I don't play much that isn't by queer composers."

Beaming, she gushed, "You're an activist!"

It was a new thought; I wasn't sure how comfortable it made me. "Well, a cultural activist, maybe. I guess."

"Wait till I tell the guys. I don't think they have any idea."

"Nobody does." I quoted Danilo. "Our history is kept hidden. They don't want to know the truth about us. And they don't want us to know the truth about ourselves."

"You're right." She smiled a sweet smile. "Most of the guys in the group are a bit afraid of me. I tell their futures."

"In this country, that's not too hard."

"I mean it." Again she smiled. "I'm two-spirit. I have the power."

She had to be joking. Activists. I decided to change the subject. The talk drifted into gossip about people on campus we both knew, which professors were sleeping with which athletes, that kind of thing. I decided I liked Joe. She told me she always made a point of spelling it with the final *e*. "Josephine—what kind of name is that for a dyke?"

That night Paul slept over. Our lovemaking was restless. Mostly, the problem was with me. Too much had been happening to me of late.

I dreamed. Danilo and I. Making love in the shadow of the Great Pyramid. He stood there, naked, powerful, He spread his beautiful wings and carried me high into the night sky. It seemed we would touch the moon.

Then we were on the ground again. The pyramid loomed over us, massive, immovable, unyielding. The entrance flew open and a cascade of blood poured out. Covered us. Thick, hot, it seemed ready to engulf us. I tried to clutch him but the river of blood carried him away from me. He was drowning. I reached out to him, clutched his hand, but it slipped away and I lost sight of him.

"Jamie! For God's sake, let me go!"

I woke. I was clutching Paul's hand, crushing it. He cried out in terrible pain. It was his bow hand. Horrified at what I'd been doing in my sleep, I pulled away from him and stood in a corner of the room.

"Jamie, for God's sake, what happened?"

"I had a nightmare." I barely whispered it.

"It must have been terrible."

"Are you all right, Paul?"

He was rubbing his hand, massaging it. "I think so. You could have broken it."

"I'm so sorry. I didn't mean to—"

"No, of course." He got up and put an arm around me. "Are you sure you're all right?"

I hadn't realized it, but I was shaking, quite badly. "I had the most awful dream about my old lover."

"The one who left you this house?"

I looked at him. I had never told him about Danilo. "How did you know?"

"People talk, Jamie. Everybody knows about you and your Egyptology professor." He pointed at my hand. "He gave you that ring, didn't he?"

For some reason it surprised me. "Do they know how much I loved him?"

"Have you ever heard gossip about love? You were on the make, or he was a predator. People don't want things to be more complicated than that."

I pressed myself close against him. "We were in love, Paul."

"I know."

"How could you?"

"Because I think I'm in falling in love with you, and I can feel you holding back. I knew there was someone else."

This was not a conversation I ever expected to have. I stepped away from him. "I'm sorry, Paul. I—"

"It's all right. I guess." He hesitated. "What happened to him?"

"I don't know." I was still shaken from my dream, and I felt tears coming. I had never talked about this with anyone before. "Paul, he just…left. Vanished."

"But he provided for you, Jamie. He must have loved you."

I think I needed Paul to hold me. But the spell was broken. He made an excuse, got dressed and left.

Love.

Blood.

Where was I?

The play was not good. Amateur theatrics; worse, yet, amateur *campus* theatrics. I sat through two rehearsals, making notes. There was a piano reduction of *The Nutcracker* in the music department library; that would work for most of it. Easy enough playing; it would be fun. I was glad Joe had asked me; a diversion would be good.

The auditorium was decked out for Christmas, trees at either side of the stage, wreaths on the wall, twinkling lights everywhere. Overdone, for my taste, but then Christmas had never meant much to me anyway.

Joe played James Dean and did a pretty good job. A drag queen named Bill something played Barbara Stanwyck and did a lousy one. A really cute guy name Tom Ilgenfritz played Rock Hudson; he wasn't good, but he was so attractive no one cared. Another woman in drag played "Tom Scrooge," which was also the name of the piece.

The posters went up a week before the play, and my name was featured more prominently than any of the actors. I found it a bit embarrassing. But Joe called me a day before the first performance and told me that having me do the music had sold a lot more tickets than they were expecting. The run was sold out.

Roland was amused by it all. His generation did not do such things; and I don't think he quite knew what to make of it. But I promised him a pair of tickets for opening night.

When the night came, Heinrich and his ACM crowd were there, protesting noisily, handing out brochures to everyone who went inside, or trying to. Joe was a bit alarmed, but I told her not to make a fuss or she'd only generate publicity for them.

"But Jamie, they'll scare people away."

"Take a good look. Most everybody's laughing at them."

She realized I was right. End of crisis. Minor crisis. They don't come much more minor.

Despite the lame acting and the mostly improvised music, audiences loved the show. I had no idea why. But I enjoyed doing it more than I'd expected to; at least it took my mind off a lot of other things. Too many other things. I actually found myself wishing I'd bothered to compose something original for the play.

At the opening night party Tom Ilgenfritz hit on me; I was tempted, but after what had happened with Paul...

Paul came. So did Kurt. I noticed them keeping their distance from one another. Lazar Perske was there. "Another wonderful performance, Jamie. It's not much of a play to be the star of, but even so." He made a funny face.

"I've been wanting to catch up with you, Dr. Perske."

"Call me Lazar."

"Lazar, then. I want to talk to you about Vivier. I want to hear everything you remember about him."

He frowned. "He was a good composer, but a terrible man. A complete whore. Slept with everyone he could. Students, faculty, hustlers... He should have been more discreet. He'd be alive today."

"You're blaming him for his death?"

"He was too open. He was asking for it."

"But Lazar, the guy who killed him—whoever he was—could just as easily have been the first trick he'd ever picked up."

"Survival is a matter of hiding our natures, Jamie. There's no other way. I mean, the way you kissed Kurt Sivers onstage…" He looked around, as if we were discussing something secret and he didn't want to be overheard. "Look at what's going on outside. Pastor Heinrich and his group. We have to be discreet."

For a moment I thought, that's just his generation talking. Roland had said pretty much the same thing to me once or twice, though not quite so bluntly. But Roland at least seemed to appreciate what the new generation had done. Perske seemed lodged in an earlier time.

He asked me if I'd given any thought to playing his concerto for him; I hadn't.

But I had a thought. I had also had a bit too much to drink. "Suppose we strike a bargain?"

He laughed. "What do you have in mind?" Every time we talked, I found myself trying to place his accent, but I never could, quite. Somebody said he was from Latvia or Estonia. Who knew?

"I've been giving a bit of thought to composing. Suppose you tutor me, and I'll play your piece in exchange."

He rubbed his chin. "My schedule's pretty full. I'm not sure I could—"

"That's the deal. I want to compose. I want an intensive course."

"Let me think on it for a few days." He looked around again, a bit distracted. "Suppose we talk after the holiday break."

"I'll be in your office first thing."

Over the two years since he had left, I'd spent as much time as I could going over Danilo's papyri. Not the ones at the campus museum, the private ones, the ones he kept for himself alone. Spells, rituals, incantations. Absurd as it must sound—absurd as it seems to me myself—I thought I might be able to use them one day. Do for someone else what Danilo had done for me. He had rescued me from the land of the dead. Perhaps, someday…

The final night of the play, the house was sold out. It meant a great deal of money for the club, and I was only too happy to help them. Lazar Perske showed up again. He came backstage and told me he simply had to hear me play one last time before the end of the semester. "You're the reason there are so many people here, Jamie. Not this silly play."

"That isn't true, Dr. Perske."

"Call me Lazar. And it is true."

I told him I didn't think so. I didn't want to believe it.

"I hope you thought about what we discussed last time. This kind of thing, this *activism*"—he said the word as if it tasted foul—"never accomplishes much. People prefer us to be quiet and not make waves. Why do you think I write the kind of music I do?"

"It may be a bit silly of me, but I thought art was supposed to be about what we prefer, ourselves. This is our night."

There was no point arguing with him. I thanked him for coming again, reminded him I'd be talking to him about a crash course in composition, then told him I had things to do before the performance began. His reaction was hard to gauge, something between disapproval and bewilderment, I thought; but he left.

The Christian Morals people were there again, protesting, handing out leaflets. One of them was about me and the way I'd supposedly sold my soul. Not by name, of course—they knew enough about the law to avoid getting too specific. But their protest didn't do them much good. The people who didn't simply ignore them treated them as a joke. Which was all they deserved.

Anyway, the performance went smoothly, best of the three, and the audience seemed to enjoy it. There was a lot of enthusiastic applause. Personally, I still thought the play was a bit silly, but there's no accounting for taste.

There was another party. The club seemed to like parties. But for whatever vague reason I was feeling restless. Something, some sense, some overpowering instinct told me there was somewhere else I should be. I had no idea what to make of it, but I was in no mood for cake and smalltalk.

The night was cold and clear, one of those crisp winter nights when everything in the world seems still. The morals protesters had gone. There were a thousand stars in the sky, visible even through the city glare.

A bright quarter moon hung over Academic Tower. The campus was dressed for the holiday; lighted garlands stretched across all the streets. The campus wasn't as crowded as it would normally be on a Friday night. The semester had ended that day; a lot of people had left already, and more would tomorrow. I decided to walk home.

Once I was off campus and in Shadyside, the streets were darker and the sky seemed even more crowded. Among the glistening stars I saw Mars. Danilo had taught me about it. It was the soul of the great god Set, the contrarian deity, the Egyptian god who, as Danilo always put it, teaches us that there are no gods. Bright; red as blood.

Someone was following me. I was sure of it. I stopped, planted myself firmly in the middle of the sidewalk and waited. After a moment he stepped out from where he'd been trying to hide, behind a telephone pole. It was Kurt.

"Jamie, I wanted to—"

"What do you want, Kurt?"

"I—I don't know. To talk, I guess."

"It's cold out. I want to get home."

"Can I come with you?"

"I'm afraid not."

I had the impression my aloofness was a bit baffling to him. "Jamie, can't we be friends?"

"I don't much like closet cases."

"I have my career to think of."

"And I have mine."

"I thought I was in love with you."

"Trust me, Kurt, a man like you could never give me what I need."

"I don't know what you mean."

"I know." I smiled at him.

"Jamie. We have to hide. It's the only way to survive."

Strange. He was the second one that night to say that to me. But if I didn't want to hear it from Perske, I certainly didn't want to hear it from someone I'd slept with. I told him to leave me alone, said a terse goodnight, and walked on. At the next corner I looked back over my shoulder and he was still standing there. I walked.

It was well past midnight when I got home. Idly I switched on the TV to the local news channel and sank into my favorite chair. It was the usual. Fires, traffic accidents, interviews with talking heads who "didn't think this kind of thing could happen in my neighborhood." Then they got to the national news wrap-up.

I still remember the words.

A young gay man lies close to death tonight in the town of Spartanburg, South Carolina. Sixteen year old Adam Pilarski is in critical condition at Spartanburg General Hospital. Preliminary reports say he was assaulted by his parents and other members of their church in a town just outside Spartanburg. Local authorities described them as members of an extreme, fundamentalist sect. Details are still coming in, but there are reports he was actually nailed to the church wall. We'll have more on this developing story as details come inv.

I went numb. Despite the numbness, I started to cry uncontrollably.

I had sent him to that. I had sent him home to that, believing it was the right thing to do.

Fifteen minutes later I had booked a flight. I caught a quick nap, packed and left for the airport. It was three-thirty. The sky was black and pocked with starts. In my bags were some Egyptian vials, little bottles of potions. I hoped no one in airport security would question them. If they did, I could handle it; but I didn't want to be slowed down.

The first daily flight to South Carolina was at six a.m. It was to Columbia; I arranged for a rental car to be waiting. Two hours till I could fly. I wanted wings, like Danilo's, but I had never learned how to…I had never learned much of anything. He disappeared before he could teach me what I needed to know now. Adam. Sweet, sad, Adam.

The flight was half an hour late. Then our landing was delayed. By the time I reached Spartanburg and found the hospital, it was late morning. I wanted night; I wanted stars, gods, even anti-gods.

A small group of reporters waited in the lobby. I got out a notebook and tried to look like one of them. "What's the latest?"

He wasn't expected to live. Despite myself, I felt more tears coming. He was upstairs. There were more details than had been released to the public. They had beaten him bloody. They had stripped him naked and nailed him to the church wall upside down. Then they slit his throat and bled him like a slaughtered animal because, as they said, his blood was tainted with the devil. The parents and the minister were in the local jail; the rest of the congregation, even though they had been party to it, had been let go.

The blood.

I had to reach him, do what I could.

I got the room number. Took the elevator. There was a sheriff's deputy on guard outside the room. I focused, I concentrated, and he let me pass.

Adam was unconscious, of course. Then had beaten him more badly than I expected; his face was severely cut, bruised, swollen. I'm not sure I'd have recognized him if I hadn't known. Despite that his skin was deathly pale. There were thick bandages around his throat. A few drops of blood had seeped; there were bright red spots. He was connected to more monitors than I had ever seen in a hospital room before. And he was being fed blood intravenously. The wrong blood. I knew it at once.

I walked to the bedside and touched his cheek. And whispered, "Adam."

No response. I had not expected one. I bent down and, gently as I could, kissed him on the kips.

He felt cold to me. I looked at the monitors, and they registered nothing. Frantically I felt for a pulse, and there was none. Adam was dead. He had died there, in that place, alone and unseen. I should have let him live with me. I should have...I should have...I had no idea what I should have done. Set was the only possible god, the one who acknowledged his own non-existence.

There was a single chair in the room. I pulled it up to the bed and held his limp, cold hand and cried. Several times I tried to stop, but I couldn't make myself. It seemed like I cried for eternity.

After I don't know how long, a nurse came into the room. I looked up and saw him standing over me. He was in his thirties. And I knew at once what he was.

He put a hand on my shoulder. "Were you his…his…?"

"No." I shook my head, as if the word itself might not be adequate. "Nothing that simple."

"Then…?"

"I can't explain. It would take too long. The blood they spilled was sacred blood."

"Sacred?" He took a step back away from me. "How did you get in here?"

"Never mind that. Where is the church? Where is the place where they did this?"

"About twenty minutes west of town. Out toward the Smokies, in the foothills."

"Tell me how to get there."

He did. I did not have to compel him. He seemed to understand, on some level, why I needed to know.

"You ought to leave, now. People will be coming. I could get in trouble. I don't know how you got in here in the first place."

I stood and started to leave. Some impulse made me stop and go to the bedside again. I kissed Adam another time. Maybe, I told myself, some tiny fragment, some particle of soul was still there in him, and would feel it, and would know.

The nurse touched my shoulder again. "Please. I could get in trouble."

I left. My car was parked half a block away. There was thick morning fog. The cold, damp air seemed hardly to touch me.

I followed his directions. As I got closer to the mountains, the fog got thicker. The church was a bit farther than he'd said, but I found it, off the main highway and up a dirt road. A crude sign announced Covenant Church of Spartanburg in Jesus, Riley B. Higgins, Pastor. The place was surrounded by bright yellow police tape, Police Line—Do Not Cross. I crossed.

A deputy sheriff approached me. He seemed to be the only one there. Young, twenty-something, blond, lean. "Hey, there! You can't go in there."

"I'm afraid I have to."

"This place is off limits. You'll have to leave." Idly he reached for the revolver at his hip.

"You don't understand. What happened here touches me." I tried to smile but couldn't. "In a very direct way. I knew the boy."

"You a faggot?" He got a firmer grip on his gun. I made him stop and keep quiet. Fog swirled around him, and he was still and obedient.

I crossed to him, took the gun out of his hand and tossed it into some undergrowth. Then I looked him up and down. Deep green eyes. Handsome. I kissed him, pushed my tongue as far into his throat as I could. And whispered to him, "Remember this."

The church door was off one hinge. I wondered if it had happened in the aftermath of Adam's death or if the place was simply falling apart.

Inside it was dark—filled with dim gray light—and cold. There was the most eerie stillness. The pews were simple, rough-hewn things. There were Bibles stacked at the end of each one. And pamphlets. Idly I picked one up. What kind of mentality could lead them to do what they had done? It was a brochure from the national headquarters of the Alliance for Christian Morals. I let it drop; holding it, merely holding it in my hand, made me feel dirtier than I already did in that place.

There was the wall where they had done it. Holes pounded into it. A pair of twelve-inch spikes lay on the floor. There must have been more; maybe the police had taken them. I picked them up, ran my fingers along them, and slipped them into my pocket.

And there was blood, the wall and floor were stained with it. More blood than I expected. More than seemed quite possible. So much it was still moist. The pool of it had dried to a dull brown around the edges, but most of it was still a wet, bright red.

Adam's blood.

I took a small bottle out of my pocket. Bright, deep blue, lapis lazuli. Ancient, three thousand years old. A little stoppered bottle. I filled it with as much blood as it would hold and replaced the stopper.

Part of me wanted to taste it. But that seemed…not right, for some reason; I didn't understand why. But I pushed my fingers into the pool of it and then rubbed it onto my face. It was still warm; quite miraculously it was still almost hot.

Outside, the deputy was still standing where I had left him. Not bothering to free him from my spell, I got into my car and drove off; my face was stained with the boy's blood.

CHAPTER 7

"Why? I want to know why you did it." I made my voice as forceful as I knew how.

Pastor Riley B. Higgins faced me through the bars of his cell. "You."

I had no idea what he meant. There was no way he could know me, or recognize me.

I could have left South Carolina, gone home directly from the church. Adam was dead and there was nothing I could do about it. And yet…there was something else that had to be done, if I was to sleep that night.

Spartanburg was not much of a city, even for the upcountry South. Hills all around; not much happening. There was a main square, a little park with a couple of old, unattractive statues; a small department store, pharmacy, the kind of thing you'd expect. And bars. Lots of bars. The park wasn't well-kept; there were weeds and cracks in the cement; a soiled American flag flew on a pole at the exact center. Most of the town seemed to be built with an unattractive brownish-red brick.

Desultory Christmas decorations everywhere, trees, twinkle lights, a nativity scene, didn't help. I thought I had learned something about the place from one of my old history classes—the Klan, maybe? I couldn't remember. But it fit. Even the trees looked bigoted.

I had stopped at a gas station and cleaned myself in the men's room. There was a glory hole. A good, conservative Christian glory hole. The South.

Word about the horrible death at the Covenant Church had spread across the country, and people were descending on the place. There was more activity than the place seemed to want to handle; by nightfall the town's population had doubled. TV crews, print reporters, state and federal law enforcement people, thrill seekers...

I found a room in a small old hotel, the Kaufman House, just off the square. Lucked onto the last one available. There were cheaper places, motels out on the interstate, but somehow an old place felt more right to me, even though there was another crèche in the lobby. Baby Jesus seemed to glare at me.

I asked the desk clerk what he thought about the killing. He looked up from his copy of the Spartanburg *Times* and asked if I was a reporter.

"Nope. Civil War tourist."

"In Spartanburg?"

I shrugged.

He did too, and he said, "If the kid was just a fag, he was asking for it."

Oh. "What if he was something more than 'just a fag'?"

He glared. "Can I get a bellhop to help you to your room?"

End of discussion.

The mayor's office issued a statement calling Adam's murder an "isolated incident." The state police did the same. There was word that the governor would be coming to town. How could a politician not come and say the right things? It hardly cost anything, and saying all the appropriate warm-fuzzy things hardly implied a commitment to do anything. I was beginning to understand why Danilo had always regarded America with a kind of detached, scornful amusement.

A few reporters had asked inconvenient questions about arresting the rest of Higgins's congregation as accessories and as co-conspirators, but no one in authority seemed to want to do it, and none of them would say why. When pressed by the few news people who actually seemed to care, they made statements about how powerless the people were to stop what their pastor did. Everyone seemed to want to believe this, so they did. Myself, I kept remembering the bromide the churches kept promoting all the time, that the church is the people. Then shouldn't the people be held responsible?

Higgins and the Pilarskis were being held in the local lockup but would be moved to a state facility as soon as possible, probably the next day. I had to act quickly. My night had been a long one. I went upstairs to my room, tipped the bellhop, thanked him for his offer of drugs or sex but told him no, called down and asked the switchboard to wake me at dinnertime, and went to sleep.

I didn't sleep deeply, and there were awful dreams. I thought I could hear Adam's voice. For a fleeting moment I found myself thinking the phrase, "uncomprehending cries." But I think he must have known all too well what was happening to him. His blood would have told him, even if he didn't know it any other way.

When my wake-up call came the sky was darkening. I looked out the window, and the square was all lit up. Less than a week till Christmas. I had a quick, light dinner in the hotel café, then asked the night clerk for directions to the jail; then I told him to forget I'd asked. By night there was less activity in town. Everyone was having dinner, having sex, whatever... No more breaking news, not till morning.

It was a small building, or smallish. That same dull borwn-red brick that hadn't been cleaned in decades, from the look of it. A string of foot-tall tinfoil letters proclaimed MERRY CHRISTMAS. There were bars on the front windows but not on the door; anyone could have walked right in. I did.

Two cops sat at side-by-side desks. One was reading *USA Today*. The other was the one I'd seen that morning at the church; he had a small TV on his desk and was watching CNN. Coverage of Adam's death was on. Neither of them seemed all that interested. Long day? There must have been others on the force, but I imagined they were out dealing with the press, working with the higher-ups, whatever. A scrawny plastic Christmas tree twinkled in one corner; there weren't more than a dozen little lights on it.

The cop from the church, the one with the TV, looked up at me. He must have been a jock when he was in school; he still had the body. "Yes?" He showed no sign of recognizing me.

"I want to see them." I couldn't quite bring myself to say their names.

"No one's allowed to see them."

"You will permit me to." I had compelled him to my will once already; another time would be nothing.

His partner put down his newspaper. "Who are you?"

"I want to see them."

"Look, buddy, you've already been told once you can't. You'll have to leave."

Focusing, imposing my will was easier every time I did it. They sat at their desks and said not a word as I took a set of keys and headed to the back of the building, where the cells were.

The Pilarskis were in the same cell; I found it odd. But then the family is the center of society. The mother was the older of the two; the father must have been ten years younger. They both looked a bit numb. And they were still wearing the clothes they must have had on when they were arrested, covered thickly with dried blood. Their son's. Apparently Spartanburg justice didn't involve clean clothes. Adam hadn't looked much like either of them. They both noticed me at the same time. The mother asked who I was. Without answering I moved to the next cell.

Higgins, like his parishioners, was still in clothing stained with Adam's blood. He must have been seventy. His skin, like his hair, was gray, if such a thing is possible. But even though we had never met before, he recognized me, as clearly as I recognized him. And I knew why. He had the blood, the royal blood in his veins. Alarmed, he asked loudly, "What are you doing here?"

"Why, pastor." I smiled. "You know who I am."

"No, but I know what you are."

My smile grew even wider. "What am I?"

"You—you've come here for vengeance. The boy was your Blood Prophet. I knew it."

Danilo had always told me that I was the prophet, myself. I didn't think he could have been mistaken. But I didn't want to be any such thing. I had never felt like a prohet; far from it. And the blood had pulsed so strongly in Adam…I had let myself hope that maybe *he*…

"But now you.!" His eyes widened. Had he made a mistake, killed the wrong man? "You are the one, aren't you?"

"Yes." It seemed wise to let him think so, even if I wasn't at all sure of myself. I stopped smiling. "But now me."

I unlocked the door of his cell. Stepped inside. He backed into a corner, or tried to; he stumbled and fell onto the bunk. "Please."

"Adam must have begged you for his life. What good did it do him?"

"Please, don't do this."

"Did he know? Did he understand? Did he see that the blood that flows in your veins was the same divine blood that flowed in his?"

Higgins was trembling like the frail old man he was. I was not moved to sympathy. When I looked at his face, all I saw was evil. "Please. He was...he was...he had to die."

"Pastor Higgins, so do you."

I leaped across the room and tore his throat open. Blood sprayed. His limbs twitched. He clawed at my face weakly, then he went still.

In the next cell Mrs. Pilarski cried out, "Help! Help!"

But the two men outside didn't come.

Her husband stood up. He was six inches taller than me and must have outweighed me by fifty pounds. Like his wife, he cried out for help; he shook the cell bars violently.

They watched as I completed the sacrifice. I used the golden knife. Drank his blood, ate his organs. The blood was especially strong in him, and it gave me an enormous high. Nothing I had felt since Danilo had exhilarated me so.

When they realized no one would answer their screams, the Pilarskis fell silent and put their arms around each other. But the horror showed in their faces. Calmly, slowly, I walked to the door of their cell and unlocked it. Danilo's blood and the spells he'd used on me had made me strong, much stronger than I looked.

"Please, mister." She was crying.

He rushed at me. I knocked him down.

"Please, mister." She repeated it.

"'Please, mister,'" I mimicked her. "Did your son beg you? I'll bet you laughed at him when the nails went in."

"Please, mister."

"The Greeks used to write tragedies about people like you."

"Pastor Higgins made us do it."

"You could have stopped him. You could simply have…not gone there."

Her husband climbed to his feet again and rushed at me. I caught him by the throat and shook him like a marionette. His wife screamed.

I tore Pilarski's head off, then smashed his wife's against the stone wall. My senses told me what I needed to know—no blood for me there.

When their bodies both stopped moving I went back to Higgins's cell. He had the blood; he denied his nature, more emphatically than anyone I'd ever known. And he had slaughtered a sweet boy who knew his own, or was beginning to.

I had understood what Danilo taught me, in an abstract way. To deny your nature is a kind of death. I understood that I needed the blood of such men to sustain myself. Now, for the first time, I understood why.

There was a bit more blood left in Higgins. I drank, and his blood gave me an enormous surge of energy. Even though it tasted foul, drinking it was the most fantastic thing short of sex.

Then calmly I went to the washbasin in the corner of his cell and cleaned myself. There were a few blood stains on my clothing, but my shirt and jeans were both dark. No one would notice. And if they did…

The night clerk at the hotel ignored me. I got my things together and left.

The flight home was turbulent. A winter storm was coming down from Canada, and we were flying directly into it. It was good I had gotten out of Carolina when I did, or I might have been trapped there. There would have been more questions, more eyes examining the odd young stranger. I'd have had to try and blend in with the press crowd.

The pilot advised us all to fasten our seat belts. It was already snowing in Pittsburgh, heavily; there was a chance we'd be diverted someplace else.

I tried to sleep. And inevitably there were dreams, dark, disturbing ones. I had killed often enough before that night. But always for sustenance, always to keep myself alive. I'd look in the mirror and see myself aging, see the gray hair and the wrinkles coming, feel the stiffness and pain in my joints and limbs, and I'd know it was time.

That night, for the first time, I'd killed for another reason. I hadn't needed Higgins's blood to stay alive or young. No. I wanted it. And I hadn't killed the Pilarskis for any reason other than a desire to kill them. Vengeance is mine, said the God of the Bible. He didn't have anything on me.

I was still high from the pastor's blood. It was better than wine, better than drugs. Whoever said that revenge is a dish best served cold didn't know what he was talking about.

And yet… Higgins knew me. Not just my blood, no, it wasn't just that instinct. He seemed to know me, personally. How could that have been?

The only thing I regretted was that I couldn't see to Adam's funeral rites. His body had been taken to a crime lab somewhere. The exact location was not revealed.

Mine was the last plane to land in Pittsburgh before they closed the airport. There were already eight inches of snow on the ground, and there was no sign of the storm letting up.

It was nearly midnight. From my window I saw snowplows clearing the runway for us. By the time we landed it was already covered again. Winters in Ebensburg had always tended to be fierce, but I'd never seen anything like this. By the time I collected my bag and got out of the airport, there was nearly a foot.

My car was one of the few still in the airport lot. I started it and let the engine warm up while I cleared the snow. By the time I was finished, I was covered myself. Clouds of snow.

They had cleared part of the lot, but things finally reached the point where even the plows couldn't keep up with it. I drove slowly, steadily, and made it out of the lot and onto the parkway. I'd get home all right; just be patient, Jamie, take your time.

The snow seemed to be coming in thick waves. The wind whirled it into mini-cyclones. There weren't many other cars on the road; people had sense enough to stay in out of this. But I had to get home. I needed to feel Danilo's presence, at least by proxy. Would he approve of what I'd done?

I switched on the radio. They would have discovered the three corpses by now. How were they reporting it? But the airwaves were filled with nothing but the snowstorm—traffic warnings, school closings and the like. It was just as well; I turned it to my favorite classical station. They were playing Brahms. Annoyed, I switched it off again.

Part of the parkway was a long, descending grade. I kept my foot on the brake and took it slowly. Large, heavy flaked danced in the yellow glow of sodium vapor lights. Mine was the only car in sight. I glanced at my watch: midnight.

Suddenly he reared up in front of me: There, in the glow from one of the lights. Ten feet tall, maybe twelve. Lean, muscular body, beautiful chest and legs, but I was too frightened to appreciate them. Wearing only a white linen loincloth. Holding a scepter in his right hand. Head of an animal, that strange, unidentifiable creature with a long, pointed snout and long, long ears.

It was Set. It was the Great God Set.

There.

In front of me.

I slammed on the brake. The wipers worked furiously, clearing the windshield of snow. I looked up at him as he loomed directly in front of me.

Slowly, almost majestically, he held out his scepter. And in a deep, resonant voice he pronounced, "You are my divine son. I am well pleased with you."

There was a sudden squall, blinding white, and when it passed he was holding something in his arms. Or rather, someone. I stepped out of the car and walked slowly toward him, or them.

Adam. The great god held Adam's limp body in his arms. Adam looked like a toy there, a doll being held by a beautiful young man. When I was ten feet from them, another squall came, worse than the one before. And they were gone. The god had blessed me, had taken Adam to his bosom, and vanished. Stunned by what I had seen, I climbed back behind the wheel and drove on.

By the time I reached downtown Pittsburgh the snow seemed to be letting up a little. I was still stunned. What I had seen could not have been real. Adam's corpse was in Carolina. I was high, terribly high from the preacher's blood. That's what had given me the vision. Set was a myth; he was the god who proclaimed his own non-existence. I could not have seen him. If that was what drinking blood when I didn't need it meant, I determined then and there that I would never do it again. For life, yes. For any other purpose…I could not enter that kind of voluntary madness another time.

But what if the vision was real? What if Danilo's god really had been there, really had blessed me?

The city was blanketed, and the work crews were having a hard time keeping up with it. Main roads were barely passable; the secondary ones were not. It seemed to take forever to get home.

At least the storm was passing. When I finally reached Shadyside, the snowfall had tapered to heavy flurries. It would be over soon enough. But there was more than a foot on the ground. I had to get out of the car and leave it running while I shoveled a parking space.

I hadn't been at it more than a minute or two when I saw someone coming toward me. A man, dressed in a thick, hooded parka.

"Jamie! Where on earth have you been?" It was Paul. I couldn't have been more surprised to see him. Or, frankly, more happy.

I invented a story about having to go "home" to Ebensburg on some vague business.

"Do you have another shovel? I'll help you."

I didn't. He watched. It didn't take me long.

Inside, he threw his arms around me. "I was so worried about you."

"I'm a big boy, Paul. I can take care of myself."

"Can you? What if you'd gotten caught?"

"I don't know what you mean."

It was pretty obvious he knew something. He backtracked. "Caught in the snowstorm, I mean. You could have driven off the road and frozen to death." He smiled as he was saying it; it wasn't what he had meant at all. "Anyway, I had to see you, tonight."

I was still climbing out of my winter things. "Why, for heaven's sake? It's the middle of the night."

"When better?"

"You should be home in bed."

"The weather outside is frightful. But your smile is so delightful."

Bubastis came trotting out from wherever she'd been and rubbed herself against my leg. I picked her up and nuzzled her.

"There, you see, Jamie? I came for some of that."

"You're lying." I made myself grin at him. "But it's a nice lie. Let me put on some water for cocoa, okay? Make yourself comfortable."

But he followed me to the kitchen. While I was filling the kettle, he came up behind me and threw his arms around me. I let him. "It's good to see you, Jamie. I'm glad you got home safely. But you must have heard about the storm. Why didn't you just stay in…Ebensburg?"

I turned and kissed him. "My cousin Millie and I don't really get along."

"In a motel, then."

"This weather's horrible enough. Can you imagine sitting it out in a Motel Six?"

"There's always the Gideon Bible."

"You're a sick man, Paul."

A few minutes later we sat in the den with big mugs of hot cocoa spiced with cinnamon. Bubastis crawled between us and lay there purring happily. She seemed to like Paul a lot. But what the hell was he doing there?

We made smalltalk for a while. Lazar Perske had been all over the department looking for me, it seemed.

"Why, Paul? We're on break."

"I asked him. He said he was anxious to start coaching you in composition." Good performer that he was, he paused for dramatic effect. "I didn't believe him."

"What do you think he wanted with me?"

96

Another pause. "You tell me."

"You're being awfully cryptic, Paul."

"It's in my blood."

I narrowed my eyes and stared into his. "What are you talking about?"

"Tell me the truth, Jamie. Please."

"I have."

Quite abruptly he changed tack. "Let's watch some television."

"The weather outside is frightful, but TV is so delightful?" I reached for the clicker, but I couldn't hide my puzzlement at what he had on his mind, mixed with a touch of caution.

The set was tuned to TCM. Bette Davis in *The Great Lie*. He took the remote out of my hand and switched to CNN. As it happened, they were doing a live update on the killings in Spartanburg. A talking head stood in the main square, in what looked like two feet of snow. He explained that the murders, first of Adam Pilarski, then of his parents and the minister accused of killing him, had "rocked the town to its foundations." Trust TV news to use the handiest cliché.

No one had any idea how the killer or killers had gotten into the security section of the town lockup, he said. There had been two officers on duty, and neither of them had seen or heard a thing.

Then they ran some footage from earlier in the day. The crowd of reporters in the hospital lobby, waiting for an announcement. There among them was me. Paul switched off the TV with a flourish. "There. We both saw it."

"It was someone who looks like me." I pulled away from him. "Haven't I ever told you about my evil twin?"

"In that shirt."

I hadn't changed. I couldn't think of a thing to say.

"I want to know what you were doing there, Jamie." I could tell from the tone of his voice that he was sincere, that he was genuinely concerned.

I wasn't at all certain how to explain it, and I decided to tell him as little as I could to satisfy his curiosity. "Do you ever pay much attention to the audiences at our recitals, Paul?"

"Answer my question."

"I am. Do you?"

I had thrown him off balance. "Well, sure. I mean, I try to. Any good performer has to be in synch with the audience. But—"

"You remember a kid who kept coming to those early concerts, back at the beginning of the school year? Tall, dark-haired boy. Boyish face. A bit grimy, dressed in dirty clothes?"

"I think I know the one you mean. He used to cry a lot."

"That's him."

"But—"

"Paul, that boy was Adam Pilarski."

It shocked him. It showed.

I told him about Adam, about how he ran away from home to hear me play. Told him how he had spent the night at my place, and how I had sent him home. All I left out was the stuff he couldn't understand, the royal blood that had flowed in Adam's veins, as it flowed in mine. Blood Adam's parents and Higgins had drained away. The bottle I had filled with it was still in my pocket. I could hardly tell Paul about that.

Idly I reached into my pocket and fingered it. It was warm. It must have picked up my body warmth. It couldn't have been anything else. But the warm touch of it startled me.

"What's wrong, Jamie?"

"Nothing."

"There's something you aren't telling me."

"No."

"What do you know about who killed the parents and the preacher/"

It was making me uncomfortable. "He was a sweet kid, Paul. When I heard what happened to him… I wanted to see him in the hospital, that's all. He liked me, and I don't think he had many other friends. I thought if I showed up there, it might…it might…I don't know, it might comfort him or cheer him up or something."

"And that's why you were posing as a reporter." My story was only making him more suspicious.

"I was not 'posing as a reporter.' I just happened to arrive at the hospital when a press briefing was taking place, that's all." I had to put a stop to this. "I don't think I like being cross-examined, Paul."

He softened. "Sorry. I don't mean to sound like that. But when I saw you there, on that newscast earlier tonight… I mean, what could I think?"

I kept silent.

"All I could think was that you were mixed up in it in some way. When I heard about the boy's parents and pastor being killed in the prison…"

"They don't know who did it or how, Paul. Do you think I can walk through walls?"

He took a long swallow of cocoa. "Who do you think did it, then?"

I shrugged. "Someone with magical powers, obviously."

"Someone who's suspected of selling his soul?"

I pulled away from him and moved to the far end of the couch. "Can we please not talk about this anymore?"

"Sure." He took another drink. "I really am sorry. I was just concerned, that's all."

The footage of the crowd of reporters came on again. There I was, sticking out like somebody's broken thumb, easier to spot than I'd realized the first time.

Paul inched toward me. "I can't help being concerned, Jamie. I think I'm falling in—"

"Don't say it."

"Well, I think I am. So there."

He took me by my shoulders and kissed me. It felt good. After two years of sex, not love, it felt wonderful. I kissed him back, hard.

Then he seemed to have a sudden thought. "You do realize what this means, don't you?"

"About us? Well, I—"

"No, what it means about *you.*"

I wanted to be kissing him, not talking more. "What do you think it means about me?"

"Jamie, that kid ran away from home to hear you. To be with you. You have that much power in your music."

I wasn't following. "Yeah? And?"

He took a deep breath. "He won't be the last."

It hadn't occurred to me before, but he probably had a point. I didn't know what to say.

"He won't. Hell, I've heard you play often enough myself. I mean, I've gone out of my way to hear you. Changed plans, shirked obligations."

Joe had told me the same thing about some of the guys in the campus gay group.

Unsettling thought. Danilo had always said I held more power than I could realize. He called me the Blood Prophet, the one who was destined to restore our line to greatness. I had always taken it for love-talk, the kind of thing an older man might say to his younger lover, to keep his spirits up or bolster his confidence or whatever. The thought that it might actually be true, that I might be…that I might be whatever it was Danilo said… No, I couldn't think about that. Just keeping myself alive was burden enough.

But Paul was on a roll. "You have that kind of power, Jamie. You could rule the world." He laughed. He wasn't being serious about that, at least.

"You sound like a character in an old 'mad scientist' movie."

"Just call me Renfield." He did a pretty fair imitation of Dwight Frye in *Dracula*.

"Paul, you're an old movie buff! I never knew! Let's watch something."

He punched me playfully. "I've never known anyone so obstinate about changing the subject."

So I did Bela Lugosi. I waved my fingers like I was trying to hypnotize somebody. "Ve vill vatch a classic movie."

He kissed my fingertips playfully. "That's it. Dominate me."

I leaned forward to kiss him, but he ducked and slid down to the floor. "I want to worship you, Jamie. I want to be yours completely."

No one had ever propositioned me in quite that way before. I wasn't certain what to say, or what to make of it. But I have to admit it was a turn-on.

Paul took hold of my leg, leaned down and kissed my boot. Then he looked up at me and let me kiss him.

"I'm yours, Jamie Dunn."

For a long moment I looked into his eyes and didn't answer. That kind of domination game—I had never played it before. But, to my surprise, I found it was really exciting me.

Christmas came.

Paul didn't have any family, at least not any he wanted to spend the holiday with. They had rejected him. Apparently being queer wasn't the issue. When he told them he was going to train as a countertenor, that was too much. Not a masculine enough job for them, or something. Not that Paul was queeny; it was just his career choice they had a problem with. Anyway, we were together, happily so. I tried not to think of us as master and slave, but more and more that was they way our relationship was developing. He waited on me, scrubbed my back in the shower, cooked for me… The business of being strictly a top was new to me, and I liked it.

The holiday didn't mean much to me. It didn't hold the kind of pleasant memories it did for most people. All I could remember were my relatives giving me gifts—grudgingly—then lavishing their attention and their affection on their own kids. I was the orphan, Oliver Twist with everything but the gruel. All Christmas ever did was emphasize the fact I wasn't one of them.

Christmas with Danilo had never been a big deal. We exchanged presents, but we did that all the time anyway. They were expressions of love, not holiday observances. For Danilo, Jesus Christ was an upstart. He'd told me that Christ was part of our bloodline, but whenever I pressed him for more details about him, he shied away from the subject. The only thing he ever said about him was, "He was a pretty considerable fool."

After a while I reined in my curiosity. The god for me—for *us*—was

Set, the god who taught us the possibility of chaos, of meaninglessness, of godlessness. The god who, given his will, would have chosen that we not worship or even know him.

Anyway, Paul and I bonded. By the time the new semester started, we had begun to settle into a domestic routine. Paul kept his own apartment, but he was nearly always at my place. I played for him, Chopin, Satie, Schubert… He was especially fond of baroque music. When I pointed out that Handel had been one of us, he had me play some of his keyboard sonatas again and again. He sang some of Handel's arias, and I accompanied him. And when one of the local choirs performed *The Messiah*, he insisted we go.

When they sang the "Hallelujah Chorus," he laughed and whispered to me, "This music belongs to us."

His subservience was domestic and sexual, nothing more. He kept raising the question of what had happened in Spartanburg. It was pretty clear to me that he didn't believe my story, at least not completely. And he kept dropping broad hints that he knew, or at least suspected, that there was more to it than I was admitting.

CHAPTER 8

The winter was a rough one. There seemed to be more snow every day or two, and temperatures were arctic. That first terrible storm proved to be a harbinger of things to come. For the first time since I moved to Shadyside, I actually found myself taking the bus to school and back instead of walking. And I felt guilty about it; I spent a lot of time doing extra laps in the pool to make up for it.

Because of all the snow, the campus was more subdued than I'd ever known it. People going from one building to another, even if it was only a matter of a few feet, were bundled heavily against the weather, and they moved as quickly as they could.

Roland had trouble coping. He had developed arthritis, and the cold left him in a good bit of pain. When it was especially bad, he walked with a cane; seeing it always startled me.

But instead of bringing him down, it only made him feistier. He was grumping rather magnificently, all the time, about everything. Especially the weather. "I had an offer to go to the University of Miami. But no, I had to be loyal to dear old Pittsburgh. Why do they even build cities in places where it gets like this?"

"Be serious, Roland." I always tried to prick his balloon, knowing it was full of nothing but hot air. "There are three rivers here. This was an important trade center. There was money to be made."

"Rubbish. Someone who wants to make money can make it any-where. There's no excuse for putting a city in a place like this."

"But Roland—"

"Look. Let's say it's 1750, and you've decided to emigrate from the Old World to the New. You have a range of choices. You can go to Ja-maica, to Cuba, to the Virgin Islands…or to Pittsburgh. Why would anyone—*anyone!*—pick Pittsburgh?"

"There were beavers here, Roland. The fur trade—"

He cut me off with a loud harrumph and stalked out of his own office.

Oddly, unexpectedly, I also found myself developing a relationship with Lazar Perske. His concerto was easy enough to master, more of the same simple-minded neo-medieval, faux church stuff he always cranked out. But to my surprise he turned out to be a good, lively composition coach.

I had learned all the basics in my other classes, of course. Four years of music theory, conducting and such had given me a good groundwork. Harmonics, sonata from, modulation…

What Perske was good at was giving me a sense of architecture, of the overarching structure a work had to have. And he did it not by requiring me to study more music, but by reading novels. Classics, contemporary work, and everything in between. *Oliver Twist, Catch-22, Burmese Days, Childhood's End, The Sot-Weed Factor, The Sheltering Sky, The Time Machine…*

From our discussion about each of them I learned. And my own grasp of what I wanted to do musically became firmer and clearer.

I asked him once why he had selected the particular novels we were using. "He shrugged. "They're clear, they're well-written, and they're all brilliantly structured. Ask any seasoned artist. It's all about structure."

"I had figured that out." I smiled at him. "You're a good teacher."

"Why, thank you." He seemed genuinely surprised to hear it. "Of course, the one book that really counts is the Bible. But not for structure." For the first time, he smiled. "Only for the truth. You're not a Christian, are you, Jamie?"

"Not according to the Alliance for Christian Morals, no." The question made me more than a bit uncomfortable. Under the university's ethics policy, he shouldn't have been asking. I hoped turning it into a joke would deflect it.

"You should be washed in the blood of the Redeemer."

I was tempted to tell him there was a lot fresher blood I preferred. Instead I said, "That sounds so unsanitary."

But he pressed on. "The kind of music I write… Some people scoff at it. You know that. But I hope it might help fuel a revival of the great days when Christianity dominated the Western world."

"That's a great idea." I finally caved in and turned smartass, as usual. "You get the stakes and kindling, I'll bring the gasoline."

So his evangelism was getting him nowhere. Thankfully, he let go of it. "Do you have any idea what you want to compose, yourself?"

"I've had an idea at the back of my head for a long time. For a symphony."

"A symphony?" He laughed. "Don't you think you should try walking before you learn to run?"

"When I was a kid and wanted to learn how to swim, my first coach picked me up and threw me into the pool. I learned, all right."

"I'd be cautious, Jamie. Swimming, all you could do is drown. Write something bad, and no one will ever take you seriously again. You'll be that brash, overconfident kid who bit off more than he could chew. It'll color your whole career, not just as a composer but as a performer too. They'll laugh."

"I know I can do it, Lazar."

"What's it to be about, then?"

"Hadrian. I want to write a *Hadrian Symphony*."

"A—! Do you remember that conversation we had once before? You mustn't flaunt. It could be fatal. The classical music world is the world in small, Jamie."

"I see it the other way around. Denying your nature is a kind of death. And art is supposed to be the essence of life."

"The audience isn't ready. The classical world isn't ready."

"Corigliano's first symphony was unabashedly about AIDS. And it was a major success."

"Even so."

"And who knows what Claude Vivier would be writing if he was still alive? *Lonely Child* can only have been the beginning."

"No one ever plays his music. It's tainted by his sinful life. And by his sinful death." He had said things like this before, when I'd asked him about Vivier.

I decided to ignore it. "Listen, Hadrian's life falls neatly into four movements." I ticked them off on my fingers. "His youth. His ascent to the throne of the empire. His first meeting with Antinous and the passionate love that grew between them. Antinous's death, Hadrian's grief, and their mutual triumph when Antinous was made a god." I smiled, a bit smugly. "I even have a few themes in mind. I haven't really started developing them yet, but you've given me a lot of ideas, and—"

"Jamie, don't do this."

"I have to."

He scowled; he clearly thought I was committing career suicide. Or was it the closeted Christian in him that bristled at the idea?

Another time I asked him what he knew about ancient Egyptian music.

"Not a thing. Why?"

"Because Hadrian was a pharaoh." I didn't want to tell him anything too direct. "There are temples in Egypt, built during his reign, that show him in the style the Egyptians had always used for their kings. I think it must have been the only way they could think about him."

"He was an emperor, not a pharaoh."

"The Egyptians didn't think so. They honored his royal blood, as they'd honored all their kings before him. And Antinous died in Egypt. I saw the spot. I swam in the Nile there, myself."

He narrowed his eyes. "Are you still holding on to that idea for your symphony?"

"I thought trying to get a bit of the music of old Egypt into it would make my work that much richer." And it would be my little homage to another pharaoh. I still loved Danilo, and I had no idea where he was, but at least I could honor my memory of our love.

"Well, I don't know a thing about it." That was that.

I got up to leave. When I opened the door, Kurt was standing there. He tried to look casual, but it was pretty obvious he'd been eavesdropping. I smiled at him. "Hello, Kurt."

Abashed at being caught, he blushed, a rich, bright red. "Hi, Jamie. Is Lazar in his office?"

Shit-eating grin. "Who do you think I was talking to in there?"

He turned even redder, went in and closed the door behind him.

Every time we met, he seemed odder to me. Why hadn't I noticed when we first met? Or was I too overcome by his blond, squeaky-clean, Hitler Youth good looks? Not for the first time, I wondered why sex makes us so stupid.

Danilo's house fascinated Paul. Time and again I'd find him studying the portraits on the walls, or going through Danilo's books and manuscripts. It always seemed to fill him with a kind of enthusiasm.

One day when I found him studying the portraits, he turned to me and asked, "Where are the auto mechanics?" He was directly in front of signed photographs of Ludwig Wittgenstein and Friedrich Nietzsche.

I had no idea why he would ask such a thing. "I beg your pardon?"

"Where are the auto mechanics? And the trash collectors? And the refrigerator repair men? Why are there only philosophers and composers and scientists and such?"

It had never occurred to me to wonder. But the answer was obvious. The men on the walls were royalty, great figures who changed the course of human thought and civilization. There must have been scores, hundreds, tens of thousands more who lived their lives quietly and never accomplished much. And it was for them that Danilo had lived. Reviving the greatness of our bloodline would raise all of us in the world's esteem. Or at least that was what I thought. Danilo and I had never talked about it, so I could only guess.

"I don't know, Paul." I tried to evade the question. "I didn't collect these."

"But you keep them."

I shrugged. "They were Danilo's. I loved him."

He wasn't satisfied. He never was when we started talking about things like this.

I tried to change tack and asked him if he'd ever come across anything about ancient Egyptian music.

"Nope. I haven't actually read too many of the manuscripts around here. I would have thought you had. It's all those portraits that fascinate me. Why? Why would he turn this house into such a shrine?"

I wouldn't let him draw me into it. "I haven't read quite all of them. If you find anything about music, let me know, okay?"

There was one portrait in particular that seemed to hold his attention. It was among the medieval kings. Done in that stylized, almost abstract style from the Middle Ages. It was labeled "Edwarde Plantagenet."

Time and again I found Paul looking at it, studying it. "I've seen this guy, Jamie, I swear it."

"I doubt it. He died eight hundred years ago."

"No, I've seen him."

"Paul, all the kings in these look pretty much alike. It's medieval art."

"Not this one. I've seen him."

"You must be a secret dope fiend, or something."

"I'll figure it out. By the way, did you know your old boyfriend's been hanging around here?"

For a moment I thought he meant Danilo. "What?!"

"Kurt Sivers. I've seen him outside three or four times now."

"He must be passing on his way to school or something."

"He lives on the North Side."

"Oh." And he'd pretty clearly been following me on campus, too, at least that time at Lazar's office. I didn't want to think about it. Two years earlier I had seen what horrific things jealous ex-boyfriends were capable of. I didn't think Kurt could be another Greg Wilton, but... I let the subject drop.

In the basement of the house was the room where Danilo had revived me when Wilton cut my throat. In the center was a gleaming alabaster sarcophagus. All around were other objects taken from Egyptian tombs. Authentic things; magical ones. I kept it carefully locked.

One afternoon when I was late coming home from campus, Paul was nowhere around. It was almost dinnertime. His things were there, as usual, his backpack and such, but there was no sign of him. Then I noticed the door to the basement was wide open. As quietly as I could, I went downstairs.

Paul had forced the lock on the room. Inside, torches and candles were burning, dozens of them.

I stepped inside. At first glance there was no sign of him. And then I saw him. He was lying in the sarcophagus, arms crossed like a corpse or a mummy. It was the oddest moment.

"Paul." I kept my voice soft. The objects in the room were sacred; this was a holy place.

Startled, he sat up. "Jamie! I—I—"

"What are you doing here?"

"I—I—" He stammered and groped for something to say.

"I had this room locked, Paul. You shouldn't have broken in."

"I didn't break in. I picked the lock, but it still works."

"That doesn't make it any better. Please get out of that thing."

Abashed, he did so. It was hard to tell by the bright orange light of the torches, but I thought he was blushing a bit. He stood beside the sarcophagus and dusted his clothes off.

I needed to be the master for real, this time. "Please go upstairs."

Silently he did so. I extinguished all the flames, pulled the door shut, made certain it really was locked, made a mental note to get a combination lock and went up.

He was sitting at the kitchen table. When I entered, he avoided looking at me.

I tried to make my voice as stern as I could. "Well?"

He looked up at me. "You mean you can't guess?"

"This isn't a game show, Paul. I want to know why you've been pretending to love me and what you were doing downstairs."

"I have not," he said loudly and firmly, "been pretending to love you. I do." He waited for me to say something, but I kept quiet. "Really, Jamie, I do."

Still I remained silent.

"And Jamie, I loved Danilo, too."

"What?!" I lost my composure. If he had told me he was the living incarnation of Mickey Mouse, it couldn't have startled me more.

"I had him for Egyptology 101. Spring semester, freshman year.

Right before you took that summer course from him."

"Why haven't you told me so before?"

"I fell in love with him. We even…well, it was a tiny bit mutual."
This hurt.

"But only a tiny bit, Jamie, honestly. We…we slept together once or twice. He brought me here, and told me about the portraits on the walls, about how they were all queer like us, and we made love."

"That's all he told you? Just that they all loved men?"

He nodded but didn't say anything.

I was numb and getting number. I sat down at the table opposite him. But I couldn't make myself look at him. "So what has this been about? You've been using me to be near Danilo's things?"

"It started that way, yes. I really was in love with him. Hopelessly." He tried to reach across the table to take my hand, but I pulled away. "And I really am in love with you, I think."

"You think." I made my voice as cold as I could.

"I used to see him with you around campus. At first I was jealous. Then, later…"

"Yes?"

"Then later I wanted you both."

This was coming at me too fast. I had no idea what I wanted to let myself think, or feel.

"He broke it off with me, Jamie. And it hurt more than I can tell you. He said he thought I was the one, but now he knew I wasn't. He had found the one, the true one he had been waiting for. At the time I thought he meant his true lover, but he meant more than that, didn't he?"

I was lost, completely lost.

"When you asked me to sing *Lonely Child,* my first impulse was to say no. But then I realized it would bring me one step closer to Danilo."

"Silly me. And I thought it was the music."

"It was. The first time I read through it, I knew. And then there was you. When you conducted, when you coached me, I could almost hear Danilo's voice. He may have left you, but part of him is still in you,

Jamie. That was when I started to—"

"I don't know what you expect me to make of all this."

"I don't know what to make of it myself."

He reached for my hand again. This time I let him take it. I had no idea why; I didn't really want to, but...

"How well did you get to know him, Paul?"

"Not nearly as well as I wanted to."

"He brought you here. What did he tell you?"

"About what?"

I'm afraid I raised my voice and yelled. "About himself, damn it. About this house and why he has all those pictures. About the blood of kings."

Softly he responded, "I don't know anything more than I said about any of that. I only know what I feel. And I know there was more to him than he ever told me." For the first time he looked directly at me. "And I know there's more to you. And I know it's the same thing."

I let go of his hand. Got up and went around the kitchen, straightening things. No one was supposed to know. No one. "Should I make some tea?"

"Don't try and change the subject. Jamie, I want to know."

"I have some good Earl Grey."

"Jamie!" He almost shouted it. Then he caught himself and said softly, "Please."

I have to admit that in that moment I was terrified. If I didn't tell him enough to satisfy him, he would keep at it. That was clear. And if I told him too much and he panicked and went to the authorities… Weakly I said, "There's nothing to tell, Paul. We were lovers, that's all."

"No."

I stared at him.

"Do you think I can't see? Danilo used to age, then turn young again. He tried to tell me it was my imagination, or a trick of the light. But it was true. I even tried to joke him into telling me—I said he was like Orson Welles in *Citizen Kane*, older in one scene, younger in the next. But he kept telling me I was imagining it.

"And I finally decided maybe he was right. I was in love, I wanted my lover to be mysterious, so I dreamed up this mystery. But when I met you—started to get to know you—and saw the same thing…"

As forcefully as I could I told him, "It's your imagination all over again."

"No, it isn't. I have photographs. They take pictures at the parties after all the recitals, remember? Sometimes you look like you're in your thirties. Tonight you don't look any more than fifteen or sixteen."

"Flattery will get you nowhere."

"Don't try to turn this into a joke."

We were sitting, facing each other across the kitchen table. There was no way out. "What do you know, Paul? Or what do you think you know?"

He buried his face in his hands. "None of it makes sense. That's why I need you to explain it."

The telephone rang. I had never been so grateful to hear that sound.

"Hello?"

"James Dunn?" It was a woman.

"Jamie Dunn," I corrected her. "Yes?"

"This is Officer Nowack with the State Police in Cambria County."

Cambria County. Ebensburg. My relief at having the phone ring vanished like that.

"I'm afraid I have some bad news for you, Mr. Dunn. Your family have all been killed."

"There must be some mistake." I had no idea what she could mean. "I don't have any family."

"You are the cousin of Mildred Beranoski?"

Millie. "Yes."

"I'm terribly sorry to have to tell you this, but she, her husband and their two children all died when their farmhouse burned down early this morning."

I'm afraid I went a bit numb. Not that I had ever felt close to them, but I was used to them—used to the idea that they were there, and a part of my past. Paul must have seen my reaction. Maybe I went a bit pale, I don't know. But he crossed the room to me and tried to take my hand. I pulled away from him.

"What happened, officer?"

"The forensics people are still at the farm. At this point it looks like some kerosene must have gotten spilled somehow. The house was engulfed almost at once."

"The kerosene was stored in the barn."

"We found a dozen cans of it in the basement."

Oh.

"You are the next of kin, Mr. Dunn."

"No!" I felt myself shaking. "I mean—I mean—there's another son. Bobby."

"He's in a federal penitentiary in Florida. Convicted of murder."

I hadn't known. Last I'd heard, he'd been jailed on a drug bust, but— "What do you need from me?"

"The bodies are in the county morgue, You'll have to claim them and arrange for burial."

"Can't you just—?"

"There are some legal concerns, too. I believe they were heavily in debt."

Every farmer in North America is heavily in debt. If they weren't, I don't know what they'd talk about. "Fine. I'll be out first thing in the morning. Who do I see?"

She gave me names and phone numbers, just in case.

Paul put a hand on my shoulder. I let him.

"Jamie, what's wrong?"

Part of me wanted to tell him. Another part— "I need to be alone, Paul."

"Is there anything I can do?"

"Just leave." I lowered my voice. "Please."

"If I can do anything at all…"

I looked around. The house was quite empty; having only Danilo's things, not the man himself, would never be enough. I had never liked my relatives, and they had never liked me. I was the queer cousin, the fag, the cocksucker. Yet learning they were dead left me feeling…I didn't know what. I gave Paul my spare key, asked him to keep an eye on the house, and he left.

Ebensburg.

Ugly place, hateful place, empty place full of empty people. It had always seemed like that to me, and it had not changed. But it was my turn: to do for them the bare minimum, and to do it grudgingly, as they had always done for me.

So next morning I called Roland to explain what had happened; he'd notify my instructors. Then I drove to the county coroner's office in Johnstown, the county seat. A larger, dirtier Ebensburg. When I was a kid it was "town" and going there had always seemed a big deal, not exactly exciting but at least a change. Now…

The coroner had also been my biology teacher in highschool. He gave me the same kind of cold, barely civil reception everyone there did. I didn't bother covering up what a nuisance this all was for me, which seemed to confirm his worst thoughts about me, but fuck it.

He gave me the death certificates and the name of a local mortician who had a crematorium. And told me I was expected there. There were fairly obviously working together—kickbacks most likely, but in that kind of place the corruption isn't always the most obvious kind.

The corpses were in body bags. It seemed odd that there were no child-sized ones; the kids were in large ones, but you could tell they weren't anywhere near full. I wanted them all cremated; I wanted not one trace of them left. The mortician's assistant picked up the bodies, two adults, two children, crammed them all into one hearse, and I followed him to the mortuary. Once I'd written a check, they disposed of them quickly. Oddly, he put the ashes into four little pine boxes instead of urns. It didn't much matter.

Then I headed to the farm. It was white—a dirty white. The snow lay a foot deep on all the fields, but here and there clumps of sod had been turned up for some reason, by someone. At random places the snow was streaked with mud. From the kids playing? Who knew? Closer to the farmhouse it had all been tamped down by the firefighters, and there was quite a lot of ice. The house itself was nothing but charcoal, a few beams still standing but charred and brittle. I poked a finger into one and it crumbled. Where had my bedroom been? The only safe place I'd known as a boy, and even it wasn't all that safe.

There was some light wind, not as much as I'd have liked, not enough to make the day colder than it was already. I got the ashes out of my car, one at a time, and scattered them, and the wind took them. But it didn't take them far. I moved around so their remains wouldn't all end in one little pile. It was probably romantic of me; I assumed the children had disliked their parents as much as I had.

Just as I was finishing, a car pulled up. A young man in a business suit. I recognized him, Jack Tilden. He had been a senior on the swim team when I was a freshman; we had known each other in the most nodding way. Blond, straight, starting to go a bit to seed the way high school athletes do. He smiled one of those practiced professional smiles. "Jamie?"

"Yes." I did not smile back at him.

He said his name, I told him I remembered him, and we shook hands. Uncomfortable moment, shaking hands with Ebensburg High.

"I was the family's lawyer."

I must have registered surprise.

He looked a bit abashed. "Just out of law school. Setting up my first practice."

"Oh."

"I work cheap, so a lot of the farmers around here…" He didn't have to finish.

"You're not going to tell me there's an estate, are you?"

He laughed. "Good God, no. But there was a bit of insurance."

I showed him my check stub from the mortician's. "Enough to over this? And their debts?"

"Just barely. With a few hundred left over."

"Give it to Bobby's defense fund."

"And there was a safe deposit box."

Oh. Wind was kicking up; I pulled up my collar. "Do you have any idea what was in it?"

"No, not a clue. How could I?"

"Well, they can't have had anything valuable. They couldn't."

"You never know. You hear these stories about little old bag ladies who die and it turns out they were worth two million dollars."

I smirked at him.

"Shall we go and look, Jamie?"

"Can't you just open it yourself and send the contents to Bobby? Whatever it is, it'll be something that doesn't matter to me. My great-grandmother's string collection. A family Bible with a swastika on the cover."

He laughed and glanced at his watch. "We've still got time to get to the bank. Come on. This won't take long."

There was more wind; and it was starting to snow again. The roads between Cambria County and Pittsburgh would be terrible. The thought of spending a night there— But the bank would be fine, if it didn't take long. "We can get everything done quickly, then? I have to be back in Pittsburgh tonight." White lie.

He nodded and got into his car. "The will's pretty simple. Everything to Bobby."

"Then why—?"

"But there's apparently something for you in that box."

"Oh."

The bank was on Main Street. By the time we got there the snow was coming down steadily. Everyone in sight seemed depressed, or maybe their blank expressions just indicated stupidity, I don't know. The ones who recognized me didn't seem happy I was there.

That included the bank manager, Bruce Johanssen. He was an uncle of Tim, my first lover. He minced and swished like no one I'd seen in months; but since he never troubled the stout hearts of Ebensburg with an actual admission he was queer, and never would, that was perfectly fine. Tim and I used to laugh about him, used to call him "Aunt Bruce" back before Tim decided that yes, Uncle was living the right way. Seeing him brought up horrible memories. My stomach was in knots. I wanted out.

Tilden had a brief talk with him. They glanced my way a few times, neither of them looking happy. Finally Uncle Bruce disappeared for a moment and Tilden gestured that I should join him.

The next moment we were in the vault. Since there was no way we could have Millie's key, a maintenance worker was brought in to drill the lock. "There will be a slight fee for this, naturally." Uncle Bruce smiled a tight smile.

"Bill the estate."

The box was one of the very large ones, bottom row, almost two feet square. It could have held anything. I half hoped we'd find body parts in it, or stolen emeralds, or the corpse of the Lindbergh baby, something, anything, to smear Millie's memory with the townspeople.

But inside was a stack of books, all identically bound, burgundy leather. I got down on one knee and touched the top one, as if it was a completely alien thing. This was wildly improbable—Millie and books had not occupied the same universe—and my surprise must have registered. Tilden asked me what was wrong.

"Nothing's wrong, exactly. It's just that...well, I can never remember seeing Millie with any book in her hand except the Bible."

"She was a woman who walked with God," Uncle Bruce told me helpfully.

"Of course." I looked up at him and smiled the widest smile I could. "That's why her son is in jail for murder."

He stiffened. Telling the truth never went down well round Ebensburg.

But I couldn't resist adding, "Millie always seemed to think that the Bible is not only the Good Book but the Only Book. A lot of good it did her."

Tilden decided to get between us. He reached down and took the first book out of my hand. When he flipped the cover open and whistled softly, he said, "So this is why she wanted you to have these."

I picked up the next one and opened it. It was filled with handwritten pages. Bright blue ink, somewhat faded, badly smeared here and there. The title page read: Journal of Samuel Dunn, D.D.

My father.

My father's journal.

Once again I was caught off balance. I had never known him, and I had always assumed I never would. To have his journal... I wasn't at all certain how it made me feel. Not that I wasn't used to trafficking with the dead, by now, but... My father, my long-dead father...

I looked up at Uncle Bruce. "Get me a box or something to put these in."

"This is a bank, Mr. Dunn. I'm afraid we don't—"

"Get me something!" I shouted it so loudly he was shocked into action. He went off and a moment later came back with a large cardboard carton. Slowly, carefully, I stacked the books in it. There were fourteen of them. I had a lot of reading ahead of me.

Then at the bottom on the box there was a thick, battered, wrinkled old manila envelope. Sealed. I looked at Tilden, he nodded, and I tore it open.

It was full of old photographs, faded, yellow things, maybe sixty or seventy of them. I recognized my parents from the pictures Millie had shown me once. One or two were of people from the town, ministers, ward-heelers. Most were quite unknown to me. But there was writing on the back of each one, careful penmanship, not the same as the writing in the journals. Perhaps it was my mother's; there didn't seem any way to know for sure. I put them carefully back into the envelope, put the envelope in my box with the journals and got to my feet.

"Is there anything else?"

Tilden assured me that was all. He'd submit the insurance claims and make certain I was reimbursed for the funeral expenses.

I told him, "You can take whatever your fee is out of the insurance money, then send the rest to Bobby, okay?"

I shook his hand; Uncle Bruce wouldn't let me shake his. Dear, dear Uncle Bruce. What could a creature like him make of a man who never lied about himself? His nephew had been like him, and had died for it. Hiding your true nature is a kind of voluntary death. I looked briefly into Bruce's eyes, and they were empty, as vacant as lunar craters.

The journals were heavy; the box was a bit awkward to carry. Outside, the snow was coming down quite steadily now, large, heavy flakes. But unlike the other cars on the street, mine had no snow on it. When I got to the curb, I realized someone had vandalized it. The word Sodomite was spray-painted, in bright green, around the front, from the passenger-side door to the one on the driver's side.

Uncle Bruce was standing at the doorway of the bank, smiling. I couldn't resist. "Why Bruce, someone's mistaken my car for yours."

He stiffened. "Don't you think it's time for you to leave this town once and for all?"

"Sure. That way, they'll be sure and get the right car next time."

He harrumphed and stomped back into the safety of his bank.

Tilden had listened to this exchange with undisguised amusement. "You people never stop tearing each other down, do you?"

"You'd be surprised what I tear. Goodbye."

But Uncle Bruce had been right, in a way. Every time I left Ebensburg, I told myself I'd never go back, never see it again. This time, maybe I'd be lucky enough for that to be the case, finally.

Snow came more and more heavily. Since it started, more than four inches had fallen, and there was no sign of it letting up. I remembered Roland's grouchy comments about Pittsburgh and winter. Maybe he had a point. Maybe the disagreeable climate had worked its way into the inhabitants' blood.

The roads were bad, and it was getting dark. I decided to stop and spend the night in a motel. There was one just outside of Greensburg, a Best Western that didn't look too bad. The desk clerk asked where my luggage was. "Don't have any. I was out in Cambria County on some family business today. Hoping to get back to Pittsburgh by nightfall. But…" I gestured to the front window and let the snow tell the rest of the story.

The room was a motel room like every other motel room. Polyester drapes and bedspread, particle-board furniture, carefully neutral color scheme, cable. I got a bit of dinner at a fast-food place next door, went back to my room and showered.

My father's journal. What could be in it? I had a sinking suspicion it would be full of drafts for sermons, church accounts and so on. Not edifying reading. The desk clerk told me the nearest bookstore was in a mall three miles down the road. I tried cable. Bad sitcoms. There was a porn channel—there is always a porn channel, this was America—but even it had nothing I wanted to watch. Just those god-awful made-for-cable soft-core things where women with plastic breasts pretend to make love to obviously gay actors.

So it was the journal or sleep.

I remembered the envelope of snapshots. Opened it, shook them out onto the bed.

There seemed to be no pattern to what had been photographed or saved. Some random shots of the town; random shots of its people. The handwritten notes on the back of them didn't do a thing to explain why my father had thought them worth taking, or keeping.

About a dozen of them were pictures of his church. Small, even by small-town standards; white clapboard. Sign out front—First Covenant Church of Ebensburg, Samuel Dunn, Pastor. He was in a few of them, in his clerical drag; most of them were just architecture. Plain man, almost aggressively ordinary looking, even in those preposterous getups ministers wear.

There was Millie as a little girl, standing side-by-side with her mother, my mother's sister, who looked as unpleasant as her daughter turned out to be. A picture of her in her wedding dress, no husband in sight. It occurred to me that there were no pictures of my own mother. Odd.

I rummaged through them all fairly quickly. As I'd expected, none of them struck me as particularly interesting. Until—

Just as I was about to put them back in their envelope, one of them caught my eye. My father was standing shoulder-to-shoulder with another man; their heads were leaning together, cheeks touching. It was much too intimate a pose for who and what he had been. Is it possible he had been—?

I looked at the note on the back. Sam and Larry, Church Picnic, August 1980.

Sam and Larry. They sounded like a couple. They looked like a couple, or a reasonable approximation of one. I flipped it over and examined it again. No, it hadn't been my imagination—their cheeks were touching, and my father was smiling tenderly. Suddenly I knew I had to read the journal. If my father had been... I could almost hear Danilo's amused voice: *"Well, you got the blood from someone, right?"*

Volume 1 was on top. I picked it up. The books were heavy—good paper, rich bindings. Small-town ministry didn't pay much. This journal had meant something to him. And so I looked into my father's world for the first time.

He was from Philadelphia. Hated small towns, but Ebensburg was the only ministry he'd been able to find. The fact that he was not married worked against him—congregations wanted a preacher with a wife, two church workers for the price of one. But he was determined to make the best of his job.

It wasn't exactly gripping reading. But I kept looking for some indication that he took his "faith" seriously as something other than a job. There was none.

I tucked the photos back in their envelope. I'd have to take a closer look sometime soon, especially of that one. By chance it fell onto the bed. And then I noticed something I hadn't before. I had studied my father, studied his body language and the expression on his face. I hadn't given anything like that attention to his "friend" Larry.

Now I did.

And what I saw made me freeze.

"Larry" was Lazar Perske. Not a Lazar Perske twenty-five years younger, but Perske as I knew him today.

There was no doubt of it. I kept trying to tell myself it had to be someone who only looked like him.

But it was him.

CHAPTER 9

So I read.

Outside, the snowstorm turned into a full-fledged blizzard. I don't think I'd ever seen snow fall quite so heavily, quite so relentlessly. At eleven o'clock I turned on the news channel; the smiling heads were predicting a foot and a half. Highways were being closed, people were warned not to drive. It was a good thing I'd stopped when I did.

For the twentieth time I stared at the photo of my father and— It couldn't be Perske. But it was; it had to be. A bit younger, but only a bit; a bit less lined, but only a bit. The resemblance was too close. Even the body language said so. This was not simply someone who looked like him.

Fourteen volumes, most of them wildly uninteresting. I skimmed the early ones. My father wrote about establishing himself in Ebensburg; about how much he missed his friends in Philadelphia, one in particular; about how difficult it was to get the townspeople to accept him. "This isn't what they told us to expect in seminary. Men of the cloth…" The entry tailed off there, as if whatever he was going to write was too obvious to bother with.

There was one routine entry after another. "What should my Xmas sermon be about?" "The organ needs a new wind chest—where will I find the money?" "The roof is leaking over the choir loft." And on and on. I found myself skimming more and more quickly.

Oddly, among it all, I couldn't find the least hint that he believed in what he preached. There were no prayers, no mentions of the Bible, no indications of piety at all. Once or twice he even talked about various parishioners as gullible. I remember reading about a study once, done by some historian—I forget who, exactly. But he examined all the letters he could find that had been written home to England by British soldiers in the trenches during World War I. And to his surprise, he found that there was virtually no mention of God, of Christ, of prayer, of anything identifiably Christian. This was true even of letters written by military chaplains. They had survival on their minds, nothing more nor less. There are, it turned out, atheists in foxholes.

And in pulpits, it appeared. My father never invoked the name of his "Redeemer" even once, that I could find. He was too busy hustling donations, writing properly pious-sounding sermons…and telling people how to run their lives, when he obviously didn't have much idea how to live his own.

There was unfriendly gossip about him. Why was he not married? There were eligible single girls in the congregation—why wasn't he courting one of them?

And so he married my mother, out of social and professional obligation, not out of affection or even respect, it seemed. Dated her, got her pregnant with little me—I think he thought an unplanned, "accidental" pregnancy might dispel any unhealthy rumors about his sexual tastes— married her. The word "love" was absent almost as conspicuously as the word "Jesus."

My mother was barely mentioned again. Now and then her name would crop up, working on the parish books or polishing the stained-glass windows, but she didn't seem to figure at all largely in the thoughts or the world of Pastor Samuel Dunn, D.D. Most of the time he called her M instead of using her name, Mary.

Then an uncharacteristically wealthy farmer died and left an endowment to the church. It was for a professional organist, enough to pay a decent part-time salary. My father placed want-ads in the newspapers of all the surrounding towns and cities. Almost at once an ideal candidate presented himself, an instructor and Somerset County Community College. His name was "Larry Perske."

This was in the thirteenth volume of the journal. I had read till the small hours. Two A.M. Outside, there seemed to be a foot of snow; and the wind was blowing viciously. My car and the others in the lot were vague humps; they might have been snowdrifts, nothing more. The wind tore white streamers from them that spiraled into the air and vanished quickly. I must have been the last to reach the motel; there were no footsteps in the snow. Most people had more sense than me, it seemed. I drew the drapes and tried to forget about the storm and the night.

Despite the journal, and despite the truth I was learning about my family, I was tired. It had been a long, unpleasant day. Against my will I was yawning. But I wanted to know everything there was to be learned from the journal. It would, perhaps, give me unpleasant dreams, but that didn't matter.

The night clerk was at his desk watching the porn channel. Young guy. Under other circumstances, I might have… "Is there a coffee machine?"

He nodded toward an alcove off the lobby. Soda, ice, hot drink machines. I got a large coffee. As I was heading back, he asked me idly why I was still up. I smiled. "I like pornography too."

He laughed and winked, and I went quickly back to my room

The coffee was pretty foul but it warmed me up and woke me up, and I went back to reading my father's journal.

Fourteenth volume, the last one. "L and I have become so close," he wrote, "unnaturally so. He says he loves me and needs me. He has been so much help to me, running the church, more than M has ever been."

"His kisses," he wrote, echoing David's lament for his lover Jonathan, "are more to me than the kisses of women. More than M's, certainly. More than hers could ever be."

"His love…" Yes, that was the word he used.

They were lovers, my father and "Larry Perske." It was inescapably clear.

"He tells me about our love, and he compares us to Jesus Christ and his Beloved Disciple, and he tells me about how special it makes us. I don't really understand what he means, and I'm not sure I want to, and I suspect there is something about him, himself, that is keeping him from giving himself totally to me."

Conscience struck. "I want to tell M. Divorcing her is the only decent thing to do. But L says no, we must keep our love a secret, hidden from everyone but just us ourselves. We must not disturb the order here."

My mother was a dutiful wife, a dutiful *preacher's* wife, and went about her duties at the church without complaining. "I feel so terrible, cheating on her. But every time I'm with L, I feel so alive, so strong. I could not have dealt with this town and its people otherwise. He is my life."

And so he told her. She cried. She made a scene. But she was not, it appeared, strong enough to leave him. A woman's place is in the home. What God has put together, let no man put asunder. "Every time she sees us together, she looks completely crushed. One of the farmers in town routinely beats his animals. I've seen them. M has that same hurt air. Poor woman. I've used her so terribly."

Perske wasn't happy. "Larry is furious that I told her. Worse, people around town are wondering what's wrong between her and me."

And finally, "I've made the decision. I'm going to tell the congregation the truth about myself, give M a decent divorce and move somewhere far away. Maybe I'll be able to start a new life. I've made enough of a mess of this one."

He quickly came to regret his decision. "L is furious. He threatened me. Says he'll lose not only this job but his one at the college. He rage was so violent, I'm still quite shaken."

Three guilt-ridden pages later, the journal ended. It was around the date when he died; I knew that much from Millie.

My father had been queer; he must have been *blood* queer. It made sense—I got the blood from someone.

My father and Lazar Perske had been lovers.

And it was impossible not to suspect that Perske, good, saintly, Christian Lazar Perske, had killed him.

For a long time I lay on the bed, in the dark, trying to make sense of all this. The noise of the storm outside got louder and louder, then started tailing off. Sex, love, blood. Once I was born, my father barely mentioned me. Why? After a time I fell asleep without wanting to.

But something woke me, a loud rattling sound. Not just the wind.

The room was quite dark, only the faintest light coming in at the sides and bottom of the drapes. It took me a moment to remember where I was, and why.

Something was scraping at the window.

Wind. It had to be the wind. Branches scratching against the windowpane. I got up, stretched and walked to the window. The drawcord for the drapes was stuck; I gave it a stiff tug and they opened. White world. Illumination from the lights in the parking lot.

There was a boy outside. Clawing frantically at my window. He was naked. His throat had been torn open, his eyes ripped out, genitals severed, his fingernails pulled out. Blood poured from him; the snow was red for yards all around. His bleeding fingers streaked the window. He called to me, "Help me! Jamie, help me!"

Through the blood I recognized him. It was Kurt.

How can he have been there? How could he have known where I'd been, and where I was?

Kurt, beautiful boy, horribly mutilated, begging me for help.

I cried out, I don't remember what.

Ran from my room, down the hall to the lobby. The night clerk was asleep. I shook him awake; he stared at me groggily.

"There's someone outside, a boy. He's been hurt. Call 911."

I left him sitting there, not quite awake yet, and ran outside.

The world was nearly quiet. My footsteps crunched in the snow, and the wind blew, not loudly now; that was all. I listened. No voices, nothing, just the wind.

The snow was more than a foot and a half deep, and there was ice under it. I slipped and fell, hitting my elbow quite painfully. It was still coming down quite heavily; I could see just how heavily in the cones of light around the parking lot. But when I looked along the side of the motel to my room there was…there was nothing, no one. No blood, no footsteps, no boy.

Stupidly I gaped. Had it been a dream? A hallucination?

Even more stupidly, I stood there, staring, trying to make sense of it. Nothing. No one.

A strong gust of wind shook me out of it. I walked quickly back inside, as quickly as I could without falling again. A gust of wind seemed to cut right through my clothing; I was shivering when I got back inside.

The clerk was holding the phone to his ear. He looked up at me.

"Where is he?"

"Gone."

"Gone? In this?"

There wasn't much I could say. "Maybe I was dreaming."

"Yeah." He smirked. "Anyway, the phones are dead." He held out the receiver, as if seeing it would show me.

It didn't make any difference. I imagined. I apologized for bothering him, and it sounded pretty lame, but what else could I do?

My jeans, shirt, socks, and shoes were soaked, and I was freezing. "I'm going to get a hot shower."

Again he smirked at me. "Or a cold one."

I apologized again.

I had always had such vivid dreams, but this didn't feel like one of them. My dreams tended to be about passion—about Danilo and the Pyramids and the gods—not about mutilated boys.

I switched on the light in my room. The curtains were still open. The journal was gone. Half the volumes had been in their box, the rest spread out on the bed. They were gone.

My photographs were scattered. I gathered them together and realized that the one of Perske and my father was gone, too.

I sat and forced myself to concentrate.

Perske and Kurt were...what? Collaborators? Master and student? Lovers?

The lawyer had told them what we'd found in the bank. No, on second thought it made more sense that it had been Uncle Bruce. He would have known Perske from my father's time. It wasn't hard to imagine the scenario. Perske would have approached him with a sad story about his closet being violated. "Please, Bruce, if anyone ever finds Sam's journal, let me know right away, will you?" Bruce would have thought he was doing Perske a big favor, and he probably thought it would help him, himself, to keep securely closeted. How could he know that Sam never even mentioned him?

Perske. Kurt.

I did not understand what was happening, but for the first time in my life I felt completely vulnerable.

As tightly as I could, I closed my eyes and tried to conjure up an image of Danilo. I needed him there, to love me and shelter me. *Lonely Child* had never resonated more deeply for me.

But once I was asleep, I dreamed about Danilo, and the dream terrified me more than anything else. He was bound to a chair with what looked like barbed wire. He was naked, thin, pale, and the wire cut into his flesh everywhere; he was covered with open wounds, some of them very deep. Desperately he looked to me, agony in his eyes, and whispered hoarsely, "Jamie, please."

I took a step toward him but my legs seemed frozen in place,

And again he begged, "Jamie."

I slept till nearly eleven the next morning. The drapes were still open and the world was blinding white under a brilliant sun. Shaken from that dream, which had recurred every time I closed my eyes, it seemed, I lay in bed and tried to make sense of what had happened. None of it was possible, not the journal vanishing, not Kurt, naked and bleeding in the snow, not the vision of Danilo wounded and helpless.

I got up, stretched, and walked to the window, as if looking again might show me something. There was no sign Kurt or anyone else had been there. Not one drop of red blood on the white snow, not a single footprint. Across the parking lot I could see where I had gone myself, and the spot where I'd fallen. That was all.

The night clerk was out on a snowplow, clearing the lot. As I watched, a plow from the state highway department passed on the highway. I'd be able to leave soon enough.

Another clerk was on duty, a middle-aged woman. She was full of chat about the storm and how hard it had been to get to work, but I was in no mood for smalltalk. I settled my bill and went back to the room to get my things.

One last time I paused and closed my eyes, trying to make sense of it all; and that vision of Danilo, bound and desperate, came to me again. Slowly, slowly he was bleeding to death. Or, more precisely, being bled.

It was not a dream, not the usual kind, I knew that now. I was seeing him, somehow, somewhere, and I knew that I had to find him or my life would never be complete, would never even be good again.

Outside, the air was quite still, not the least breath of wind, and it had that crisp, almost metallic tang it sometimes gets after a snowfall. The calm after the storm. The guy on the snowplow, the night clerk, smiled at me, than laughed. He shouted something over the roar of his machine, but I couldn't make it out.

The highway was pretty much cleared of snow, and salt had been scattered. Once I got back to the interstate, I made good time. Here and there I could see road crews pulling cars out of snowbanks or ditches along the side of the road. The news station on the radio had almost nothing but stories about the storm, people stranded, people missing; a woman in Johnstown had gotten lost in it and froze to death. But they did report one non-storm-related piece of news: There had been a murder during the night in Ebensburg. Bruce Johannsen, bank manger, had been murdered and mutilated in the night. So I had been right.

What could they do to me, Perske and Kurt? Danilo had given me his blood. I was, at least in theory, immortal like him. The blood of the sacrificed kept me alive and young. But my new life, Danilo's gift, had never really been tested. What could they do to me?

Back in Pittsburgh two hours later, I was surprised to see that my driveway had been cleared. Inside I found a note from Paul. He had waited up all night for me; then in mid-morning he had to get to campus. He hoped I was all right. It was signed with his name and "XOXOXO."

Bubastis gave me her usual greeting, and I picked her up and nuzzled her. Home felt good.

But there were things I had to know. I took a quick shower, changed into warm clothes, and went online. The Cambria County site. Coroner's records.

The site wasn't easy to search; I'd have expected the state to have provided support to all its counties for state-of-the-art software, but this database was antiquated. Everything was filed by date rather than subject's name, which struck me as unwieldy and near-useless. Once I finally got the hang of it, I searched for the date of my father's death. And there was the autopsy report.

Dunn, Samuel. Age: 41. Status: Married, one child. Profession: minister. Cause of death: Murder.

In the section titled "Notes" was additional information: *Mutilated—eyes, heart, genitals severed; blood drained.*

This was exactly as Danilo would have done. And exactly as I had done myself, to all the men I'd sacrificed.

Precisely one year later, on the anniversary of his death, there was another entry: *Dunn, Mary. Age: 29. Status: Widow. Cause of death: Suicide.*

Millie had never told me. It was easy enough to guess why. Scandal—spare the boy. Don't trouble him with the shameful facts—how could he understand? How could she have guessed that her silence, her secrecy, would ultimately lead to her own death, and those of her children?

Of course, I was only guessing that that was what happened; but it seemed the likeliest scenario. People were dying around me, divers, Egyptian embassy officials, and I was more and more certain that Lazar Perske was at the center of it all. Why? Who could he be?

Perske. He had taught me. That much, at least, I owed him. Through all of this, the themes for my symphony had taken much more concrete from in my mind. I sat at the Bechstein and played them, began to work out the ways they would develop together. Hadrian and Antinous. Danilo and Jamie. I played till, exhausted, I finally fell asleep.

Roland was supportive and understanding, as usual. "You need to go to Florida? Why, for heaven's sake?"

I told him about the deaths of Millie and her family. "Her son Bobby, my cousin, is the only one left. I have to see him. I mean, a card would hardly be right." The fact that I wanted to do more than simply express my sympathy, I could hardly explain.

He arranged to cover for me with my professors. "They'll understand."

"I hope so."

"Don't worry, Jamie, even college teachers have trace amounts of humanity."

"Most of them are hiding it pretty well." As I was leaving, I had a thought. "Roland?"

"Hm?"

"Don't tell Perske where I've gone, okay?"

He seemed puzzled, but since Perske wasn't "officially" one of my instructors, he agreed. Perske had to know I still had a surviving cousin, so he might guess, but there was nothing to be done about that.

I booked a hotel online and caught a flight that afternoon. The flight attendant cruised me, and he was cute. But sex was the last thing on my mind. After a Pennsylvania blizzard, the warm weather in Miami seemed a bit miraculous. Palm trees, flying fish. When I looked away from the ocean and ignored the humidity, it might have been Egypt. Well, a bastardized, Americanized Egypt.

I checked into my hotel, asked for a room that didn't face the ocean, tipped the bellhop. Than I called a taxi and headed for the Dade County Correctional Facility.

It must have been the only building in the county that wasn't Art Deco. Gray walls, gray steel gates—a prison, in fact. The last time I'd been inside one, it was to meet Greg Wilton, who had tried to murder me.

The young bureaucrat in the warden's office was polite but firm. "Robert Beranoski?" He checked the file. "I'm afraid he isn't allowed visitors."

"I'm his cousin."

"Even so. I'm afraid—"

"Has anyone given him the news about his family?"

This caught him off guard. I explained what had happened. He excused himself and disappeared into an inner office. A few moments later he came back to tell me they were checking with the Ebensburg police. He went off a second time, then came back to tell me I could have fifteen minutes with Bobby.

I was expecting the usual kind of arrangement, some sort of barrier between us. But I was led to a simple gray room, a table, two chairs, metal grille over the window. All three pieces of furniture were stenciled with the facility's name and with ID numbers. I sat in one of the chairs, stared out the window and waited. I was wearing a green shirt; the contrast with all the gray made me self-conscious. I hadn't seen Bobby in years.

The door opened. There he was, in a prison uniform as colorless as everything else in the room. His hands and ankles were shackled. We were close to the same age; he looked ten years older. For a moment he stood and stared at me. "Jamie."

It was an odd moment, for more reasons than the obvious ones. Bobby was taller and heavier than me; his hair was blond, his eyes blue; under other circumstances I'd have found him attractive. But he had always resented the fact that the family orphan had moved into his bedroom and he was expected to share it. Bobby was a good Christian; sharing didn't come easily to him. My life with him and his family had never been more than bearable.

For a long instant I stared at him. "Hello, Bobby." I kept my voice muted.

A guard entered just behind him and stood in a corner, as unobtrusive as he could be under the circumstances, I guess.

Nothing showed in Bobby's face. "What are you doing here?"

"Please, come and sit down."

"What the fuck are you doing here?"

"Sit down, Bobby." I made myself smile, but it was faint. "Please."

He shambled across the room to the other chair, started to sit, then thought better of it. We had never been close. It was obvious that he resented me, even now. He narrowed his eyes. "What's wrong?"

"Bobby, your parents and the kids…" It was difficult to know what words to use.

"What happened?" Finally he sat.

I told him about the fire. "I'm sorry, Bobby."

For a moment he didn't say anything. "It's too bad they had to go that way."

"Bobby, I know this is a bad time, but…"

He looked at me.

I had to ask. "Did Millie ever tell you anything about my parents?"

He shrugged. "Not much. Your old man was a fag." He said the words pointedly. "Like you."

"Did she ever say anything about how he died?"

Loudly, unexpectedly, he laughed at me. "He was a fag. Somebody took care of him."

"Bobby, please, I—"

"Somebody sliced the cocksucker." More laughter. He turned to the guard. "Get me the fuck out of here." He stood, rattled his chains in my face in what he must have thought was a menacing manner. The guard caught him by the arm and steered him toward the door. Just as he was about to leave, Bobby spit on me. The door slammed shut.

For a long moment I sat there, wiping my face dry, more shaken by our encounter than I wanted to admit to myself. Then the door opened. It was the guy from the warden's office. "Are you all right?"

I got to my feet. "I guess so."

"Come on, I'll show you out."

We walked. The corridors seemed even longer than they had before. He tried to make smalltalk. "We keep him in solitary. He's tried to kill three other prisoners."

"I—I never—we aren't really close."

"So I gathered."

"Who did he kill?"

"A street kid. Beranoski paid him for sex, fucked him, then slit his throat."

"Oh."

So much for the last of my family.

There was a newspaper in Ebensburg, for the few inhabitants who saw any point to reading. The *World Guardian,* no less. I called them and asked if I might gain access to their archives. There would have been news stories. A murdered minister, his suicidal widow…

They told me that issues over two years old were archived, sent to a document storage facility in an old mine in northeastern Pennsylvania.

"You don't store them digitally? Or even on microfilm?"

"Be serious. This is Ebensburg." And no, they weren't willing to help me find the old news stories.

"But this is my family. My parents. I need to know what happened to them."

"I'm sorry," said the woman on the telephone.

"What about your staff? Do you know who might have covered those stories?"

"Are you kidding? This is the Ebensburg *World Guardian*. Kids work here, recent journalism grads, frantic to work for the *New York Times*. The minute they get anything better—*anything*—they're out of here like a shot." She laughed and added, "I'm leaving for St. Louis next week myself."

So that was that. Given the unfriendly reception I'd gotten in Ebensburg, from the first time I went back, it didn't seem likely I'd find anyone there who could tell me more. "Larry" Perske, by chance or by design, had left no footprints.

That night I was hungry. I should have fed while I was in Florida, comfortably far from home. I went to East Liverpool, Ohio, hit a sleazy bar—a straight one, they were always the best hunting grounds when I wanted easy prey—found a married engineer who was looking to have some fun on the side.

"My wife doesn't understand me," he told me, clearly wanting sympathy.

"That's all right," I cooed, "I understand you perfectly." I showed him that I really did by giving him exactly what he deserved. Sometimes it can be fun to be undead. He didn't have much blood in his veins, and his organs hardly amounted to anything at all, but he was enough.

Back home, though, I couldn't sleep. For the hundredth time in my life I was lost and alone. Nothing that had happened made sense to me, and I didn't know how I could make it make sense. I needed Danilo.

Next day I headed back to campus. Roland asked me to stop by his office, and he gave me his condolences a second time.

I thanked him; but my loss was not a matter of simple grief. Millie had known. And she had never told me.

"Roland, I know you're busy, but…" I couldn't make myself look him in the eye.

"Hm?"

"This individual study thing with Perske, it's not working out. I need to you to coach me in composition."

He looked up from the paperwork on his desk. "What's the problem?"

"Nothing I can quite put my finger on." I lied, conveniently. "We're just not clicking. There's something about him, I don't know what, that…" How could I ever have explained?

"You're not the first one to say that about him. But Jamie, I just don't have the time."

"Make it. Please."

I think he must have heard in my voice how important it was to me. He weakened a bit. "But look, Jamie, whether you're 'clicking' or not, Perske's an internationally known composer. He can do you a lot of good."

There was no way to explain the problem. "We're just not in sync, that's all. I don't know how else to explain it. It doesn't feel right." Pointedly I added, "I just don't trust him."

His eyes narrowed. "You're trying to wrap him around your finger, the way you did your Egyptologist. And the way you do me. Aren't you? And he won't buy it."

This hurt. "No, Roland, that's not even close to the truth."

"I have a conference in a few minutes. I'll have to get moving." He glanced at his watch and stood up.

"Roland, please. I have a symphony inside me. I know it."

"Perske's the best composer we have here." He shrugged. "Or at least the best-known, the most successful. That comes to pretty much the same thing. Stay with him."

That was that. He left.

It was the first time he'd ever really rebuffed me, and I wondered what might be behind it. Was my ineffable boyish charm failing me? Glum thought. But I was being silly. Roland really was busy.

I looked around the office. Roland usually kept his file drawers unlocked. There was one labeled Personnel. Perske's file would be there.

Quietly I closed the door and locked it. I half expected Perske's file to be missing. But I pulled open the drawer, careful to make no noise, and found it.

It was a standard personnel file. The C.V. listed all his published compositions and all the ones that had been performed, along with the dates and orchestras. He was, it said, fifty-five years old. He looked it. Born in Israel. Came to America in the late 70s. Taught at a series of colleges, including Pennsylvania State University. He had been teaching there when my father died, it said. A lie. He came to West Penn as composer-in-residence a year ago. There was nothing else in it. No mention of my father, of Ebensburg, of Cambria County Community College, of anything else in the journal.

As I was leaving Roland's office, I saw Kurt at the other end of the hall. Needless to say, he was quite intact, eyes, throat, hands all in perfect order. I had asked myself a dozen times whether what I'd seen had really been him, or a dream, or perhaps even a phantom summoned up by…by whoever.

He saw me from the corner of his eye; I could tell. At first he looked away; then he seemed to make a decision to confront me. He put on a big, wide grin and headed straight for me. "Jamie!"

"Kurt." As always, I couldn't read him. Did he have the divine blood? It was like trying to look inside a stone. I had always found it odd; now it was genuinely disturbing.

When he reached me he took my hand and shook it energetically. "It's so good to see you."

I stared at him. "Why?"

This threw him. People like him always count on everyone else observing the social niceties; it was what made their existence possible. "Well…we're partners."

"That ended, remember?"

"But…well…I mean, Jamie, we played so well together." He lowered his voice to a confidential whisper. "And I don't mean just music."

I had the impression he was trying to be seductive. Did he—or Perske—think I was that big a fool? "How are your hands, Kurt?"

He looked at them, puzzled. "Fine. Why?"

"I heard you'd been having trouble with them. Bleeding."

"No. I—" Suddenly he looked around, apparently alarmed. "Why? What happened?"

"Why, nothing at all." I glanced at my watch, as if I needed to be somewhere. "I heard something about trouble with your fingernails or something, that's all."

He flushed. Kurt had the most beautiful peaches-and-cream complexion; when he was self-conscious he turned the brightest red. Then, apparently baffled, he looked down the hall, to Perske's office. "Where can you have gotten that idea?"

"Oh, nowhere, really. It was silly of me. Just a notion I picked up while I was rooting around in an old closet."

Kurt took me by the arm and led me into an empty classroom. "Jamie, I don't know what this is about. But I want you. I think I love you."

Gorgeous man; talented man. Under other circumstances he might have made a good match for me. But now, knowing what I knew, or thought I knew, or was beginning to know… "You're the one who ended it, Kurt."

"Listen, Lazar's a success in this business. He's the only one I've ever known who was, really. And he keeps telling me the only way to become a success myself is to do what he does and hide who I really am." He looked away from me. "You too."

"Where were you during the blizzard, Kurt?"

It caught him completely off guard. "What?! Jamie, I'm talking about us, I'm trying to make you—"

"You don't have to make me do anything. I won't live the way you want me to."

Again he looked around; again he spoke softly. "Jamie, I'm afraid. I don't know what's happening to my life. But I'm miserable." Weakly he added, "We're not safe."

"You're the only one who can change that."

He looked straight into my eyes. "Jamie, please. I—"

"Let Lazar fix things for you."

I walked out of the room, leaving him there. And I have to admit I felt a bit of a heel. But he had made his choice.

As I was walking down the hall, I passed Perske's office. He was sitting at his desk, staring into space, apparently lost in thought. His desk was full of some kind of paperwork. He noticed me.

"Jamie." Forced smile. "Come in."

I stopped. "Hello." Cautiously I took a step inside his door.

"I haven't seen you for a few days."

"No. I've been reading." He knew that I knew.

"Fiction or non?"

"Non, I'm afraid."

"You should be careful what you read. People who confuse fact with fantasy don't usually end well."

"Nobody ends well, Lazar. Isn't that what gives life its meaning?"

"Through Our Lord, Jesus Christ, we can—"

I was in no mood for this. "Save it, Lazar."

On the wall was a very large map of the Middle East. There were colored pins stuck in it at various places, I couldn't make out exactly where. There were black ones, green, blue, purple and, quite noticeably, a bright red one stuck into a place midway between Cairo and Luxor. From a distance it looked like it might be indicating Amarna. The capital city built by Danilo's father, Akhenaten. The place where our bloodline began—and where Danilo had initiated me fully into it.

Perske changed tack. "When are we going to get back to work on your symphony?"

"I've decided to switch teachers. You've expressed too many doubts about what I'm doing."

The conversation was dangerously ambiguous. But he had to know I'd read my father's journal, or at least enough of it to have some idea what had happened to him. Perske scowled at me. "You're young. You'll make your own foolish mistakes. Young people always do."

I had had enough of this. I put on a tight smile. "You know what they say, Lazar. There's no fool like an old fool."

He went back to whatever paperwork he'd been doing, ignoring me as pointedly as possible.

CHAPTER 10

When I got home, Paul was in the house; he still had my spare key. We hadn't seen each other for a few days, not since my trip to Ebensburg. He saw me, his face lit up and he threw his arms around me. The encounters with Kurt and Perske had drained me more than I realized; I was too tired, or maybe too numb, to respond. There was music on the stereo, a recording of our performance of *Lonely Child*. I kissed his cheek. "Hi, Paul. Good to see you." I meant it.

"Let me make you something hot to drink."

"Tea. I need the caffeine."

He headed off to the kitchen. A moment later, I followed him. "What are you doing here, Paul? How did you get in?"

"You gave me your spare key and asked me to keep an eye on the house, remember?"

"That was while I was out of town." I sat down. "Something strong. English breakfast."

He got the teabags. "I've been here half the morning. I had nightmares; I was terrified something might have happened to you." He started to take my hand but seemed to think better of it. Tentatively he asked, "That's all right, isn't it?"

"Sure." I made myself smile at him.

"I've been reading in Danilo's library."

I wanted the tea water to boil. "Anything interesting?"

"A history of the Plantagenets."

This was quite unexpected. "If you wanted something dry, why didn't you just eat some dust?"

He laughed. "The place could use a good dusting."

"I'm a pianist, not a housekeeper."

"And everyone says you're so versatile."

"Everyone?" For some reason, it surprised me to hear it. I had been sexually active, really active, since Danilo left and once I lost the first shock of his going. But it had never occurred to me I might have a

140

reputation.

"Everyone." He said it emphatically.

"Swell."

"They all say you're fantastic in bed, too." The kettle whistled and he poured the water. "Which you are. At least in my limited experience."

He handed me my cup and I thanked him. "Where's the cat?" I hadn't seen her since I got home.

"Sleeping someplace."

Almost as if she'd been cued, she walked in, looked at me lazily, yawned, and stretched. Then she trotted across the room and rubbed herself against my leg.

"So." He poured his own cupful and sat down across the table from me. "The Plantagenets."

"What about them?" The tea was still steaming, but I sipped. I was in no mood for a history lesson; maybe the tea would energize me.

"You tell me. You have enough of their pictures around here. I thought you'd know something."

"Henry II, Richard Lionheart…" My fingers were still cold; I wrapped them around my cup.

"And Richard II, and Geoffrey of Brittany." He was pleased with himself.

"Old news. What about them?"

Slowly, pointedly, he said, "And Edward II."

"And Edward II." I repeated it just as slowly. One of our most tragic forebears. When he was a boy he fell in love with Piers Gaveston, a slightly older boy assigned to his court. He later he saw him beheaded by the bishops and the barons who hated Edward's open life. They complained about 'too much sodomy,' whatever that was supposed to mean. Then he was killed himself, by a red-hot poker forced into his rectum. One of the martyrs. My ancestor. It was all in the official histories.

"The mainstream historians all call him one of England's weakest kings, Jamie. He loved another man. So *naturally* the Scots rebelled, *naturally* the treasury was drained empty, *naturally* his wife, her church and the barons led a series of revolts against him. Naturally."

It had been a long, unsettled day; even Paul had been disturbed by dreams. "Look, I'm not sure I'm up for this kind of thing right now, Paul. Okay?"

He went ahead anyway. "The establishment historians all take that view. But most of the problems of his reign were inherited from his father."

I resigned myself to listening. "Okay, fine."

"But if you go back and read the chronicles from his time, a different picture of him emerges. Unlike the nobles and the bishops, the common people loved him. Absolutely adored him. And they had reason to. Did you know he was the first king to let the commons take part in Parliament?"

"Yeah, I think I did."

"When he died, the nation mourned. The people had lost their king. Not just the nation's king, Jamie, but *theirs*. His tomb in Gloucestershire became a place of pilgrimage. People from all over the country went there to pray."

I hadn't known any of this. I said so.

"And that's not the best of it, Jamie. There were stories of miracles happening at his graveside. The blind saw and the lame walked. A whole cycle of myths sprang up abut him. He was immortal. He was going to return from the dead one day and lead his people back to glory."

I hadn't heard any of this before. And I should have. How many more of our forebears had been…what Danilo was, or something close to it, even if it was only in legend? But I could hardly discuss that with Paul. There was no way he could understand, or even begin to. I shrugged and tried to sound nonchalant as I said, "Stories, that's all."

"There were miracles at his graveside, Jamie. People knew; people believed it."

"Just because people believe something doesn't make it true."

Paul reached across the table and took my hand. "What if 'his people' were not the English but *us,* Jamie?"

"Then they were legends about *us,* that's all. Fables. They said the same things about King Arthur, remember?"

"Arthur was a myth. Edward was real."

I pulled free of him. "They were legends, Paul."

"And what if they were true?" He stared right into my eyes. "Jamie, I want to know the truth about Danilo." He waited for me to answer, but I kept silent. So he added, "And you."

My tea had cooled enough for me to drink it. He fell silent, waiting for me to answer him. Slowly I asked him, "How much do you know, then, or think you know?"

"I've seen both Danilo and you age, turn young, then age again. And again, and again. And please don't try and tell me it's a trick of the light or my imagination. I have photos."

My guard was up. "And what do you make of it?"

"I make death of it. I knew a few of the men who died two years ago. Closet cases."

"What of that?"

"I knew—I noticed once—that Danilo's name was phonetically the same as an ancient pharaoh. Semenkaru, Smenkhare. Ancient Egyptian, like ancient Hebrew, didn't use vowels. *Smenkhare* is a modern guess how the name would have been pronounced. Semenkaru is just as good."

I had to persuade him this was all coincidence. "You're letting your imagination run wild, Paul. Danilo, an ancient Egyptian?"

"The killings started at the same time he came to West Penn."

I fell silent, completely lost for what to say.

The doorbell rang. I had never been so happy to hear a sound, any sound. I suppose I'd always been aware that someone might guess the truth about Danilo, and about me. But it always seemed an abstract possibility, nothing more. I could compel Paul to forget, but…I don't know, for whatever reason, part of me didn't want to do that. Opening up to someone, finally having a friend I could confide in and trust…if I could…

I got up. "Let me get that."

Bubastis trotted after me to the front door. The cold blast when I opened it sent her running off again.

It was Kurt. Dressed, not naked, eyes and throat intact. He was bundled against the cold, but he was smiling. "Hi, Jamie."

I was stone. "What do you want?"

"Lazar wants to talk to you again. He has a proposition for you."

Sweet smile. "You can't always get what you want."

"You ought to see him. He'll be on campus the rest of the day, in his office." He smiled back at me. "He's writing an oratorio about death and resurrection."

"More and more I think Lazar Perske is a fool, Kurt. And so are you. You're not welcome here anymore. Please don't come again."

I closed the door on him and went back to the kitchen. Paul was just sitting down at the table again. Had he been eavesdropping?

He picked up his teacup, sipped and then smiled at me. "Jamie?"

"Hm?"

"Let me help."

I made my voice neutral. "I don't know what you mean."

"Let me help you find Danilo. Please, Jamie. I know someone who might be useful."

"Useful? In what way?"

"Look, none of it adds up, Jamie. I'm not stupid. Danilo leaving you his house, his weird disappearance…"

"The police say he was a victim of the serial killer."

"The police are wrong, and we both know it, don't we? All these things in his house—your house—these legends about immortals rising from the grave to lead us back to greatness. Please don't treat me like a fool, Jamie."

"You're doing what all the people in crackpot cults, do, Paul." I finally sat down again; my tea had cooled. "You're taking a bunch of unrelated facts, stringing them together in ways that only *seem* logical, and then you're drawing wild, irrational conclusions."

"'The road of excess leads to the palace of wisdom.'"

"Good god, where did you find that?"

He laughed. "It's from Blake. *The Marriage of Heaven and Hell!*"

"I've never read it." Blake was a half-mad visionary; more to the point, he was not one of my bloodline.

"You should. You might find it has a lot to say about your own marriage."

Suddenly Danilo's ring seemed to weigh on my finger. I decided to call Paul's bluff. "Okay, fine, you know someone who can 'help.' Have him come around sometime and we'll see."

"Not him, her."

"Her, then."

Bubastis let out a loud cry. I realized I'd forgotten to feed her before I left for campus that morning. I gave her an extra ration of moist food, and she chowed down happily.

Late that afternoon I had an appointment with Roland. He had agreed to tutor me in composition, even though he didn't really have the time. So he listened as my symphony progressed and give me feedback.

And he loved what I'd done so far. He found the themes rich and melodious, the development—what I had worked out of it—lively and interesting… I was pleased. I knew Roland well enough to know he wouldn't simply tell me it was good to make me feel good; he meant it.

As luck would have it, I ran into Perske as I was leaving. He smiled, and it was the phoniest smile I'd seen in months. "Why, Jamie."

"Hello, Dr. Perske."

"Dr. Perske? Are we back to that? I thought you were calling me Lazar."

"Lazar, then. Please excuse me, I have to get home."

"No." He said it quite forcefully. "We have to talk." He gestured to the open door of his office. A bit reluctantly, but aching to know what he might say, I stepped inside. He followed and closed the door. I opened it again. "If you don't mind, I'm feeling claustrophobic."

He shrugged. "Roland tells me he's taken over your tutoring in composition."

"Yes."

"That's a pity. I thought we were working well together."

"I didn't." I saw no reason to be anything but blunt. Even if, by some fantastic chance, he hadn't been the "Larry" of my father's journal, he had most certainly had Kurt following me around and eavesdropping on my conversations.

"You should hear the piece I'm working on, Jamie. I'm calling it my *Resurrection Symphony.*"

"Mahler already did that."

He chuckled. "So he did. But Mahler didn't know death and resurrection the way we do, did he?"

"I don't know *what* you know, Lazar." I was on edge. Talking to him at all had been a mistake. But I made my manner breezy. I stood up to go.

"Don't!" He shouted it; it was an order. Out in the hall a few students stopped and looked, startled.

"You don't have any authority over me. I'm leaving."

"Not legal authority, no. But there is such a thing as moral authority, Jamie. You must submit to it."

Appalled at hearing this from the man I believed to be my father's killer, I sat again. Peered at him. "You are the one who did it."

A benign, fatherly smile appeared on his lips. "Young people are always so confrontational. Why is that?"

"You can't hurt me. You have to know that."

"Are you sure? How deeply have you cut yourself? Have you tried throwing yourself off a high building, to see what would happen?"

He was admitting it. I stared into his eyes without saying anything, hoping I might find something there. They were cold and hard as granite.

"Jamie, think. You read the journal. It's too bad I couldn't get to you before you did, but…" He shrugged as if to say, those are the breaks. "The blood was strong there, in Ebensburg. I thought I had found him when I found your father."

The question must have showed on my face, even before I asked it. "Him?"

"The Blood Prophet." He spoke the phrase slowly, carefully, emphatically, every inch the teacher. "When he wouldn't see reason, I— But you've guessed that already. I never thought it might be you, not your father."

"Who are you?"

He waved a hand casually up and down the length of his body, as if it was the most obvious thing in the world. "You read. You must know and understand."

He wouldn't tell me any more; somehow I knew it. I had only skimmed the journal, stopping here and there, when something interesting had been going on. If I had read it all—but there hadn't been time for that. He thought I understood more than I actually did. "I'll be going now. Thank you for the lesson. And for the warning."

"You must believe in God, Jamie. You must."

"I believe in the Great God Set, the one who instructs us there are no gods."

"That's nonsense."

"No," I smiled and adopted the tone of a preacher. "It is a mystery. Like the trinity, or original sin."

He sighed. I wasn't playing his game by his rules. "Jamie, join us."

"Who exactly is 'us'?"

"I believe you know. And I believe you know we're right. Come to the side of truth and decency and enlightenment. I found your father before Danilo did. *He* found *you* first. But he's gone, and we're here."

I took a step toward the door. "You killed my father, didn't you?"

He shrugged.

"And that is the side of decency?"

"'I come not to bring peace, but a sword.'" He chuckled. "That's from the Gospel of Matthew."

"I know it. He was more honest than you."

I turned to go. Kurt was standing just outside the doorway. I wondered how much of our exchange he had heard. Most or all of it, I guessed. He moved to try and block me. I pushed my way past him and left the building as quickly as I could.

I tried not to think about that exchange for a few days. Paul kept hanging around. We made love a few times. He was sweet. If I hadn't known Danilo, Paul might have…but what's the point of a thought like that?

Days passed slowly. I knew I couldn't trust Perske anymore, or Kurt.

But every time I looked over my shoulder, one or the other of them seemed to be watching me. They couldn't actually hurt me, or at least I didn't think so; I had Danilo's blood in my veins. I had returned from the land of death. What could they do to me? And yet…how could I be sure? Despite Paul, despite Roland, I felt quite alone, and I felt Danilo's absence more deeply than I had since he first left.

Then three nights later I was at the keyboard working out the development for my first movement. It was snowing, a pretty substantial storm, large heavy flakes; but nothing near as bad as the blizzard had been. The door opened—I made a note to get the key back from Paul; I should have done it already—and in he walked with another guy on his arm. The guy was carrying a parcel wrapped in what looked like purple crepe.

No—I realized almost at once that it wasn't a guy at all. It was Joe Maggio, the lesbian from the campus group. Her drag was getting better, or her acting was. If I hadn't recognized her, I'm not sure I'd have known.

They both smiled at me. Paul waved and said, "Hi! I told you I have a friend who can help."

I closed the keyboard and stood up. "Joe."

"You two know each other?" Paul looked at her, puzzled.

She smiled back at me. "Just slightly, Paul. Jamie helped us with the music for our Christmas play."

"That's right. I should have remembered."

I crossed the room and shook hands with her, then kissed Paul on the cheek. "Let me take your coats. What can I get you to drink?"

Paul wanted cocoa; Joe said she'd like anything caffeine-free. Mysteriously she added, "I have to keep my channels open."

I invited them to make themselves comfortable and headed to the kitchen. Just as I was leaving the room, Bubastis trotted in, to check out the new arrivals in her territory. She looked from Joe and Paul to me, then back again. Her eyes widened. For a moment she seemed torn by indecision, the way cats sometimes do; then she turned and ran out of the room.

Paul followed me to the kitchen. I was more than bit annoyed. "You might at least have told me you were bringing her."

"I did." He was defensive. "In a way."

"Remind me. When did that happen?"

"I'm sorry, Jamie." He paused tentatively, then found the nerve to go on. "She has second sight. Everyone around campus says so."

"Does she use a crystal ball, or should I brew some tea and let her read the leaves?"

"When Danilo and I were…involved, I asked her to do a reading. She told me he didn't love me."

"He could have told you that himself."

"But she did. Jamie she knew, or she saw."

I made the cocoa and brewed some herbal tea for her. We all sat around the dining room table and drank and made smalltalk. Joe was graduating this term. She couldn't wait to get out into the real world. As she was saying this, she unpacked a Ouija board and placed it carefully on the table.

"The real world." I was wry.

"Yes." My irony was lost on her. "Of course, the world doesn't look the same to us two-spirit persons as it does to more mundane types. Shall we get started?"

I bit my tongue. The Ouija board was a large one; I had the impression it might be an antique. It was decorated with Egyptian gods and symbols around the edge —Thoth, Isis, Anubis, a line of ankhs and hieroglyphics—elaborately drawn and colored. I was going to point out that the glyphs were nonsense, that they didn't make any real Egyptian words. But it seemed better to stay quiet and get the damned silly thing over with. The script on the board, the "Yes" and "No" and the two rows of alphabet, were printed in an elaborate calligraphy, vaguely Arabic; it must have looked "Oriental" to people in the 19th century. I noticed, in very small print at the bottom corner, "1878."

Next, from her parcel she took what seemed to be an incense burner. From a small plastic bag she got what seemed to be some grayish-yellow gum, placed it precisely in the center of the burner, then lit it with a Bic lighter. The gum burned with an almost ghostly blue flame, and she closed the top of the burner. Its aroma was unpleasantly pungent. Her seriousness through all this struck me as funny. "Do we really need incense?"

"It isn't incense," she said in hushed, almost somber tones.

"Then—?"

"It's opium."

"Really?" I almost laughed but restrained myself. Absurd as it all was, it was goofy fun, too. I stared at the stream of smoke rising from it. "Opium."

"Mm-hmm." She giggled, pleased with herself. At our first encounter, doing the play, she had always struck me as no-nonsense, feet-on-the-ground. Now...

Finally she unpacked the planchette, the "pointer" for the Ouija board and placed it at the center. The ones I'd seen in the past had been roughly heart-shaped. This one took the form of an Egyptian god; his upraised arm was the pointer. And it was Set. Danilo's god. And mine. Coincidence; it had to be coincidence.

Joe seemed to read my thoughts. "There is no such thing as coincidence, Jamie. I've been using this board for five years. I saw it in a little occult shop, and something made me buy it. Now, tonight, I know why. It was for you."

Again I held my tongue. This kind of thing, this mystical hocus-pocus... I could as soon have believed in Bigfoot, or Atlantis... I knew enough about real ancient mysticism not to be taken in by this modern hokum.

I began to relax. The world suddenly seemed sweet to me, sweet and pure. I looked at Paul, and the expression on his face was pure bliss. So it really was opium. I wondered briefly where you'd go to get it. It seemed like something out of old movies, Limehouse, Chinatown, white slavery, the insidious hand of Fu Manchu...

"There's too much light in here." Joe interrupted my little reverie. I got up and dimmed the chandelier; then I went around the room turning on the little Tiffany lamps, for color, for mood and atmosphere.

Paul's eyes were closed; my lighting effect would be lost on him. When I sat down again I nudged him, but he was gone, high as that kite people talk about.

"And some music would help." She looked at me and her features were stone serious. "Something contemplative."

I went to the den, turned on the stereo, switched on the speakers in the dining room, and put on a CD. It was our recording of *Lonely Child*, Paul's and mine. Claude Vivier's sad, pensive, haunting music filled the air. It seemed to suit perfectly the atmosphere Joe wanted to create.

The room took on the most uncanny stillness. We might have been floating in some timeless place, in hell or Olympus or the Castle of the Holy Grail. Suddenly, there in my dining room, it seemed to me that anything was possible. Or nothing at all. It didn't seem to matter which.

Joe placed her fingers lightly on the planchette. I followed suit. Paul was out. She took his hand and positioned his fingers. My own hands seemed to weigh a ton and seemed to weigh nothing at all. Opium. I told myself that was all it was.

"Let us," she whispered, "begin now."

"Do we invoke the gods?" I asked and giggled.

"It doesn't matter that you don't take this seriously, Jamie. It will work none the less."

"Of course it will. Get us much higher and we'll turn into committed swamis for the rest of our lives."

"I am two-sprit, Jamie. And you…" A slight smile flickered on her lips and vanished, like the flame of the opium. "You are more than that, even."

She knew, somehow she knew, or thought she did, which came to pretty much the same thing. It was unsettling, it was dangerous, but I was too high to care.

Again as if she could read my mind she said, "No, there is no danger among the three of us. Not here, not tonight."

Suddenly the planchette moved under my fingers. I wasn't pressing on it at all heavily, and Joe didn't seem to be, either. And Paul's fingers weren't even quite touching it. Slowly it moved across the board. It seemed almost to glide. It rested at the word "No."

What was it responding to? To her claim that there was nothing dangerous? Or was it a more general "no"?

Joe looked at the planchette, at where it had come to rest, and her eyes widened slightly. "Check the windows and doors, Jamie. Make certain they're locked."

A bit reluctantly, feeling more than slightly foolish, I got up and went around the house, securing everything. Did she—did her Ouija board—somehow know about Perske and Kurt?

When I rejoined them in the dining room Paul seemed to be completely lost in his trance. Eyes wide open, now, staring blankly in front of him. His hands were stretched out over the board, hanging an inch or so above the planchette. Joe seemed to be almost as far gone. I sat down between them. Our fingers touched above the planchette.

"Someone is there," Joe intoned.

The planchette moved to "Yes."

"Who?"

It crept across the board to the alphabet. And came to rest at "D."

Danilo. I told myself not to get caught up in this. Joe glanced at me quickly, then refocused her attention on the board. "You have a question, Jamie. Ask it."

"D," I began, feeling quite the fool, "are you Danilo Semenkaru?"

Quickly the pointer moved. "Yes."

"Really?!"

It shook, it shuddered, and it made a large circle around the board, coming to rest again on "Yes."

Joe spoke. "You are dead, then? In the spirit world?"

It spelled out the word, "Half."

Joe and I looked at one another. I had to ask. "You are half dead and half living?"

The pointer moved to the alphabet again. "As always."

"Where are you?"

"Here. With you. Soul here." It spelled the words quickly.

I remembered Danilo explaining once that the soul and the body do not have to occupy the same space. The lights in the sky, the ancients knew, were the souls of the gods, whose physical selves moved here among us on earth. The planet Mars is the soul of the Great God Set.

"Where is your body, Danilo? Where are you?"

For what seemed eternity the planchette didn't move. Then, slowly, it pointed to the A. Then the M.

"Am— Where? Where are you, Danilo? And why did you leave me?" I felt tears coming. It was the opium.

Joe squeezed my hand. "One question at a time, Jamie. Don't rush him."

"A-M-A-R-N-A."

"Amarna? You are in Egypt?"

"Yes," said the board.

"Danilo." Tears were pouring down my face; I couldn't help it. I told myself it was the fucking drug in the air. "You said you loved me."

"I do."

"Why did you go?"

I felt Paul squeezing my hand, very hard. He spoke. But out of his mouth came Danilo's voice. "Jamie, you know why. I left to protect you."

Hearing his voice come from Paul's lips, I felt a dozen conflicting things. Danilo was there with us. He was not. This was a joke. This was real, it had to be.

Slowly, softly, terrified of the answer, I asked, "And why, Danilo, why have you never come back to me? For God's sake, why?"

The table shook, I looked from Paul to Joe, but they were both deep in an opium trance. The shaking became more violent.

I shouted, "Danilo, why?"

And the world turned to stars and comets, spinning madly about me. When they parted everything was dark. I was falling. I reached out, groped for something to hold onto, anything. There was nothing. Only night.

Then the blackness began to dissipate.

There was a mountainside. Into it was cut a tomb. Not an Egyptian tomb, not clean and square and sharply cut. Not with carved decorations. This was simple, rough and crude. A gaping mouth had been hacked into the stone. I stood and watched, and for a long, long time nothing happened.

Then a voice thundered, "Come forth!"

A figure appeared at the opening, haltingly, reaching for the light. A man. Wrapped in a winding-sheet. He stumbled to the opening out of the darkness. The shroud fell away. Naked and filthy he stood there, gasping for breath, groping for…for what? Life? Humanity?

Again darkness fell. My head spun and went numb. I tried to find something, anything to hold onto. There was nothing. Through black space and time I hurtled.

And was in another rock-cut place, another tomb or a temple. This time an Egyptian one; there was no mistaking it. Gods and demons lined the walls; torches burned brightly. A brazier burned incense or, I wondered, was it more opium?

In the center of the room, bound to an ancient throne, sat a man, soaked in blood.

And it was Danilo. Slowly, tentatively, I took a step toward him. His mouth was gagged with purple cloth. And it was not rope that bound him, it was something like barbed wire. It was coiled around him from head to foot, wrapped tightly across his face, his hands… The barbs dug into his flesh, and his blood poured out, soaking him, the throne, the floor, everything. More blood than seemed possible. It was the same vision, or dream, I'd had once before.

His eyes were contorted with pain. He saw me, seemed to recognize me. He struggled wildly against the barbed wire, which only made it dig more deeply into him. His eyes pleaded with me: *Release me, Jamie, free me.*

I felt a heavy blow to my face.

And woke up, at my dining room table. Joe and Paul were standing over me; Paul had me by the shoulders and was shaking me.

Something was wrong. I could feel that I was wet, soaking wet; my clothes were drenched. Stupidly I looked at Paul. "What happened?"

He gestured down at my body.

I looked.

Blood. I was covered in blood. At first I thought it must be Danilo's, somehow. Then I tried to move. There was pain. Pain everywhere I could feel. My body was covered with gashes, exactly like the ones that covered Danilo in my dream, or vision.

I tried to stand, but the piercing pain was too much. Involuntarily I screamed. And fainted. The last thing I remember was *Lonely Child,* still playing on the stereo.

CHAPTER 11

My sleep was tormented by dreams of Danilo, bound and suffering. There was fire; there was blood, his and mine flowing together. In that dark dream world it seemed to me there was no difference. When I woke, on what seemed a bright afternoon, I was still quite exhausted. It had not been the kind of sleep that gives rest.

There was no one else in the room. I tried to get out of bed. Unsteadily, holding onto the bedpost, I got to my feet. I was naked, and my body was covered with cuts, scores of them, some deeper than others; they were starting to heal, it appeared, but they were all painful. When I touched one, it stung horribly.

Paul came in. He was alert and smiling. All he had on was a sweatshirt, a pair of shorts and white sweat socks. "I thought I heard you."

"What day is it?"

"Don't worry. I called Roland and told him you have the flu. No one's missed you."

"How long was I out?"

"It's been three days."

"Jesus."

"No, Danilo. You've been calling out for him in your sleep. It was because you stopped calling that I knew you were awake."

There was music in the air, soft music. I recognized it. Scarlatti, one of the sonatas. Another of my forefathers.

Paul saw me listening. "I thought something baroque—something precise and mathematical—would be the thing, after the other night."

"It is." I put a hand on his arm to steady myself. "Get me some clothes, will you?"

He grinned. "I like you naked." But he went to the dresser and got me some underclothes, then got a pair of slacks and a flannel shirt from the closet.

Pulling them on, I winced. The cuts were still tender, very much so.

"Careful, Jamie. You lost a lot of blood."

"What did you do with it?"

He laughed at the question's oddness. "I cleaned it up. What else?"

"You didn't save any of it?"

"No." He was lost. "Why on earth…?"

"Nothing. Never mind."

I went to the mirror. My face was older than I had ever seen it; I looked forty or more. It was covered with cuts, tiny ones, enough to make me look grotesque. I hoped vaguely there wouldn't be scars.

"You should have seen yourself the other night. They seem to be healing really quickly, though." It pleased him.

I was hungry. Paul helped me to the kitchen. On the way he said, "I wanted to take you to the ER, but you kept shouting at me not to. And Joe agreed. She said they'd never understand what happened."

"She was right."

"She's been calling every day to see how you are. Jamie, what did happen?"

We went to the kitchen and I sat down at the table. Paul put on water for tea, then opened the refrigerator.

"Nothing too heavy, Paul. I couldn't."

"Just cereal?"

I nodded. He whipped up some hot oatmeal, sliced some strawberries. I dug in. The spoon seemed to weigh a ton.

"What happened to Joe?"

"She left, terrified. I don't think anything like that had ever happened to her before. Not surprising. She used to do tarot readings and such all the time. Now…" He looked over his shoulder at me. "She was shattered when she left. I don't think it ever occurred to her that her two-spirit nature might open up anything like that. Like I said, she's been calling."

"She should have stuck to telling her friends how their dates would go."

Paul sat down across from me. "Jamie, I want to know what happened."

I stared at him for a moment. I had to trust him. I had to trust someone, and Paul was all there was.

"Paul, I know where Danilo is, I think."

"You think."

"Yes. I'm going to Egypt."

"Then I'm coming, too."

I wanted to tell him, no, it's too dangerous, you don't know what you're getting into.

But before I could say anything he went on. "I'm not dumb, Jamie. I've made sense of a lot of this, I think."

I watched him but kept silent.

"This house. These portraits on the walls, all these artists and emperors. They were *us*. They were our forebears. And they didn't hide, at least most of them didn't."

Still I said nothing.

"I mean, they had the power not to have to. Didn't they? And look at us. From kings and philosophers to…" He left the thought unfinished, and he changed tack. "Power isn't something you *have,* Jamie, and it's not something you're given. It's something you *take*. I think you and Danilo have taken it."

It was inevitable that someone, someday, might guess what we were, might somehow divine the power we held. I almost laughed at that "we." Danilo was the one; I was only his follower.

"Jamie." He spoke with quiet emphasis. "I want that, too. I want that power."

I knew that he meant it, and I didn't see any point to arguing with him. He had the blood. He had the right. "You said you want to know the truth about Danilo and me."

He nodded.

"Then tonight…" I wasn't sure I could trust him, but I had to. "Tonight, you'll see me regain my strength. And you'll understand a bit more."

I wasn't sure what reaction to expect. But he was quite sober, quite serious. "All right."

"We have one more thing to do. I know where Danilo is, I think, but there's something I can check to make certain. Will you help me?"

Again he nodded.

"We're going someplace dark, Paul."

"Jamie, I know it."

Paul drove. I was still weak; but that would pass before the night was over.

I had never gone to Dayton, Ohio, before. Small place; not much there but a backwater college. A religious college, staffed by Catholic clergy. Fertile ground for what I needed.

There was a bar just outside town, dingy, working-class, anonymous, no questions please. We parked then went in separately, Paul a minute or two after me. I sat at the bar, at the far end, where the light wasn't good; he got a beer and stood in a corner, watching. The jukebox played country, loudly. The place smelled like stale cigarettes and staler liquor.

The customers were nearly all in jeans and flannels, and they were a mix of men and women, mostly men. At one end of the place were the bathrooms, side by side; on the door of one, someone had scratched out Women and written in Boys. That passed for wit in Dayton, Ohio, it seemed. Two straight couples danced; everyone else watched or sat indifferent. Not many were talking. Desultory place.

I glanced at Paul. He was dressed prep and looked out of place. A guy approached him, late middle-age, sixty or so. They chatted. Paul shook his head, then shook it again more emphatically. The guy gave up and looked around for someone else.

It wasn't long before he fixed on me. A bit tentatively, he crossed the room to where I was sitting. In his late fifties at least, I guessed a bit older; eyeglasses, bad plugs, out of shape. Black polyester slacks and sweater. He smiled. "Cold night."

I pretended to be bored. "It's winter."

It wasn't funny, but he laughed. Did I look like that big a pushover? "My name's Ralph." I didn't believe it; he didn't expect me to. He held out his hand.

Still acting bored, I shook it. "Peter."

"Nice to meet you, Peter." He smiled and sat down beside me. Things were going better than he seemed to have expected. "I'm in real estate."

I took a stab. "Bullshit. You're a priest and you teach at the college."

Mild alarm showed in his face. "How—how did you know?"

"Are you kidding? You've got it written all over you." And he did. There was that same manner I had noticed in scores of other ministers, a bizarre mixture of sanctimoniousness and cringing.

"You won't—?"

"Relax, father. You're not worth the cost of the phone call to out you."

It was an insult, a calculated one, but he ignored that and relaxed. The bartender asked what he wanted, and he ordered a Scotch on the rocks. Then he turned back to me. "So, what do you do, Peter?"

"Name it."

It caught him quite off guard; he wasn't used to people being so direct, it seemed. "Anything?"

"The wilder, the better."

He looked back over his shoulder at Paul. Paul looked like a college boy; I looked forty. But you take what you can get. He drank half his Scotch in one gulp. "Do you get into S&M?"

"Like you've never imagined."

Involuntarily, I think, he broke into the widest smile. "There's a motel down the road. It's nothing fancy, but they aren't nosy."

I pretended to think for a moment. The last time I tasted a preacher's blood, it was foul. What the hell, I needed it.

"Let me pay your tab, Pete."

"Thanks." I was getting friendlier.

The bartender dropped some of the cash and couldn't seem to find it. He switched on some overhead lights, and there was an instant flurry of activity in the place. Everyone faced away. Dear me, we can't have anyone *know*, can we? "Ralph" was the worst of them; he covered his face with his hands and then lowered his head almost to the level of the bar. But in the instant before, he saw me. When the lights went on again and he recovered himself, he commented on the cuts on my face.

"I'm a careless shaver. What of it?"

It was good enough. He wanted me, or rather he wanted sex.

"One thing, though, Ralph."

"Yes?"

I nodded in the Paul's direction. "My friend over there."

He looked. "That kid?"

I nodded.

"He's your lover?"

"No, just a friend. But he likes to watch."

He looked from Paul to me and back again, then smiled and nodded. "This will really be kinky."

"You said it."

This time I drove. We followed him down the road a few miles. Dingy little motel, off the main highway. We waited while Ralph went in and paid for a room. Paul said the place looked like the Bates Motel.

I did an old lady's voice. "You got the guts, boy?"

"Yes, mother."

We kept an eye on the office to make sure no one was looking out, trying to see who Ralph had with him. There was no indication they gave the least damn.

Ralph came out and waved to us. We followed him to the room, and he switched on the lamp beside the bed. It wasn't very bright, which was fine. The place smelled of its last dozen or so occupants. Paul stepped discreetly into a corner, as he had done at the bar. I expected him to be nervous, but the only thing that showed in his face was anticipation.

Ralph sat down on the bed and began to undress. In the process he got a pair of handcuffs and a little toy whip out of his back pockets.

"Not yet," I ordered.

Startled, apparently pleased, he stopped and smiled at me.

I crossed the room to him and slapped him. "Wait for orders."

"Yes, sir."

Then I bent down and kissed him on the top of his head. "Good boy."

We were slipping into our roles nicely. But suddenly he broke character. "Can I tell you something, Peter?"

"Go ahead." I pretended to be bored.

"You know my vocation."

"What of it?"

"In the morning, after we've finished…"

"Yes?"

"I can give you absolution. You won't have to carry any guilt for the sin we're going to commit."

"Imagine that."

He turned tentative. "Will that be okay?"

"What makes you think I want 'absolution'?"

It seemed to be the most unexpected thing I could have said. He stammered, "I—I—I—I—"

"Are you going to yodel?"

Then he recovered and remembered what we were there to do. "I'm sorry, sir."

I slapped him again. He quivered with anticipation, or with…I couldn't imagine what.

"Get down on your knees."

He did, and lowered his eyes.

"Look up at me."

He did. He was shaking.

"Kiss my foot."

Down he went, and kissed.

"Worship me."

He looked up, puzzled. "I—?"

"Worship me. Pray to me. Make me your god."

Slowly, nervously, he leaned forward and kissed my crotch. He licked it, he made love to it.

Then he reached for my zipper.

I slapped him again, harder this time. "Ask!"

"Please, sir, I want to kiss it."

From the corner of my eye I glanced at Paul. He was aroused; it showed. And he was doing everything he could to excite himself even more. I turned back to Ralph and told him, "Beg for it. Pray for it."

"Oh, please sir." Even his voice was shaking. "Let me worship your body. Let me see your—"

From the nightstand where he had left them I took the handcuffs. Quickly, briskly I snapped them on his wrists. He was quivering so badly I thought he might have a heart attack. I had to act quickly.

There was no way I wanted to use my teeth on this one. I had brought the golden ceremonial knife. Quickly it plunged into his throat; even more quickly he collapsed onto the motel room floor. For a moment he trembled, then he was still.

I got down and went to work. Blood—it tasted awful, but it renewed my strength. Eyes, heart, genitals. My face covered with blood and bodily fluids, I looked to the corner where Paul as standing, watching. He was stimulating himself; I had never seen him so excited. When he saw me watching, he quickly reached a powerful climax. As Ralph had shaken, now Paul shook, quite violently. He didn't have to tell me he had never felt anything so intense; it was in his face and his voice. He let out a loud, satisfied sigh, or moan, then crossed the room to me quickly, and we kissed.

"Jamie, I've never seen anything more exciting."

"We aim to please, Paul." I kissed him again, even harder.

"Danilo...he gave you this?"

I nodded and smiled. "Come on, let's get out of here."

"Shouldn't we...I don't know, hide his body or something?"

"They'll find it sooner or later anyway. This isn't quite like the way I've taken any of the others, I doubt the police will connect it to anything else. Besides, he's a priest at a Catholic university. The story will get covered up quickly enough."

"Maybe not." Suddenly he was looking worried.

"Paul, trust me. Even if the police find us, they won't do anything."

"You can't know that."

"I can. Believe me." I realized I was sounding like Danilo, back when he used to tell me the university officials would never do anything about our love affair. The realization pleased me.

"Jamie, have you looked at yourself?"

I stepped in front of the mirror. I was young again. Eighteen, nineteen. All the cuts were healed. Paul stepped behind me and put his arms around me. "I just knew it," he whispered. "I knew it in my blood."

"Our blood carries more wisdom than we ever realize, Paul." I switched off the light. "Let's go." Then I noticed something. "Paul?"

"You've got blood on your lips, from when we kissed."

He licked it off and smiled at me. "Does it always taste like this?"

"Nope. It varies from man to man. It must be dietary or something." Just outside the door I caught him by the shoulder. "One more thing, Paul."

"Anything. Name it."

I held out my left hand. In the dim light from the highway Danilo's ring gleamed. "Kiss it."

For a moment he seemed uncertain. Then a wide smile crossed his face, and he pressed the ring to his lips quite eagerly.

"Let's go."

He wanted me to drive. I wasn't at all certain why.

But as we traveled the dark roads it became obvious why. He was watching me, dotingly, adoringly, like a man in love.

Now that I was strong and young again, it was time to return to Egypt. Paul already had a passport; he had spent a summer studying voice in London.

I called the Egyptian consulate in New York City and told them I had been a friend of the late Colonel Mahawi. They promised to expedite visas for us.

It took three days, and it seemed to me that in all that time the only thing I could see was Danilo, wrapped in wire, bleeding, suffering. I poured my emotion into what would be the final movement of my *Hadrian Symphony,* the death of Antinous. There would be more music, too, a triumphant theme when the dead boy became a god. But triumphal music would have to wait.

And I spent time pouring through Danilo's library. Am arna—I had searched there, twice. I'd gone so far as to explore each of the old rock-cut tombs. And there was no sign of him. Yet every indication I had pointed to him being there. Where? Where could he be?

Finally on the third day I got confirmation of our visas by email. It seemed to have taken forever. We would fly to New York, get our passports stamped with the visas, then go on to Cairo. The first time I went to Egypt it had been with Danilo, and we sailed. This time, I could not afford the leisure.

I called Roland and told him I had more family business to clear up in Ebensburg; I'd be gone for a few days, maybe a week or so. He promised to cover for me with my instructors. Paul made a similar call to the head of the voice department. Then we started to pack. There was one particular item I wanted to take with me; some instinct told me I would need it, and I made certain it was packed securely. Our flight was scheduled for first thing next morning.

That afternoon the skies turned an alarmingly dark gray. The forecasters were all talking about an impending ice storm.

Paul was living at my place now. I didn't love him the way I loved Danilo, but I loved him. One of the stranger follies of the modern world is this notion that we only have the capacity to love one other person. And Paul—he was still quite taken with his memories of Danilo, but he told me he loved me too. And he even told me he loved my power.

"Wait," I told him, "till you experience Danilo's."

"What if this storm really hits? What if our flight's delayed, or canceled?" He put on a grin. "You can't control the weather, too, can you?"

"No such luck. But we need this storm. It'll help cover up what we have to do tonight."

He looked at me, puzzled.

"I'm pretty sure I know where Danilo is. There's one thing that will tell me for certain."

It was late Sunday afternoon; it would be dark soon. The campus was usually pretty much deserted on Sunday nights; an ice storm would practically ensure there would be no one around.

"Here?" He was lost. I hadn't told him about Perske.

"Yes. Believe it or not, there's something important we can learn in Pittsburgh."

Puzzled, he followed me. We walked to the campus; it took twenty minutes or so to get there. By the time we arrived the sky was dark—not quite nightfall, but we would have a bit of cover. Streetlights came on, casting that unpleasant yellow glow over everything. Just as we reached the music department the rain started. It was one of those odd days when the ground was colder than the air. What fell as rain turned to ice as soon as it hit the street. Within minutes everything was glistening with it, not just the street surfaces but phone poles, light poles, the sides of buildings, everything was encased in ice.

"Jamie, we ought to get home. This will get bad."

"We won't be long."

"But—"

"This is important, Paul."

The front doors were locked; they usually were on Sunday nights unless there was a recital. But there was a door at the rear of the building that was almost never locked. No one knew it but me, I think, but Roland had it left open in case he forgot his keys, which he did now and then.

The place was quite empty. Low blue emergency lights along the bottom of the walls gave the only illumination, and it wasn't much—which was good for us. Paul was nervous. "Jamie, this is illegal. We could be—"

"Roland would never press charges against me. Relax."

We walked softly, but our boots made enough sound to echo. From outside we could hear the rain; it was getting heavier.

Perske's office was unlocked. I switched on the desk lamp. Paul reached for the overhead switch, but I caught his hand. "No, we don't want too much light."

"Jamie, what are we doing here?"

"There." I pointed to the map on the wall. "That will tell me for certain."

Paul got to it a step before I did. "Egypt."

I nodded. Inspected it closely. There were all those colored pins. Yes, the bright red one was stuck precisely into Amarna. Danilo was there; I knew it.

Just as important, I suddenly knew there was one who could tell me for certain. And he was at Amarna too.

Almost at once we heard something. The front door of the building was opening. It would be a faculty member, or maybe security; no one else had keys. I switched off the lamp, stepped to the door, and closed it quickly and quietly. Paul came to my side and took my hand.

There were voices in the hall. At first they were indistinct, the they came closer. It was Perske and Kurt.

We pushed ourselves into a corner. The doorknob turned and the door swung open. In the dim light from the hall we saw their outlines as they embraced and kissed. "They'll be here soon," Perske whispered. How could he know?

I had made love to Danilo a hundred times. I don't know why, but the sight of Kurt in Perske's arms turned my stomach. Their embrace finished, Perske reached for the overhead switch.

I whispered to Paul, "Let's go!" and we made a break for it, pushing past them and dashing down the hall.

There were loud footsteps behind us. I heard Perske shout, "No, Kurt! They'll be taken care of!"

But he kept coming, and I could hear him getting closer. Paul and I pushed open the door we'd come in by and ran. Behind the music department is a maze of alleys and corridors. I had explored them,; most people never did. We ducked into one. But the world was ice. Paul slipped and skidded into a dumpster. "Jamie, my ankle!"

I helped him to his feet and he tested his weight. We could hear Kurt's footsteps in one of the other alleyways. "Can you walk?"

Uncertainly he nodded.

"Come on, then."

He put an arm around my shoulder and we headed out of the alley and toward the main avenue.

"What if he catches us?"

"I can handle Kurt. I don't know why I let myself panic and run like that."

"What about Perske?"

"He's not the one chasing us."

The rain was coming down in sheets and freezing almost at once. Footing was treacherous. Just was we reached the avenue Kurt appeared behind us. "Stop!"

There was no one else in sight. Only we were mad enough to be out in it. The rain poured down heavily, clearly visible in the cones of light, and froze as soon as it hit. We stopped and the curb and looked up and down the street, to make certain there was no traffic coming. A city bus came slowly around the corner and proceeded up the street, past us.

I looked back at him. "What do you think you're doing, Kurt?"

"You broke into Lazar's office. We've got you."

"Go back inside, Kurt. You can't do anything to me. If Perke's been at all honest with you, you know that."

"I don't know what you mean. You're the burglars, not me."

Paul seemed to be getting some strength back in his ankle. He let go of me and tested it. "I think I'm okay, Jamie. The stiffness is passing."

I could have compelled Kurt to leave us alone and go back inside. But letting him know what was happening, letting him see us leave, would give me too much satisfaction. Softly I said, "There's a bus stop at the next corner, Paul. There should be another one along any time now."

We started walking; Paul leaned on me, not as heavily as he had before. Our clothes were soaked. A ferocious gust of wind blow up, and the freezing rain sprayed us like the mist from a waterfall. There was no traffic in sight. "Come on, let's cross."

We stepped into the street. It was even slicker than the sidewalk. Slowly, relying on each other for support, we headed across.

"Jamie, stop!" I glanced back over my shoulder. Perske had come out the front door of the department. Kurt was at the curb, calling after us.

"Kurt, leave them go." Perske looked agitated. He could do more to us than Kurt. Why was he so upset?

From nowhere, and at breakneck speed, a car came tearing along the street. It seemed to come out of nowhere. I realized it was heading directly for us. "Paul, run!"

We moved as quickly as the icy street would let us. The car approached at horrifying speed, coming straight at us. The driver must have been mad—or else he was targeting us.

But at the last moment the car skidded out of control and hit Kurt. I heard him scream, then he went down. By the yellow streetlight I could see his head was crushed.

The car plowed into a phone pole. The driver gunned his engine, but the tires skidded and began to smoke. The air was filled with the smell of burning rubber and the awful screech of the wheels. Finally they caught some traction and the car headed off up the avenue, veering wildly from side to side. In the moment it had been delayed, I had a chance to see it clearly. In the rear window was a sign announcing Alliance for Christian Morals. Returning America to God's Own Truth.

Yes, they had been targeting us. And they were in alliance with Perske. I was furious at myself for not realizing it before.

Paul was terribly shaken. He pointed to Kurt. "We should see if we can help."

"He's dead, Paul. Just look."

"Please, Jamie. We can't just leave him lying there."

I stayed where I was while he went to the middle of the street and stood over Kurt's body. Blood was pouring onto the ice. Even at a distance it was possible to see the edges of the pool freezing, beginning to turn to bright red ice. But Kurt wasn't moving. Paul looked down at him, then back at me.

"Jamie, we have to do something."

"What?"

"Call the police. Call 911."

"You didn't want to call them for Ralph."

He looked numb. Slowly he came back to where I was standing. "This is different. I know him. We—" He caught himself, but he didn't have to say it. It showed in his face. He and Kurt had had an affair.

"Come on, Paul, we have to go."

The rain seemed to be letting up. But it was still turning to ice on the street. I asked Paul if he'd noticed the sign in the car. He hadn't.

There was no sign of Perske. Paul thought he must be inside, calling the emergency number. I told him I didn't think so. "Just wait till you see the news tomorrow morning. Hit-and-run killing, no clues, no witnesses."

He looked at me, and he knew that I knew. Perske had sacrificed his disciple. By accident, certainly, but the loss was nothing to him, or not much.

We saw another bus coming up the avenue. The driver saw Kurt's body lying in the street, stopped, picked up his phone to call it in.

The campus library was just beside the Music Department. We stepped into a sheltered doorway and watched. After a few minutes the police arrived and talked to the bus driver; then an ambulance came and took Kurt's body away.

CHAPTER 12

Kurt was dead, and we both felt terrible about it, but there was nothing to be done. Paul and I discussed whether we should call the police and tell them what we'd seen. But there was no way to explain why we'd been there, out in the driving ice storm. And no one had seen us, except Perske and the murderous driver himself... It seemed a safe bet it was us, or at least me, he was really trying to hit.

This was troubling to me. Danilo had given me to understand I was immortal, that I couldn't die except by choice. And I had thought about it, from time to time. But if Perske and his cohorts thought they could kill me... I had no idea what to make of it, but it was more than mildly alarming.

On the news, the story of the hit-and-run killing on the West Penn campus was a footnote to all the other storm coverage. Then the anchor interrupted another story with "breaking news." Pastor Heinrich of the Alliance for Christian Morals had telephoned police to tell them that his driver had done it; he would be turning himself in to the police, and Heinrich would accompany him to make a statement. Icy road, poor visibility, they both panicked...prayers for the dead boy's soul, assurances that he was in heaven now...their confession was self-serving and strictly according to a lawyer's script. If they were prosecuted at all, the driver would take the fall.

I decided to check my luggage. There was that one special item I had to take. I had no idea what impulse told me I would need it, but... I had not looked at it or touched it in months. It was still warm.

Late that night the storm began to taper off. By 3 a.m. it had stopped. Paul was still shaken by what had happened to Kurt. We sat on the couch in the den and held each other and slept on and off. Together, we still felt alone. Bubastis curled up beside us and purred herself to sleep. Our New York flight was due to leave at ten, if it wasn't delayed by the awful weather.

For some reason we both woke at the same moment. We gaped

sleepily at one another, stretched and yawned. Paul got to his feet and looked around; he was feeling lost, I could tell. The cat jumped down and headed for the kitchen, where we kept her food.

"I've never seen anyone die like that before, Jamie."

"There was Father Ralph, or whatever his real name was."

"That was different. He was already dead, in a way."

"Kurt was hiding his true nature, too. Perske persuaded him to do it."

"I don't understand this at all. What does Perske have to gain in Kurt—or you or me—hiding our nature?" He sat down again and shook his head. Things were happening too fast for him, I knew. "Now, suddenly, death is everywhere I look."

"It's at the bottom of everything, Paul. How many baroque oratorios about the suffering and death of Christ have you sung?"

"I need life. That's all I'm saying. Seeing anything hopeful would be wonderful. Perske…" Whatever he was thinking, he left unsaid.

I crossed to the front window. Ice covered everything. Nothing in the world seemed to be moving but the two of us and Bubastis.

"Come outside with me, Paul."

"What? Why?"

"There's something I have to show you."

He couldn't have looked more baffled; but he followed me through the kitchen and out the back door to the yard. Bubastis waited patiently; she was a good cat and never tried to get out.

Ice crunched under our feet. The freezing rain had stopped but there was still a frigid wind. Paul wrapped his arms around himself. Idly I flicked a shrub with my forefinger; the ice on it cracked but didn't fall off.

"What are we doing out here?"

I wasn't entirely certain, myself. "The last person I showed this to, died."

Puzzlement showed in his face.

I got down on my knees, and almost at once I could feel the ice through my jeans. Making a fist, I punched through the ice on the ground in front of me and begin to dig with my fingers. The earth was frozen; clawing through it was work.

"Jamie, what on earth are you doing?"

I didn't answer; I was quite intent on finding soft clay. A foot down, I hit it. And took a handful. And then looked up at Paul.

He didn't have to ask again; I could see he was bewildered.

I took the clay and formed it into an animal, a stout little thing like a hippo. It was crude; the clay was too cold to be very pliant. But then I warmed it in my hands and breathed on it.

My little creation moved. Stiffly it raised its head and looked first at me, then at Paul. And it let out a little bleat.

"Jamie." He moved close, to see; he stood directly over me. The animal, of no definite species, made a little circle in my outstretched palm. "Jamie, this isn't…this isn't possible." He caught himself. "Yes, it is, isn't it?"

"Here." I held it out to him.

He opened his palm and let the little thing walk onto it. "This is magical, Jamie." His breath was icy smoke. "You have magic in you."

"I don't know what I have in me. I only know I can make life where there was none. Danilo did it to me, when I was dead." Kneeling there in front of him I told him, "Paul, I'm terrified."

He touched the animal on its back, as if feeling it would make it easier to believe in. "You're afraid, and you can do this?"

I nodded. "I don't understand how, though. I only know I can do it. I don't know if I can really create life, or if I'm only giving this animation. Does it have a soul?"

"Danilo gave you this…this gift."

"Yes."

He got down beside me and put a hand on my shoulder. "I can't tell you how I wish it was me he had chosen, me he had taught."

"Then I'd be here comforting you."

"Is that what I'm doing?" He didn't seem to know what to do with the animal. He looked around for a place to put it down, but everything was ice. "I don't feel like I have anything I could possibly tell you."

"Merely having you here with me is a comfort, Paul. I'm so scared."

"Of what, exactly?" he asked it very softly.

"I'm afraid Danilo will teach me what this magic means. And I'm afraid he won't. I'm terrified I won't find him, yet I know that finding him means more and more of the darkness and the unknown. I'm afraid I won't be able to help him, Paul, and afraid that helping him will make my life even more chaotic. He always told me that I'm a prophet. He called me his Blood Prophet. I'm so frightened of learning what that means."

He got to his feet, then held out a hand to help me to mine. "The kind of chaos you just described, Jamie, is love."

"Is it?" I was lost. "How can love feel like that? It should be clear. It should be simple. Unambiguous."

"You've seen too many old movies, that's all. Clueless as I am, I know the voice of love when I hear it." He looked at the animal in his hand. "What do we do with this?"

It brought me back to reality, at least for the moment. "I've always just let them go."

"There are more of these things running around?"

I nodded.

"You'll make Bubastis jealous."

"Here, let me have it."

I took it, held it to my lips, and inhaled. I drew the breath of life out of it. It was suddenly inert, a poorly molded lump of clay, no more.

Paul stared at it. "Poor thing. To know life so briefly."

"Maybe that's more of a blessing than we know." I picked some ice off a shrub. "Paul?"

"Hm?"

"If we can't find Danilo, I'll die."

"I thought you couldn't."

"Not if I don't want to. But without him…" I threw the clump of clay that had been the little animal into some bushes. "Without him, I can't imagine there'd be any point to living."

He led me back inside, closed the door firmly, then took my hands between his and warmed them.

"We should get some sleep, Jamie."

"Ever since he left, I've been making my life up as I go along, Paul. I want him. I need him. What on earth will I do if I can't find him?"

Bubastis came in and jumped up onto the kitchen table, meowing for attention. I reached out a hand and stroked her.

Paul picked her up and nuzzled her. "Is she fixed?"

I shook my head and told him about what Greg Wilton had doe to her. "She had been through so much else, I just thought…"

"You should breed her, then. This house needs new life."

"She's a mutt. A 'mixed breed.'"

"Even so."

Paul gave her a treat. She waited happily for more. But it was time for us to get some sleep.

He left me in my bedroom. "I'll sleep downstairs tonight." Wise boy. I thanked him, kissed him goodnight and started to undress.

But he lingered at the door and watched me. "Jamie?"

"Hm?" I kicked my shoes off and looked at him.

"What you said—that could be me, too."

I didn't know what he meant.

He smiled at me. "We all make our lives up as we go along. We even invent our own histories. That's all life is, just improvisation."

It would never have occurred to me to think that. But I saw his point. It helped my mood, at least slightly.

I got up, crossed to him, kissed him goodnight a second time. Bubastis came in and jumped on my bed. It was time for sleep.

Late, very late, I woke again. Something was wrong. I could feel it, even though I didn't know what it might be.

Without bothering to dress or even put on a pair of shoes, I went quietly downstairs. The house was dark, but light came in from the street. Most of the windows were glazed with ice; light came in, but it wasn't possible to see much.

Just as I reached the den, Paul sat up on the couch. "Something's wrong."

"I know it. I had to come down and see."

The living room windows weren't caked with ice; they faced east, away from where the storm had come. We stood and looked out. There was something moving, a shadow, nothing more, creeping in and out among the shrubs and hedges.

"I'm going out to see who it is."

"Jamie, don't." He caught my arm.

I looked at him.

"Think, Jamie. It was you they wanted to kill before. They'll try again. Whoever is out there—"

"Or whatever."

"Whoever or whatever it is can't be friendly. Not tonight. Not here."

"It could come in and attack me—us—just as easily."

"No. I don't think so. It would have come in already. It would have taken us asleep. But this is Danilo's house."

Even gone, he was protecting me. I took tight hold of Paul's hand, and we looked outside again. There it was, dark as midnight, shapeless as sin, creeping about.

"It's looking for a way in, Jamie."

"It won't find one,: I said. "This is Danilo's house. We're safe here."

We went back to the den and sat in the night, holding hands like the frightened boys we were, and listened.

Nothing else happened.

Nothing.

Morning. Sunlight gleaming on all the ice, almost blindingly so. Whatever dark thing had been there in the night was gone. We shared a light breakfast, just hot cereal and juice.

I found myself feeling foolish. "It was a cat, Paul, nothing but a stray cat. We let it spook us."

"Do you think it was anything like the cat that crushed Kurt's head?"

Point taken. We didn't talk much more. Soon enough, it was time to leave for the airport.

Uncharacteristically, the city cleared the roads efficiently. We got to the airport quickly. The place was near empty; most people must have expected worse roads, and delays. Our flight was held up; the storm hadn't quite left the east coast yet.

Waiting, pacing, wanting to be off, I called the neighbor who was looking after Bubastis. She had a male cat. I told her that if Bubastis came into heat while I was gone, I'd like her to breed them. She seemed a bit puzzled but told me she'd do what she could.

So we waited, and our flight finally took off, two hours late. Then we were stacked up over LaGuardia for nearly another two hours. By the time we reached the Chelsea Hotel and checked in, it was mid-afternoon. The desk clerk knew me; I'd been there often enough. Trying to make chitchat, he told me the police had never found whoever had killed Col. Mahawi.

"That's too bad. Can we have my usual room?"

"Of course." He looked Paul up and down and seemed to approve of him. They have high standards at the Chelsea; later I told Paul so. He seemed pleased but not quite certain what to make of it.

We had missed our appointment at the Egyptian consulate. I called and rescheduled for first thing the next morning. If things went smoothly there, we would leave plenty of time to make our flight to Cairo. The last traces of the storm had passed, and the evening promised to be a bit warmer than usual.

That night we had a good dinner at my favorite Italian place, then took in a Broadway show. It was one of the plastic, corporate-made messes. The audience seemed to love it, except for us. We left at intermission. Paul had never been to the city before, except for quick stopovers, so we walked around, taking in the sights, Rockefeller Center, Times Square, Lincoln Center, Central Park…

More than the sights, Paul liked the men. "This is almost as good as London. All the eye contact everyone makes. What an incredibly sexual city." He gawked at everything like a tourist.

That night we slept side by side, and it felt good to have him in the bed; but he seemed to sense that, now that I had some prospect of finding Danilo, lovemaking between the two of us was over. I was grateful not to have to deal with the issue. The only other true friend I'd ever had was Justin Hollis, and he died horribly. Paul was a good man; I knew it.

There were not many people at the Egyptian consulate next morning. It hardly needed to be said that political conditions there had discouraged tourism. At any rate, we didn't have to wait long.

A young man approached us from behind a desk. He was tall, lean, handsome in the way so many Egyptian men had always seemed to me. Gray business suit, gleaming white shirt—to all appearances, a typical bureaucrat.

When we saw him approaching, Paul leaned close and whispered to me, "He has the blood, doesn't he?"

I nodded. "It's not strong in him, but it's there. You're learning."

The man approached us, hand extended. "Mr. Dunn and Mr. Koerner?" We told him yes, that's who we are, and he smiled broadly. "I'm am Magid el-Lahas. We spoke on the telephone, I believe."

"Mr. El-Lahas." I shook his hand energetically.

"You were friends of Colonel Mahawi?" He gestured us to a pair of chairs in front of his desk.

"Not friends, exactly. I spoke with him a few times. About common interests." I waited to see if this would get a reaction from him, but he stayed quite impassive in that way Moslems can do so well. "We had an appointment to meet when he…"

"Yes." He turned suddenly businesslike. "You are traveling to Egypt."

"We are."

"For what purpose?"

"To see the country. I've been there three times before, and it's my favorite place on earth. I wanted Paul, here, to see it too."

It was obvious he saw through the lie. "You know the old saying, I'm sure. 'He who drinks of the waters of the Nile will soon return.'"

Paul smiled. "I love the sound of that. It means I'll be going back, too."

El-Lahas seemed to want no social niceties. "We are pleased that you feel that way. May I have your passports, please?"

We handed them across the desk and without bothering to check them, he endorsed them both. That was that.

And it seemed that the time for business ended abruptly. He lost his bureaucratic manner and told us, "Sayeed Mahawi was my cousin."

"Oh." It shouldn't have surprised me, I guess. "You have my deep condolences for his death."

"He has gone to Allah. That is enough." He lowered his voice and looked around the office. No one was paying any attention to us. But if anyone overheard…same-sex love was quite illegal in his homeland, and quite actively prosecuted. "Sayeed and I were…close." I took his meaning. "Please be discreet. No one must know."

"Of course not." Paul looked around, too; I wasn't certain what for. "You can rely on us, Mr. El-Lahas."

"We had no secrets. I know precisely why you are returning to my country, Mr. Dunn."

Neither Paul nor I seemed to know what to say.

"I wish you luck in your endeavor."

"Thank you. Might I—might I ask a small favor?"

"Please do." For the first time his smile turned warm.

"Your cousin…" How could I explain that I'd taken a map from his room? "I have a certain document of his." El-Lahas watched me. "A map."

"May I ask how you obtained it?"

"He left it for me at the hotel desk." Convenient lie.

"I see."

"It's annotated. I presume the handwriting is his. Might I ask you to translate what he wrote?"

"Of course. Not here. I shall meet you for lunch."

"I'm afraid we'll have to leave for the airport rather soon."

"Oh." Again he looked around. "I am due for a break in twenty minutes. Might we meet outside the building then?"

It would be fine. We made a show of thanking him and shaking his hand, like good prospective tourists, then we left the office.

It was a cool sunny morning. We waited on the sidewalk, chatting and people-watching. Ten minutes later El-Lahas joined us. He had a smile that was something between foxy and shamefaced. "I took my break early."

I pulled the map out of my shoulder bag and handed it to him. Quickly he scanned it. "This"—he pointed to a jotting at the top of the page—"is the telephone number of a young gentleman, it appears." He looked to us and frowned. "He had many such. We always fought." Back to the map. "And this is the address of a delicatessen. America corrupts us in so many ways." He laughed at his own little joke.

I pointed to the place where he had circled Amarna. "What does this note mean?"

The writing wasn't clear. He squinted at it. "It says, 'Temple of the Sun,' I think. Does that mean anything to you?"

It did. "And do you have any idea why he might have sketched these dogs in the neighboring space?"

He squinted. "Doodles, nothing more, I imagine."

Something in his manner made me suspect they might be more than that. But it hardly seemed important enough to make an issue of. He had been so helpful; knowing about the temple—that was the most important thing.

"Mr. Dunn, Mr. Koerner." He lowered his voice and looked around still again, as if to convince himself no one from the consulate was with-in earshot. "There are those of us, Egyptians, I mean, who are fully in sympathy with your goal. Our past is so much richer than our present, and you are helping to recover it."

"It is our past too, Magid."

"Exactly. The climate for us is not good at home. In the diplomatic service we have so much more freedom. Sayeed and I both understood perfectly. Perhaps in time, and with the help of men like yourselves, things will change again to what they once were."

We thanked him again for his help and I gave the map to Paul. It was time to get back to the hotel, check out and head for the airport. Our flight was at 2. When we left him, El-Lahas was smoking a formidable-looking cigar and eyeing young men as they passed him on the street. Strange life he must have led, outlaw in his homeland, free man when sent to represent it abroad.

We had packed before we left the hotel. The concierge flagged a cab for us, and we were on our way.

Our flight was delayed; that same storm had moved over the Atlantic and was disrupting the usual flight lanes. And there was another storm blowing in from the west; we'd be lucky to get out of New York ahead of it.

When we finally took off, two and a half hours late, we were told we'd be taking a longer route than usual. Our Egypt Air flight was bound for DaVinci Airport in Rome for a refueling stop, then on to Cairo.

The flight was uneventful, no storm, no turbulence. That was good. It was easy enough to suspect there was more than enough turbulence to come. We settled in and chatted, watched the ocean pass beneath us, tried to imagine what would happen to us in Egypt.

I had never told Paul Danilo's history. It was clear he understood that the man was special, mystical, magical in some way, but he simply accepted it without asking difficult questions. I was grateful. It had been hard enough telling him what I'd already revealed about our bloodline and the power it carries. It wasn't that I doubted I could trust him; it was simply the oddness of it all. Danilo would explain it all in good time, and he would do it better than I could.

We talked about or own lives, more than we had before. Paul was adopted; I hadn't known. His adopted family were loving and supportive of him, till they began to realize how different he was from them. "They were...well, rednecks would be too strong a word. But they lived in a lower middle-class suburb. People like me, men who talk like men but sing like women...there was no room for me."

"Have they ever heard you sing?"

He shook his head. Obviously it was a tender subject with him. And it was too bad, really. He had the richest, most expressive talent of any singer I had known. A month earlier, he had sung the title role in Monteverdi's *Coronation of Poppea*. His portrayal of the sad wife of the mad emperor Nero brought tears to people's eyes.

I asked him if he'd ever tried to find his birth family.

And again he shook his head. "What if they turned out to be like the family I already knew?"

So we both were, or had been, lost children, not quite abandoned, not really wanted.

Paul didn't fly comfortably. He took tranquillizers and slept most of the way. I daydreamed, about Danilo and Egypt and love, till in time I fell asleep and had real dreams about him.

Because of our late start, we didn't reach Rome till well after midnight. There was to have been a three-hour layover for refueling; they were shortening it to an hour and a half. Time for those of us who wanted to to leave the plane and stretch our legs in the airport for a few minutes. Paul was sleeping soundly. I decided to take a walk.

The hour was late and the airport not crowded or busy. I had stopped over there on one of my previous trips; by day the place was thronged with loud, active people. I'd have hardly known I was in the same place.

There was security everywhere. Uniformed soldiers carried what looked to be semi-automatic rifles. Cameras watched everything. The few people in the terminal came and went unsmiling, perhaps tired, perhaps intimidated, perhaps simply bored.

I sat in one of a row of those "modern" chairs that seem to be used only in airports. It wasn't comfortable; probably it wasn't meant to be. A young man came and sat next to me. I glanced at him, then looked away. Dark, Italian I thought, very nice smile, rather well dressed. But I didn't pay much attention. My thoughts were on the journey still to come.

"Hello." He had a sweet, mellow voice; his accent was quite mild.

I nodded.

"You are an American." It was a statement, not a question.

"Yes."

I turned my head to look at him and realized he had the most piercing blue eyes. His smile was terrific. At the same time I realized he did not have a drop of royal blood in him. He reached over and put his hand on top of mine, and I pulled lightly away.

"My name is Giovanni."

I didn't much care. "Hello, Giovanni."

"What is yours?"

His attention was annoying. "Sam."

"Sam." He seemed to like the sound of it.

It appeared we were going to have a conversation whether I liked it or not. I resigned myself. "You're a Roman?"

"Yes. I am a member of the Swiss guard." He beamed, obviously proud of himself.

"Are you queer?"

The question shocked him. "Good heavens, no!"

"Then do me a favor, Giovanni, and go away."

"I—I thought we might be friends."

"I have enough friends, thank you."

"Not like me." He smiled, and it was a lascivious smile. "Here. I have a photograph of myself in my uniform."

He produced it. Even in the snapshot his smile and eyes beamed. He was dressed in that preposterous costume, blinding colors, broad stripes medieval helmet. I looked at it and handed it back to him. "You know that Michelangelo designed these uniforms, don't you?"

"Oh, yes. It is a fact of which we are all very proud."

"And at the same time the church was persecuting men like him. Arresting them, torturing them, burning them alive."

"'Men like him?'" The thought seemed to horrify him. "Oh, no. He cannot have been like that." Once again he put his hand on my leg; I pulled away.

"And the popes he served—they liked boys, too."

"Impossible!"

"Uh…you do know what *queer* means, don't you?"

"No, but I—"

"It can mean a lot of things." I decided to give him a little lecture. "In some contexts it means the same thing as *hypocrite*."

"My English is not that good."

I had had enough of him. We'd be taking off again soon enough. I decided to use the nearest men's room, then get back on board. "Good night, Giovanni."

Not at all to my surprise, he followed me. Standing at the urinal, I looked over my shoulder. He was watching me hopefully.

"Go back to the Vatican, will you? Or do I have to call security?"

He registered disappointment. "You misunderstand me, Sam. I am assigned to Santa Maria Maggiore."

"So what?"

"We could not have a scandal of that sort."

"Then if I were you, I'd back off."

I zipped up my fly, pushed past him, and headed back to the plane. As I was going through security, the soldier who scanned me with a metal detector noticed Giovanni, who was still watching me. She laughed. "We call him Officer Sodoma. The Sodomite. He is here all the time, after dark."

"Does he ever get lucky?"

"Not that I've seen. Have a nice flight, Signore."

When I got back to the plane, Paul was still sleeping soundly. I wanted to tell him about "Officer Sodoma." Two thousand years of history behind him, and he hadn't even managed to become a good closet case.

CHAPTER 13

Cairo. We landed just before dawn.

The airport there is, well, functional. Paul said he'd never seen an airport that looked so much like a hastily converted warehouse.

At that early hour the place was not busy. The passengers from our plane were the only ones in the customs line. A soldier in a white uniform with khaki trim checked my passport. "American?"

"Yes."

"You have been here before."

"Yes, three times." I smiled at him. "I love your country more than anyplace else I've been."

"We are glad. The purpose of your visit?"

"Pleasure." I smiled again and added. "I hope."

He opened my carry-on bag and rummaged through it. "This, sir, is a problem. This appears to be an authentic antiquity."

"Yes, it is."

"It is forbidden to remove such objects from the country without permission."

"I'm not removing it, I'm bringing it in."

It seemed to puzzle him; obviously he hadn't encountered such a situation before. He conferred quickly with a colleague, his superior I think, then let me go. Paul was already through customs; no antiquities in his luggage. We went quickly to the main entrance and got a taxi.

The Cairo traffic was hair-raising as always. I had braced myself for it; Paul was completely off guard. The third time our driver pulled up onto the sidewalk, scattering pedestrians in our path, he took my hand and held it tightly. I couldn't have enjoyed it more—both the chaos and Paul's touch.

The sky began to lighten. The city was covered with clouds. I had never seen it overcast before. On my previous visits, Cairo had always been washed in blazing sunshine. To see a sky gray instead of deep blue seemed…not right. As if the world was trying to tell me everything was out of joint. Our driver nearly collided with a donkey cart, cursed at its owner and stepped on the accelerator.

We opted for Shepheard's Hotel. A big, rambling Victorian place—literally, it dated from the 1800s. In its day, it had been the destination of choice for European and American travelers and archaeologists. Now... well, it had seen better days. But we wanted the history. Even more than that, we wanted to avoid too many tourists. Shepheard's was hardly the sort of place pampered Americans would choose for themselves.

The lobby was a study in faded grandeur, in elegance gone to seed. Crystal chandeliers caked with dust; once-plush brocade furniture, now threadbare and frayed. It seemed a fit place for us; we were pursuing life-in-death.

The staff were in wine-red livery, also faded. The desk clerk remembered me from my previous visits and smiled in a way that seemed genuine. I couldn't imagine the place got much repeat business, at least not from young Americans. A young bellhop saw us to our room, propositioned us—this was the hospitality industry, after all—feigned polite disappointment when we refused his offer, then left, happy with his baksheesh.

Paul stretched out on one of the beds. "Do we have time for sightseeing?"

"Later. After we've found Danilo." I had told him about the vision of him I'd had that night with Joe. Wasting time would not be a good idea. He understood. I added, "With Danilo as our guide, we'll see things most tourists never dream of."

"Jamie?" He turned serious. "What if we can't find him?"

It had occurred to me a dozen times, of course. The possibility was both real and terrible. I had tried to force myself not to think about it, but it was no use. "Mahawi's map... And that vision I had... He must be there."

"At Amarna. What if your vision was false?"

"Please, Paul. Let's not talk about it this way. Danilo... You don't know how lost I am. I have this life he gave me, and I don't know what to do with it. Without him..."

Paul had tasted the blood of the sacrificed and felt its power. And he had seen it restore my youth and strength. "We can face it together, Jamie."

"When you're an old man and I'm still young, drinking the blood of hapless fools…?"

"I see what you mean. But everyone in the world is alone, Jamie. Have you ever read Plotinus?"

I hadn't. I said so. "But he was one of us?"

"He was. And he defined life as 'the flight of the alone to the Alone.'"

"Wise man. Sad man."

"Aren't we all? It comes to pretty much the same thing."

"Paul, this is all abstract. Danilo is here. I know it. Down in my bones, I know it. And I need him. Perhaps we were alone in Plotinus's day. The classical world was dying, the world of Homer and Hadrian, and the Christian world was supplanting it. But now…" I looked at him and could see concern in his face. Was Jamie coming unhinged? Had he always been that way?

"Jamie, you know I'm in love with you."

I nodded.

"Plotinus was telling the truth. I know how I'd feel if I lost you. So I can guess how you must feel without Danilo. I only want you to know I'm here, that's all."

"You missed your calling, Paul. You should have been a therapist."

He grinned. "I thought that's what I was."

For a moment or two we stood and held each other. Then it was time to move.

I had to go to the Nile, to arrange our travel on the river. Paul asked if I'd mind if he'd take a few hours to visit the Egyptian Museum. He wanted to see King Tut's treasures. "Now that I'm here, I just can't pass up the chance. To be that close to the tragic boy king…" He smiled and looked a bit shamefaced. He nearly always did, when he let his emotions take over.

I told him I didn't mind. "But once we reach Amarna, you will find yourself closer to Tutankhamen than you ever thought possible."

"I know it was his father's city. But, Jamie, don't be silly."

"You'll see."

He changed and left, obviously excited to be in the country. The museum was only a block away, on Liberation Square. I got into a pair of khakis and a safari shirt and headed for the river.

There was no sign of the clouds breaking. Under them, the Nile looked a dirty gray, not its uszzzzzzzual brilliant blue. River traffic was heavy. Tourist boats, small freighters, barges, even police boats seemed to be everywhere. I wondered why. The Nile was usually busy, but I'd never seen it like this.

The place I wanted was just downriver from the iron bridge Gustave Eiffel built. My boatman—or to be precise, Danilo's—always anchored there. Today, he was gone. It wasn't surprising; his felucca, the *Cleopatra*, was one of the sleekest on the river, and tourists clamored for it. Finding him would only be a matter of waiting.

I sat and watched the river and the city. Of all the cities I've seen, Cairo is the most fascinating. There are spanking new buildings, high-rises, office blocks, apartments. And then there are the old ones, medieval mosques, ancient tombs… Everything that isn't brand new was hundreds of years old, or thousands. The contrast—the very old in the midst of the modern—never failed to captivate me. It was, in more than one way, like my own life.

It was several hours, well after noon, before the *Cleopatra* returned to its mooring. Mohammed saw me on the dock and waved, then smiled a wry little smile and nodded at his passengers. He had been ferrying an American family around Cairo, a yuppie husband and wife and their two horrible children. As he tied off, the husband spotted me. "You're an American too?"

I told him I was.

"Well, you need to watch out for this guy. I think he's a thief."

Helpfully, petulantly, his wife added, "Isn't that what all Moslems are?"

I listened, quite entertained, as the husband explained the difficulty they'd had with him. He didn't speak English. He kept getting their "orders" wrong, taking them to places they had no interest in seeing. It was a lot funnier than they realized; Mohammed spoke perfect English. They disembarked, flagged a taxi and bundled themselves in.

"I gather," Mohammed told me with a grin, "that they haven't experienced the traffic here yet."

"It's all right, Mohammed. I'm sure they like their vacations to be memorable. They'll be dining out for months on stories of what terrible people you Cairenes are. And their neighbors will lap it up."

He laughed and held out a hand to me. I stepped into the felucca, and we sat facing one another.

"It is good to see you again, Mr. Dunn."

"You too, Mohammed. Are you free for the next few days? I need to travel upriver."

"Again? You are still looking for Doctor Semenkaru?"

I nodded. "I think I know where he is, now."

He looked up at the dark, overcast sky. "I hope so. For all our sakes. More of us have been arrested. The world needs great leaders again, Mr. Dunn, not politicians and bureaucrats."

"Let's hope it gets them."

"I have a charter. Another American family. I can do without them." He reached up and held his nose.

We chatted for a few minutes, caught up on one another's lives. The Egyptian government's crackdown on men who love men had slowed a bit, but several of Mohammed's friends had been taken into custody over the last several months.

"Are you afraid for yourself?" I had to ask.

"I have a cousin high up in the police force, and my wife's brother works in the Interior Ministry."

"I see."

I told him about Paul.

"Another one like you, Mr. Dunn? And like Doctor Danilo?"

"I think so, yes."

"This will be a memorable journey then. Not memorable like the one

I just gave that family, but still…"

We laughed together, and I offered to buy him lunch. Not, I emphasized, at a tourist restaurant. I wanted Egypt.

And so we dined on succulent beef and shellfish, more delicious than the processed food at the places tourists usually visit. No McEgypt for me.

Mohammed told me about his family. He had never really opened up to me in a personal way before; I was growing in his esteem.

He was married, had three sons, one of whom had been arrested, then released. But the police had beaten him.

There was, he told me, a long underground tradition of bisexuality in that part of the world. No one ever acknowledged it loudly or publicly—not with Islamic law the way it is—but it had always been there. "Why," he asked mischievously, "do you think we invented the harem? Wives can be so inconvenient."

I was flattered that he opened up to me. It was hardly the usual thing. For the first time I felt I had a friend, a genuine friend in Egypt.

Paul wasn't back at the hotel when I got there. I checked at the desk, and he hadn't been back at all. When he wasn't back at dusk, I began to be worried. He wouldn't have been so foolish as to do something that would get him arrested, would he? The police seemed to be so busy. Just as I was beginning to think perhaps I should have Mohammed ask his cousin to make inquiries, Paul showed up.

At first glance I thought he must be drunk. Then I realized it was Egypt that had made him high.

"Jamie, this is the most marvelous place. The Museum, the bazaars, the mosques. And the people! So friendly and yet so mercenary. A silversmith in the souk offered me his teenage son—as near as I can tell, it was a matter of business courtesy."

"Gosh, Paul, I don't think we're in Pittsburgh anymore. Was the son cute?"

"Beautiful. But I explained that I was only window-shopping. Both the father and the boy looked at me like I was crazy. And the Museum! I wasn't there fifteen minutes when one of the security guards lured me behind a canvas drop cloth and tried to kiss me and grope me. Never mind Israel, Jamie—this is the Promised Land."

He hadn't eaten all day. We decided to have supper in Shepheard's dining room. The food was nowhere near as wonderful as what I'd had for lunch, but the service was excellent. I told Paul we'd be leaving for Amarna that night, told him a bit about Mohammed.

"Our own Nile boat. Jamie, this is fantastic. It just keeps getting better."

I smiled. "Egypt."

"It's like being a dress extra in *The Ten Commandments*."

I loved his enthusiasm. "Personally, I prefer shattering the commandments."

"But can't we please stay in Cairo for anther day or two? There's so much more to see."

"This is the largest city in Africa, Paul. We could stay a month and not exhaust it. But we're here for a purpose."

Glumly, he agreed. We got our things together, arranged to leave our other luggage at the hotel, and headed for the river.

It was after dark. Mohammed waited for us at this usual spot by the iron bridge. I introduced the two of them, we stowed our things, and Mohammed cast off. The traffic on the river had eased off some, but it was still heavy. A police cruiser sped by, and the *Cleopatra* rocked in its wake.

We headed south, and the great city, lit up brilliantly, rose around us. Public buildings were floodlit for the night and the tourists; the windows of high-rises glittered with illumination. Overhead the sky was still cloudy, and the bottom of the clouds reflected the city light faintly.

At one point, just as we rounded a particular bend in the river, Mohammed told us to look over our shoulders. In the far distance behind us, there were the Pyramids, glowing golden in their nighttime floodlights. Paul let out a little gasp. "I didn't realize they were so close. I'd have gone to see them."

"They are," Mohammed told him cheerfully, "almost ten miles away."

"They are that huge?"

He didn't bother to answer.

We reached the outskirts of Cairo, and the river traffic diminished quite markedly. There seemed to be nothing but sailing craft now, mostly feluccas but a few more westernized craft as well. Paul made the same comment everyone does their first time in a felucca, about the astonishing sensation of riding almost weightlessly, with almost no sense of motion at all.

There were a few drops of rain. Not heavy, and not much. I looked to Mohammed. "Rain?"

He emphasized the obvious, that we were in a desert country. "Last year, it rained here for almost ten minutes. The year before that, not at all."

"So these clouds are as unusual as I thought?"

He nodded. "I have never seen it like this, not for twenty years or more."

"What causes it?"

He shrugged. "The Christians believe that violations of the natural order are a proof of the divine."

Paul seemed a bit confused by this exchange. I reminded him that Egypt exists in the heart of the desert. The Nile fertilizes a long, narrow strip of green; beyond that is the Sahara. Away from the river is a desert climate. No rain, or very little, and only fair-weather clouds.

He looked up. A raindrop hit him in the eye, and he wiped it away.

The rain came more heavily for a moment; a shower swept over us, then passed. Mohammed adjusted his sail, and we sped up in the wind that drove the rain. Once it was over, we could see that there was a large gibbous moon behind the clouds, illuminating them.

I pointed out the landmarks to Paul as they drifted past, ruined temples, ancient shrines... As he always did, Mohammed stopped at the vast oasis called the Fayum and gathered fresh fruit for us, then we journeyed on.

The moonlight behind the clouds grew brighter. Eventually they parted and we caught a glimpse of its face. On the west bank something like a mountain reared up. I explained to Paul it was the collapsed ruins of the Meidum Pyramid. The landmarks were familiar, Egypt was unchanging. It should have reassured me, but for some reason it didn't.

The gentle motion of the boat lulled Paul to sleep. Sleeping, he curled up against me, and it felt good. The rain had given me a slight chill. In time, I slept too. I had wanted to show him the ruins of Antinopolis, the city Hadrian built for his young god Antinous; but we slept past it.

There were ghosts and demons around us in the Egyptian night. I saw them on the shore, men and women with the heads of animals, a seemingly endless series of them; some of them waved at us, some glowered, some watched impassively. Djinni hovered around us in the cool night air, whispering things I couldn't understand. Warnings? Blessings? Curses?

I thought I heard a voice whispering something to me, something I couldn't make out. But somehow, in it all, I could hear love. And fear.

In the midst of the ancient, magical landscape, with Paul curled up in my arms, I leaned my head against his and slept. And dreamed Egyptian dreams.

The sight of these two American boys in one another's arms bothered Mohammed not at all. When I woke, he was watching us and beaming. It was still night, but the moon was gone and the clouds and grown heavy again. The world was as dark as I had ever seen it.

I felt a raindrop. Then another. Then, with startling abruptness, the clouds broke and rain poured down on us heavily. And there was ferocious wind; the *Cleopatra* rocked violently. It woke Paul; he looked around in a bit of a panic, not knowing where he was or what was happening. He must have been having dreams as disturbing as my own. I took it as a bad omen. I looked over my shoulder to Mohammed; he was in the process of lowering the sail.

I called to him. "This is terrible. We should anchor and find shelter."

"There is a place I know, not far from here."

The current grew swift, and the wind kicked up even more. The Nile Valley was especially narrow there, and the river flowed quite rapidly.

Mohammed had difficulty getting us to shore. It took him a few minutes, but he finally managed it. The boat had three inches of water in it. Overhead, lightning flashed. He tied three lines to trees on the shore. "I wish I had more rope."

Not far from the river was a line of low cliffs. Mohammed led us there. I realized that there were tombs cut into the rock. Small ones, nowhere near as impressive as the ones in the Valley of the Kings. We sheltered in one of them and Mohammed lit a flashlight. We were completely soaked. Through the stone door we saw the rain coming down in torrents.

Paul was even more shaken by it than I was. Now that we were safe, Mohammed was unperturbed. "This will pass, gentlemen. Everything passes."

"We could have drowned." Paul pressed himself against a wall, as if its solidity reassured him.

I stood at the doorway, looking outside. "Have you ever seen anything like this before, Mohammed?"

"Once, when I was a boy. That was not so bad as this, though."

"What can be causing it?"

He shrugged. "One of the old stories says that it rained and thundered when Set killed his brother Osiris. Perhaps one of the gods is dying."

I thought immediately of Danilo. "No, that can't be it." This was not the time to be talking about unpleasant myths.

"Of course not."

It occurred to me to wonder where we were.

"At a place called Beni Hasan. It was a center of the Middle Kingdom. Nothing here is sufficiently impressive for tourists, so it is little known."

I had heard of it. He was right—it was far enough off the usual routes that I had never been there and never even met anyone who had. Not even Danilo had mentioned it.

There was more lighting, and the earth shook with thunder. A bit of dust worked loose from the roof of the tomb and cascaded down in little streamers.

Through the downpour I could see that the Nile was rising. "Will there be a flood, Mohammed?"

He shrugged. "If Allah wills it."

He had given me the impression he worshipped something older than Allah, at least in private. I said so.

And he turned cryptic. "Old beliefs are stubborn, Mr. Dunn." So I was back to being Mr. Dunn; I had asked too intrusive a question.

But I had to know. "What is your relation to Danilo?"

He bristled at the question. "The gods do not die easily." I knew that he wouldn't tell me any more than that.

I took Paul's hand and looked out the door of the tomb and waited for what seemed like the end of the world to pass.

Eventually we slept. It had grown late, and we slept for along time. But when we woke there was blazing sunlight coming in the door of our little tomb. Mohammed was gone. I looked outside, and he was at the river, bailing out the felucca.

Paul stirred and yawned. When he opened his eyes, the bright light made him squint and hold up an arm to cover his eyes. Groggily he said, "Jamie."

"Good morning." I bent down and kissed him lightly on the forehead. "We seem to have weathered the storm all right."

"Where's Mohammed?"

I pointed outside. "I saw him tossing all our fruit into the river. It must have gone rotten. I don't know what we'll do for breakfast."

Paul got to his feet. The cold stone of the tomb had made him stiff. "After a night like that, I'm not sure I'll want to eat soon, anyway."

For the first time, now that it was daylight, I noticed the walls of the tomb. There were the usual reliefs; some of them still held their color. Gods, pharaohs. In a cartouche I saw the name of one of the Middle Kingdom rulers, Mentuhotep II. I pointed it out to Paul. Things were familiar again, after our terrible night, and I needed to make it feel as concrete as possible, both for Paul and for myself. The world was the world again.

"Why would a pharaoh have a tomb as small as this, Jamie?"

"It wasn't his. This would have belonged to one of his servants, or to a palace official maybe."

"Let's go and help Mohammed."

We made our way quickly down the low rise from the cliff and crossed the ground to where he had moored. There were still six inches of water in the boat. And the Nile was still running swiftly.

He was bailing determinedly, and he seemed to find our presence intrusive. "Go and look" He pointed to the northernmost in the line of tombs. "That one will interest you. *Cleopatra* will be ready when you come back." She was his ship; we were not to be permitted to care for her.

And so we went back up to the cliffs. For a moment Paul didn't seem to want to enter another tomb. After waiting for him for a moment, I went in. He followed a minute later.

There was more than enough light from outside; and it was no bigger than the one we'd sheltered in.

One wall was taken up with a huge relief, much larger than the usual tomb decoration. A row of boys, their adolescent "sidelocks" showing clearly, processed across the wall. They would have been young, perhaps twelve or thirteen, and they marched in the usual posture of figures in Egyptian art. But there were two differences. They were smiling, in a quite uncharacteristic way. And the genitals of these boys were exposed; they each had a prominent erection.

It couldn't have caught us more by surprise. Paul grinned. "So the Egyptians went in for porn."

"Everyone goes in for porn. But I don't think that's what this is."

I pointed to the figure at the front of the line. It was a priest with his head shaved and wearing the leopard skin of his rank. He was on his knees in front of the first boy in the row. And he was brandishing a large ceremonial knife. I recognized it; it was quite like Danilo's golden knife, the one he, and I, used for sacrifice.

Paul was alarmed. "Jamie, he's castrating them."

"No." I looked at him and grinned. "This was an important rite of passage. He's circumcising them."

"What!?"

"Boys were circumcised at the start of adolescence. It was a happy ritual for them. See how they're smiling?"

"But—"

"The Jews got circumcision from the Egyptians. Despite what the Bible says."

Paul was uncut. He moved a hand to cover his crotch, not consciously, I think. The longer he looked at the tomb painting, the more uncomfortable he seemed. "Let's get out of here."

"You liked it when all you could see was the boys."

"Don't be sick."

He rushed outside, and I followed. The brilliant sunlight dazzled our eyes, and it took a moment for them to adjust. Mohammed had emptied all the rainwater out of the felucca and was raising the sail. It was time to go on.

"How," he asked us with a sly grin, "did you like the picture of the Sem priest?"

Paul ignored the question and got in the boat. Mohammed winked at me.

It seemed a good idea to change the subject. The river was still running much higher than usual, and much swifter; I commented on it. "Will it be all right?"

"I have steered *Cleopatra* as far south as Nubia and the great cataracts. We will be fine."

When we cast off, it took him a moment to steady the boat. Then the wind caught the sail, the ship glided forward, and everything seemed all right again.

Or rather, nearly everything. The landscape was soaked. There were puddles everywhere, some of them quite large. And the Nile was muddier than I had seen it. I commented on it to Mohammed.

"It will not take long for the earth to absorb the puddles and the Nile to return to its usual brilliant blue."

I knew he must be right. But this Egypt was not mine, not the one I had known.

I let a hand trail in the water, and the current was stronger than I expected. "This must be what it was like in the old days, before they built the High Dam, when the Nile used to flood every year."

"Do you know about the Nile crocodiles?" Mohammed was working to keep us in the center of the river.

There were no more crocodiles in Egypt; encroaching human civilization had driven them all upriver, into the Sudan and beyond. But in ancient times there were numerous, and quite dangerous. There were scores of paintings of them— large organized hunts, prayers for children eaten alive... "What about them, Mohammed?"

"They knew the Nile. They understood it in special ways."

"It was their home."

"They knew the flood, Jamie." I was glad he was calling me Jamie again. "They understood—no one knows how—precisely how high the next year's flood would be. And they always laid their eggs just above the flood line. How they could be so exact, no one ever knew."

"A myth, Mohammed. Just folklore."

"Like the story of the immortal pharaoh?"

I was lost for anything to say.

"It does not become us to sneer at the ancient myths, Jamie. And the lesson of the Nile crocodile should not be lost upon us."

He lapsed into silence, and so did Paul and I.

CHAPTER 14

The morning passed. The sun was brilliant, the shores green with vegetation. We passed ruined shrines and small temples. I was quite enthralled; Egypt was my second home, or my spiritual one. Paul, on the other hand, seemed to get bored after a while.

"Isn't there another way to get where we're going, Jamie? A train or something?" He whispered it, not wanting to offend Mohammed.

"There's a narrow gauge railroad. But it doesn't run regularly. And there's no privacy. Anyone could see us and follow us." It seemed a good idea to remind him there were people who were not at all friendly to us.

"Besides, Mr. Koerner," Mohammed chimed in, "The tracks will be flooded. Look at the land."

Paul looked slightly abashed, I think, that Mohammed had overheard him. But Mohammed was right. Parts of the shore were still quite drenched.

It was just before noon that we reached our goal: Amarna. City of Akhenaten and Smenkhare. City of the Sun—and of Set. Empty now; ruined; barren in the blinding sunlight.

I pointed out the enormous boundary markers Akhenaten had set up; they were all that was still standing, presumably because they were too massive for time to have tumbled them.

The plain stretched out before us. Mohammed moored at the place where the ancient dock had been; it was still possible to see traces of it.

Paul, like every visitor, took a few moments to begin to see what was really there but not obvious. The outlines of streets and buildings were still discernible, just barely. It was necessary to look, to focus, to find the small details.

"In its day," I told him, "this was the greatest metropolis in the world. But its day was so brief. After only a generation, the priests ground it back down into the desert dirt." I took his hand. "I have the blood of its kings in my veins, Paul. And so do you."

There was so much to take in, he seemed overwhelmed. "This is where Akhenaten worshipped the sun, then?" He squinted and shaded his eyes; the "heretic pharaoh" had chosen the site for his city only too aptly.

I nodded. Mohammed had gotten our things out of the boat and lined them carefully on shore. I told him I didn't think I'd need much except one backpack; but I asked him to accompany us, as he had on my first visit there.

Amarna. It was the place where Danilo had given me his ultimate gift, one I still had to understand fully. When he was with me, it seemed the richest gift in the world. Once he was gone… I had always been a lonely child. But not until Danilo left did I understand how complete loneliness can be.

Paul took another backpack with some packaged food and some chocolate bars, Mohammed stripped off his galabea and wore nothing but sandals and a loincloth, and we headed off through the city.

It is a huge place. The fact that so little of it remains, that it looks for all purposes like nothing but a stretch of barren land, can be so deceptive. With no clear reference points for perspective, the city looks nowhere near as large as it is in fact. After we had been walking for a while Paul commented on it.

"I should have worn a good pair of boots."

"Do you want to go back?"

He looked at the ruins spread out ahead of us, then back to the river. I think we had come farther than he realized. "No, I guess not. But I'm hungry." He opened his pack, got out a candy bar, and we moved on again.

There was a slight breeze, not quite enough to cool us under the desert sun. After twenty minutes we came to the largest of the remains, the royal palace and, beside it, the Temple of the Sun. It was the place indicated on Mahawi's map. And it had been the center of Akhenaten's religious reforms—the public ones, at least.

Danilo was there. I wanted to believe that. No, I had to. Of all the places in the world, it was the one that made sense for him.

And there was nothing. The outlines of the great buildings, the bases of a few columns, the remains of a broad, low staircase. There were no buildings, not even a shack; no entrances to anyplace underground. Nothing.

I had been to Amarna on both of my previous searches. Seeing it—seeing the absence of anything at all—made me want to cry. I almost called out Danilo's name, as if he might hear me from wherever he was, and answer.

There was nothing but the soft wind, like the breath of a ghost.

I sat on the ground and buried my face in my hands. Paul got down on a knee and put his hand on my shoulder. I had been so certain I'd find him, or find *something*.

Time stopped for me. I could have sat there for centuries.

It was Mohammed who brought me out of it. "Perhaps, Jamie, it is time to consult the one who can tell you what you want to know."

I looked up at him. And I knew at once that he was right. I had lost sight of it, but back in Pittsburgh I had realized where I could learn, if I could learn anyplace in the world..

He nodded slightly in the direction of the cliffs beyond the city, of the tombs that had been cut into the rock there. Then he stepped forward, took my hand and pulled me to my feet.

"Doctor Danilo's father."

We moved on. Paul was quite lost. He looked from one of us to the other but didn't seem to know, even, what he should ask.

"In the cliffs, there, Paul." I pointed. "Tombs were cut for the royal family and their officials."

"No one has ever found Akhenaten's mummy, Jamie. You must know that."

"Come on. You'll see."

But before we could set off, Mohammed froze. He put a hand on my shoulder and pointed back to the palace and temple. There were dogs, a pack of wild dogs. Mahawi had sketched them on his map. They were watching us.

"It is a bad sign, Jamie. They are death."

Then I realized: they weren't dogs at all. They were jackals. Guardians of the necropolis. Devourers of the dead.

They were far enough away not to pose a threat to us, at least not immediately; but we'd have to watch them carefully. As we watched, they ran off.

We set out east across the city, to the cliffs. I told Paul about the twin tombs of the priests of Set, their names and their resting places joined in death as the men themselves had been in life. I told him about the Kissing Kings. But that was all. He had enough to digest already.

Mohammed pointed to where the jackals had been. They were gone. There was no sign of them anywhere on the horizon.

We walked in silence for a while. I had always wanted to ask Mohammed about his connection to Danilo and the ancient religion. He had always found my questions intrusive. But I asked again. He smiled and didn't answer.

Paul caught my shoulder and pointed. The jackals were back again, at least two of them were; and it was clear they were watching us. "I saw them come up out of the ground, Jamie. They must have a burrow there."

"I don't think they're burrowing animals, Paul."

"I saw them."

Mohammed told us that, no, jackals did not live under the ground. So, where were they going?

He shrugged. "It is a mystery."

"You sound like a Catholic priest, Mohammed."

"Do not be rude, Jamie."

As we walked, I kept my eye on them. There seemed to be about a dozen in all. And as Paul said, they were disappearing under the earth, then re-emerging. And they were definitely keeping their eyes on us, not in a friendly way.

In my backpack was the sacred object I had brought. I opened the pack and fingered it, for reassurance. It was warm. The heat of the day, I said to myself, the heat of the desert…

Danilo must be there, where the jackals were. Mahawi had thought so. And I had seen it in my vision at the séance. But I had to consult with the one who would know for certain, and who could warn me what to expect there. At least I had to try. There were three of us and a dozen jackals, maybe more; if they attacked us…

It took us well over an hour to reach the base of the cliffs. Paths had been cut into the rock, ascending to the rock-cut tombs. Footing was tricky; Paul almost fell a couple of times. We climbed the steep path, and Paul and I had to hold each other for support; Mohammed was quite balanced, quite self-possessed.

Then we reached the line of tombs. One after another of them gaped before us, pitch black inside. I read the inscriptions for Paul. Akhenaten, Nefertiti, Meritaten…all the members of the royal family were to have been buried there, before the priests revolted and destroyed the dynasty.

The last tomb, the one at the southern end of the cliff, was the tomb of Per-Nefer-Set and Set-Hotep. I showed Paul how their names were joined: the inscription over the lintel read "Per-Nefer-Set-Hotep."

"They were lovers?"

"Yes," I said quietly. "Like Akhenaten and his son, Smenkhare."

He fell silent, but I could see that he was thinking. Perhaps the truth was starting to come together for him.

Mohammed got three flashlights from his pack and handed them out to us. And we went in. Bats, alarmed to be disturbed in daylight, shrieked and flew out of the tomb. Their wings brushed our heads, and we ducked. Paul was badly shaken by it; I should have warned him.

I remembered it all so vividly. The two conjoined tombs, mirror images of one another. The single burial chamber at the far end, where the two priest-lovers were united for all time. The ornate rows of gods and demons that processed along the walls, with the great god Set at their head.

And I remembered, only too well, how to open what was hidden beyond it all.

Before us, the tomb of Akhenaten opened. Magnificent white sarcophagus. Lithe, sensual images of the pharaoh and his handsome son, locked in sexual embrace, kissing passionately. Paul gaped at it all. "I've never seen Egyptian art like this."

I placed a hand on the sarcophagus. The gleaming alabaster was so cool to my touch.

I put down my pack. It was time to act. "Come on, let's open it."

Mohammed took a step back away from us. "I must leave. I am not to see what will occur here."

Paul was lost. I told Mohammed we might need him to help move the sarcophagus lid, and reluctantly he stayed.

And need him we did. Paul and I tried to shift it, but it was too heavy for us. The first time, I had been with Danilo. Now, I needed more human help. The three of us budged it, just barely; slowly, and with enormous effort, we managed to slide it aside.

There he was, the heretic pharaoh, much more a heretic than even the priests who hated him could have guessed. The great champion of the contrarian god Set, the god who teaches us that gods have no existence. And the father of Danilo Semenkaru, who was known, and lost, to history as Smenkhare.

I had seen Akhenaten only by torchlight at night. Now there was a bit more light entering the tomb from outside. He looked older, or perhaps more badly decayed, than I remembered. The blank, withered face gaped at us. Empty eye sockets stared into eternity, or perhaps into the face of the god Set, who does not exist yet gives us power. Dry fingers clutched the scepter of his imperium. It seemed to me the mummy looked in worse shape than it had the first time I saw it. Had opening the sarcophagus and exposing it to air caused more decay? I hoped not. I would not have wanted his disintegration to be on my account.

Paul stared down at the mummy. Silently he reached out and took my hand. "Jamie," he whispered, "why are we here?"

Danilo was my father, brother, lover. Akhenaten was his father. My relationship to the poor remains in front of us was so… I could not find words to explain, not in a way Paul could understand.

From outside the tomb came the bark of a jackal. All three of us froze. Mohammed took a step toward the entrance. "I should wait outside, Jamie. I do not think they will try to follow you in here—this place is anathema to them—but it is possible. Please, let me go out."

I nodded, and he handed his flashlight to Paul and left. Paul and I were alone with the dead king.

In a corner of the chamber, one bat had remained. It was too brave or perhaps too sleepy or too weak, for some reason, to have left with the others. It chittered and squeaked in the semi-darkness that surrounded it. It let out an alarmed little cry and spread its wings. Then it folded them again and fell silent. Black eyes stared at us.

Paul looked around the tomb, obviously on edge—as how could he not be? He had no idea what to expect, and I could do nothing but show him.

"I've always wondered, Jamie…"

"Hm?"

"What does a mummy feel like?"

I remembered asking Danilo that same question when we first met. "Touch it, Paul. Gently. No pressure, or you could do damage."

He extended his index finger. Very lightly, he stroked Akhenaten's dead face. "It feels like dry leather." He looked up at me. "This is really Akhenaten? *The*< Akhenaten, the famous renegade king?"

"We are all renegades, Paul, all of us. Outlaws. Gide knew it, Genet knew it. Our lives are outlaw adventures, whether we want them to be or not."

"Very poetic. Now answer my question."

It was time to do what I had come to do. Slowly I bent down and kissed Akhenaten's lips. "Yes, Paul," I said softly, "this is him."

I had no idea if it would work. I had no idea if I could bring life, real life, to my ancestor, or if I would simply animate the dead flesh, as I animated clay and mud. But I leaned very close to the dead king's ear and whispered. I breathed life into his body. I whispered the words.

And the pharaoh stirred. Just slightly, almost imperceptibly. His fingers curled and uncurled; he moved the scepter across his chest.

I felt a hand clutch mine, and for an instant I thought it must be the king's; then I realized it was Paul's. "Jamie. For God's sake, Jamie."

Akhenaten's head raised slightly, only a fraction of an inch.

When Danilo had revived him he stood, walked lived. Blood flowed in his body for the first time in three millennia. All I was able to do was bring him the slightest movement. I did not think it would be enough.

"Akhenaten." I said his name loudly.

His fingers flexed.

"Akhenaten, it is your son Jamie. The son and lover of your own son Smenkhare."

The lips parted and whispered something, a coarse grating sound, nothing more.

"You remember me?"

The mummy lay still. Paul tightened his grip on my hand.

I spoke the ancient language. "Akhenaten, where is he? Where is Smenkhare?"

With great abruptness the living corpse lurched upward and, improbably, rested on one elbow. I thought he was trying to climb out of the sarcophagus and didn't have the strength. But he stayed like that, half sitting, half lying.

Again he spoke. I pressed my ear close to his lips. The word "temple" came very faintly. His voice was like the rustle of dead leaves, or parchment.

"The temple of the sun? Your temple?"

Just slightly, he nodded.

"I've been there. There is no sign of him."

"Under the ground." His voice was a bit stronger; life was returning.

Suddenly from outside came a series of loud, agonized screams, mixed with loud barking. It broke my concentration. Akhenaten stiffened and fell back into the sarcophagus. Dust rose into the air from his body. He would tell me no more.

Paul squeezed my hand so tightly I almost cried out. "Jamie—Mohammed!"

That last, lone bat cried out, spread its wings, and flew at us. We ducked, and Paul swung at it. Then it was gone. We rushed through the tomb to the entrance. Bright daylight blinded us.

Mohammed lay on the ground, crying in agony. A half dozen jackals were at him, tearing him to pieces, eating while he was still alive. He looked to us, and in his face was helpless pleading. His blood poured out and stained the rock of the cliffside. The jackals ate greedily, as if they'd never tasted flesh before and relished it.

They saw us, stopped their meal, and assumed a menacing posture. Mohammed's body, what was left of it, twitched in the blazing sunshine and was still.

The animals seemed to be afraid of us, or of me. I took a step toward them, and they backed away. Another step, and they turned tail and ran. I had no idea why.

But Paul put a hand on my shoulder. "They eat the flesh of men, Jamie, not gods."

I didn't feel like a god, not in the least. And I said so. "A god would have seen the danger. Mohammed would be alive."

I looked at the remains of his corpse. Strange death for a skilled boatman, to be killed by desert scavengers on the side of a mountain. Poor man. Good man.

"We must find Danilo now, Paul. Then we'll have to come back to close the tomb and bury Mohammed."

"Bury him? Where? This is solid rock."

"There are all these other tombs. Some of them were cut for the supporters of the royal family. Nothing could be more appropriate."

"If we wait, will there be anything left of him?"

Excellent point. I looked again at the horrible remains of the man who had been my friend and helper. Bodily fluids oozed, trickled, stopped. "God help me, Paul. I don't know what to do. Since Danilo left me, I feel like I've been making my life up as I go along."

I started to cry, quite uncontrollably. Paul put his arms around me and held me till it passed.

I kissed him on the cheek. "Come on. Mohammed deserves a decent burial. Let's do it now."

We gathered up his body, what remained of it, and tried not to miss anything. Flesh, bone; one of his eyes was still there. It was as unpleasant a thing as I've ever done. Three tombs along, there was an empty chamber, walls decorated but not much, empty granite coffin. The inscription identified it as being for pharaoh's "good and faithful servant." We laid his remains there, and I said an Egyptian prayer I had memorized once. There was no lid for the sarcophagus; I would have to bless the place, then hope the scavengers would leave him in peace. Mohammed had gone to be with the gods, and the gods do not exist. Both halves of the paradox gave me comfort, though not much.

We stood in silence over Mohammed for what seemed a long time. Then it was time for Danilo.

Once again, the sunlight blinded us after the dark tomb. Carefully we made our way down the cliff face. My backpack seemed heavier with each step. But I couldn't leave it; what it contained was too precious. Of the jackals, there was no sign. It was high noon. The dead cityscape seemed to move under the sun's glare, shimmering like a mirage. Paul stopped and took a long drink from his canteen; I did the same. A young cobra, not more than two feet long, saw us and reared up in alarm. We stood quite carefully still, and it slithered away behind a large rock.

The ruins of Amarna had been picked over by generations of archeologists. Every last bead and potsherd had been found and taken. Here and there we stopped for rest or water or both. Paul would dig in the earth, looking for…well, for whatever he might find. But there was nothing.

"Jamie, look."

The jackals were there again, watching us from a distance they must have found safe. One of them, a young one, barked in our direction now and then. And now and then one or another of them would disappear underground. That would be the place.

At one spot was part of a toppled column, and we sat and rested on it. The sun was hotter and hotter, more unbearable with each step we took. "Jamie, this isn't possible. I saw the ruins when we landed. This place isn't that big. But we've been walking forever."

"It has been here forever, Paul. Look around us. This is eternity."

"Be serious. I'm getting more and more exhausted."

"Do you want to go back to the *Cleopatra?*"

"No, but…" He ran a hand through his hair irritably; it was covered with sweat. "I just wish we'd get there, that's all."

"We'll be there soon enough."

"I hope so."

He didn't want to be disagreeable; I knew that. It was just that the heat and the vast barrenness were getting to him. As we walked, I heard him humming. It took me a moment to place the melody. It was the vocal line of *Lonely Child*.

We were getting close to our goal, though. One of the jackals left the pack and charged at us, growling and snarling. But it stopped ten feet away. For a moment it held its ground, then slowly it backed off, turned tail and rejoined the other ones.

After another ten minutes, we reached the Temple of the Sun again. Or the outline of it in the desert earth. We looked around, and again there was no sign of anything that might be an entrance to …to anything.

A dozen jackals watched, their posture menacing, their bodies coiled and ready to spring, if we gave them the chance.

"We should have brought guns, Jamie. I have a knife, but…"

"I don't think guns would stop them. Not all of them. Besides, I've never used a gun in my life; I'd be useless."

"So would I, I guess." The realization made him glum.

"This isn't the Wild West, Paul."

"I thought you said the past never dies."

"Don't be a smartass."

"You should talk."

It had to be only a matter of time. Sooner or later—sooner, I hoped— we would see the exact spot where they were disappearing. Waiting was all. We sat on the ground and watched.

"We're almost out of water."

"Don't drink so much. We'll have to conserve."

"I'm thirsty."

"Paul. For God's sake."

And then, finally, I saw the place. One of them disappeared behind a stone, a finished block of sandstone. The entrance had to be hidden there. I pointed it out to Paul. We watched for another few moments. And another one of them vanished behind it. That had to be the place.

We moved slowly, so as not to alarm them. They watched. Now and then one of them would advance on us, but it always stopped ten or twelve feet away. Paul was right. They were afraid of us, or of me.

On impulse I let out a loud shout, and they scattered, all but one of them. It was the largest; it must have been the dominant female. She watched us closely as we inched past her. She snarled, a low, base sound that was more unsettling than I wanted to admit.

Then she let out a little yip. And from behind the sandstone block came half a dozen puppies. They trotted to her playfully; the behavior was so familiar, the sight so domestic, these might have been spaniels or terriers instead of the creatures that killed and ate our companion an hour before.

"The pack found the underground temple. She's been using it as a nest. No wonder they're being so territorial, Paul."

"Then why did they attack us on the cliff?"

Point taken. But I had to bolster his confidence—and my own. "There can't be anything supernatural about them. There can't be."

The block was four feet long by two wide and two high. Not big, but big enough. When we reached it, there was the entrance. It can't have been the original one; the jackals must have found it when they were digging. It was two and a half feet across. Big enough for us. It opened on complete blackness.

I looked at Paul. "Are we ready?"

"I think I left my flashlight on the cliff."

"I have mine in my pack. It should be enough."

I got it out, switched it on, pointed it down the entrance. It cut the darkness there hardly at all.

But I had to go on. "I can go alone, if you like."

Paul was on edge. Mohammed's death had unnerved him, as it would anyone. I knew he wanted to be elsewhere. But he took my hand. "Let's go."

I climbed in first. For about five yards the passage was narrow, big enough for the jackals, uncomfortably claustrophobic for me. I could feel Paul behind me. The earth was rough and dry. Finally, in the beam of my flashlight I saw a chamber, ten feet by ten by ten, much like the ones I had seen in tombs in the Valley of the Kings.

There were painted reliefs on the walls. Gods as always, the grotesque gods of ancient Egypt. I recognized Set and his nephew Horus; they were cut slightly larger than the others.

From a dark corner of the room came a yipping sound. I turned the beam there. Three jackal pups were curled up together, crying for their mother. Their eyes were black beads in the beam of my light. Paul crossed the room to them, got out his knife, and killed them. Their death yelps echoed. With luck it would serve as a warning to the other members of the pack: leave us alone.

It was the first of a series of rooms cut into the desert rock, much like the pharaohs' tombs in the Valley of the Kings. We moved quickly from one chamber to the next, as quickly as the dim light let us. Our footsteps echoed; when we talked, so did our voices. Other than our own movement, the place was as still as any cathedral.

Each chamber was slightly larger than the one before it; each was more elaborately decorated. I realized that the reliefs formed a series. They depicted, from one room to the next, the Great God Set's seduction of his nephew Horus, the god who was the embodiment of the pharaoh's soul. The carvings were detailed, much more so than those reliefs of the adolescent boys we had seen at Beni Hasan. These gods were lovers, frankly and unmistakably. Like the Kissing Kings, Horus and Set were locked in sexual embrace, and their passion, physical passion, was impossible to miss. Hands, mouths, genitals…

"Jamie, I've never seen Egyptian art like this."

"No."

It was clear, as we passed from room to room, that the two gods were nearing climax. We would soon reach the end of the underground temple of Set. I could only hope I would find my own fulfillment there.

Then we were there. The final chamber was vast, so high and wide the beam of my light hardly had any effect. It was possible to see, just barely, that the ceiling was painted like the sky, a dark blue field with golden stars. In the cavernous room every sound we made reverberated loudly and clearly. Paul stopped and, still again, took hold of my hand.

I pointed my light downward. There was a layer of dust on the floor; it was crossed by footprints, human boots and the paws of jackals. I pointed the light toward the far end of the chamber where, if this had been a tomb, the sarcophagus would have been.

Instead, on the far wall, was the largest relief yet. The figures were twelve feet tall, maybe a bit more. And they were the Kissing Kings, locked like Horus and Set in passionate embrace. Behind them, enfolding them gently in her wings, was the goddess Ma'at, the embodiment of truth. And behind her, blessing them all, stood the great god Set.

This was art of the Amarna period, the art inspired by Akhenaten's reforms, unlike any other in Egyptian history. The figures were full and sensual, the lines human not abstract, the faces individual and recognizable. Akhenaten and Danilo. It was possible to read peace and, more important, love in their faces. Paul let go of my hand and took a step toward it.

I lowered the beam just a bit. And there it was, at the top of a wide, low flight of steps.

A throne, carved from some black rock, probably basalt, a stone reproduction of a pharaoh's throne. It was precisely the throne I had seen in my vision during the séance. On it, wrapped in what seemed to be barbed wire, sat a mummy.

I moved closer. There were no linen wrappings for this…pharaoh? The body was shriveled and dry; pieces of skin had flaked off, and more seemed about to. The embalmers at Amarna, it seemed, were not very good.

The room, the basalt throne, the mummy ensconced on it—it was like nothing I had ever seen, like nothing no one in Egypt had ever seen or even suspected. I was irresistibly drawn to it. I had to see.

The mummy on the throne was quite naked. This was not at all characteristic; the Egyptians valued modesty. I remembered that there were some images of Akhenaten and his family naked, and of course there were the Kissing Kings, but…

Desiccated face, hands, legs, genitals. I climbed the steps to see it closely. The thorns dug deeply into its flesh. My flashlight lit the face.

And its eyes opened.

Not gaping, empty sockets: eyes. Ancient eyes, badly yellowed. This was not a corpse but an enormously old man. But in those ancient eyes was recognition.

And I knew. My vision had been perfectly accurate.

"Danilo." I whispered his name.

He turned his head slightly toward me. And I thought I saw recognition in his eyes. But the motion made him recoil in pain from the piercing barbs.

Again I said, "Danilo."

The living corpse nodded. It was him. It was my love.

Every nerve in my body told me to hug him, kiss him, hold him. But he was so obviously fragile; the pressure of my embrace would have destroyed him.

Paul was at the foot of the steps, watching. "Jamie, do you mean to say that this is…?"

I nodded. "We have to free him. Come and help me."

"But—"

"Come on, Paul."

He climbed the steps slowly, hesitantly. He could have been prepared for none of this. Danilo had been here for…how long? Unable to feed, unable to grow, he aged. He could have been two hundred, or a thousand years old. Feebly he struggled against the thorns that bound him.

"No, Danilo. Let us undo it."

He was still.

No, the stuff was not wire. It was a withe of briars, studded with thorns an inch long or more. It was coiled around his body. And the thrones dug deeply into his flesh. There were dozens of them, hundreds, and his body was covered with open wounds where they penetrated. They had seeped fluid; now it was all dry, but the mark of it was there.

There was no way this tangled vine could have been strong enough to hold him, despite all the thrones. Unless…

Near the wall behind the throne Paul found a torch. He lit it, and with that additional light we began to inspect the briars. It took a few moments to find the end of the strand, then we began carefully to uncoil them. But they were too badly tangled. I got the golden ceremonial knife and began to cut through them.

First Danilo's legs were free, then his midsection, then his chest, his arms… It seemed to take hours, but the work required patience. We pulled each thorn out of him as carefully as we could, not wanting to hurt him any more than he had already been hurt. Now and then he winced slightly or pulled away when we were too rough or a particularly long thorn went too deep.

One of the thorns pricked me. It was incredibly painful, much more than I would have expected. It felt like fire was racing through my body from the tiny cut. I trembled, and it took me a moment to recover from the pain. Danilo had been feeling that, multiplied a hundred times. Every inch of his flesh must have been in agony. Had it been going on all the time he was gone? Two years of this terrible pain?

Finally we had the last of the thorns out of him. I lifted him as gently as possible from the throne and laid him on the stone floor beside it. Paul took the briars and coiled them, carefully, so as not to cut himself, into a tight roll. Then he set them on the floor and touched the torch to them. They erupted in the most blindingly bright flames. The chamber blazed with hot, white light. When the fire died, Paul stomped on the ashes and scattered them for yards about the chamber.

Danilo's chest was barely rising and falling. So far he had not tried to speak; he must have been much too weak. But from his throat, faintly, hoarsely, gratingly, came the words, "Jamie. Love."

Paul came to my side. "Jamie, he's dying."

"He has died once before."

He didn't understand. "Can you help him? Do you know the prayers and spells?"

"No. I don't."

"Then all we can do is…?"

"Where did I leave my backpack?"

He looked around. "Over there, by the door."

I crossed the room quickly and got it, then went back to Danilo. "Give me some light."

Paul held the flashlight. I found what I wanted right away. It was the ancient bottle I had brought with me, the one whose contents I had preserved so carefully. It was warm to my touch. It had never lost it warmth. I knew what it would do. Or rather, I hoped.

My hands were actually trembling as I removed the stopper. Very gingerly I raised Danilo's head, cradled it in my arm, and held the bottle to his lips.

First, only a drop or two. He knew the taste; I could tell. A few drops more. And I felt, I swear I felt his body strengthening in my arms.

He drank more, a few drops at a time. As he gained strength, I fed it to him more and more rapidly. Finally he reached up and took the bottle from me, held it to his own lips, and drank deeply.

And before our eyes he became young again, exactly as he always did when he drank the blood of the sacrificed. And exactly as I did, in my smaller, much less extreme way. His muscles filled out and toned; his color returned; his eyes regained their deep green tint, and they began to sparkle again.

He handed me the bottle. "Here. There is some left. We may need it some day."

I placed it carefully back in my pack.

Tall, handsome, athletic, intensely alive and virile, Danilo became all that once again. And young, younger than I had ever seen him. He had the body of an eighteen year old athlete. In the light from the torch I could see the astonishing green of his eyes. Danilo was back. He stood before us, naked and smiling, then held out a hand to me. "Jamie, my love." His voice was as deep, mellow and resonant as I remembered.

But in that moment I knew that Adam Pilarski had been the true Blood Prophet, not me.

We kissed, as deep, hot, and passionate a kiss as ever. And as always I felt his strength flow through me, the most exhilarating thing I had ever felt, a surge of intense sexual pleasure.

"I knew you could find me. I had to believe. The god has not set me on this path only to..."

"Danilo, never mind the god." I couldn't help interrupting him. "Who did this? How could this have happened?"

He spoke one word: "Lazarus."

Yes. I had known. It had to be. "And those thorns?"

"His master's, yes. Each barb sanctified with his blood."

"But Danilo—"

"They have followed me for two thousand years, like vicious dogs. Ever since I raised them from the dead." He turned to Paul and spoke his name. "I underestimated you, I'm afraid. You have been good to Jamie?"

"Not as good as he has been to me, Danilo."

Danilo kissed Paul lightly on the cheek. The he turned back to me.

He caressed every part of me. His fingers undid my clothes. Naked we made love by torchlight on the stone floor of the Temple of Set. Paul watched. It was ecstasy. Sex with Danilo was as all-encompassing as I'd remembered; it pulled me completely out of myself, and for the moment I forgot about the two long, lonely, empty years without him. Paul climaxed when we did.

When we were finished, the three of us lay side by side, arms around each other, with Danilo in the middle. I think we slept awhile, but it might not have been real sleep, it might have simply been that sweet exhaustion that sometimes comes after lovemaking.

Danilo was the first to stir. Despite his young body, his movements were slow and stiff. "Come on, we have things to do." He looked down at himself and laughed. "First, I need to find some clothes."

Paul looked around for his pack. "I have some extra things with me."

"So do I. I don't know what you'll do for boots, though. But why get dressed, Danilo? You look better naked."

He slapped me playfully on my backside. "You haven't changed."

I turned into Norma Desmond. "The stars never change, and never die."

"It's too bad Paul burned the crown of thorns. You could use a lesson."

Our clothes were a bit too small for him, and he was barefoot; it made him look even sexier. I could happily have made love again, then and there, without undressing him.

He buttoned his shirt. "Where is Lazarus?"

"We know him as Lazar."

He shrugged. "The ancient Hebrews forbade eating the flesh of creatures like him. Do you know where he might be?"

"As far as we know, he's back in Pittsburgh."

"That is as good a place for him as any I can think of."

"Danilo, Mohammed is dead." I told him about what had happened. The news disturbed him; I could see it. "He was a good man, Jamie."

"And I'm afraid in the rush to find you, we left your father's sarcophagus open. We should go back and close it now."

He smiled. "So much has happened. You're right, Jamie, we should go. There is a great deal we have to do yet, so that...so that they can hurt us no more." He looked at the stone throne. "But first, a prayer of thanks."

He took up the torch and walked to the great relief on the wall. With his free hand he reached up and touched the god's foot. And prayed in the ancient language.

When he was finished he turned to us. "Now for my father."

Just outside the entrance we saw the jackals waiting, watching; they were at the far horizon. The blood of their young, it seemed, had been enough to warn them to keep away, but only so far.

We walked back through the dead city to the cliffs. Danilo talked. "I came here when I left you, Jamie. I wanted to consult with my father. He has always been my guide, my oracle. Once I had found you—you, the Blood Prophet—I wasn't certain how to proceed. Akhenaten would know. He has been my counselor for three thousand years, as wise and as understanding as any father could be.

"And when I got here, Lazarus was waiting for me. He had tried to find my father's tomb before. This time, he followed me. He had help, a disciple of his, an Egyptian colonel named Mahawi. If you ever encounter him, be careful. He hides not one nature but two—he believes as Lazarus does."

"But—but Danilo, I've met Mahawi. Or rather, talked to him. He told me he knew where you were. I was supposed to meet him, but he was killed to keep him from telling me. I thought he must have been a friend."

"No, he was a hypocrite of the worst kind."

Danilo was young, younger than me; his voice still had that same mellow richness I had always known. Young body, wise soul.

The sun was beginning to decline, but the air was still insufferably hot. There was no water. Danilo got down on a knee and struck a stone, and water flowed out of it. The three of us drank, then he touched the stone, and the flow stopped. "A parlor trick I learned once, wandering in the desert with some Jewish nomads. There was a handsome stonecutter named Joshua, who—"

"Danilo, exactly how old are you?" Paul was guessing more and more of the truth.

I couldn't resist. "A lady never tells, Paul."

"That isn't funny."

Danilo scowled at me. "I know it isn't. I don't know whether to find it reassuring that Jamie is still a brat." He began to tell Paul his true history. They walked side by side; I followed. It occurred to me that I hadn't been all that much of a brat since Danilo left; finding him again had given me the confidence to be myself again.

Over my shoulder, I saw the jackals; they were following us, but at a considerable distance. It made me nervous; I wanted them gone.

I was still puzzled about Mahawi's death. It had seemed obvious to me, and quite logical, that Perske had killed him, or had had him killed, to keep him from telling me where Danilo was. But if he and Perske had been allies… Danilo seemed reluctant to talk about it, but I pressed him.

"Do you remember me telling you, once that you were no longer alone in the world, Jamie?"

"Yes, of course I do. But—"

"There are others. Not many, and not all of them friendly—I told you once. You've learned about Lazarus and his kind." I wasn't used to hearing him called that. In my mind, he was still Lazar Perske. "I asked an old friend to keep watch over you. A king. As I said, I never expected to be gone for—how long has it been?"

It surprised me that he didn't know. But then, how could he? With no sun, no moon to keep track of the passing time… I gave him a brief account of the time since he'd vanished.

We reached the base of the cliff and climbed. When I looked down from the path, the jackals were there, staring up at us hungrily.

Something was wrong. We all sensed it. Paul was the first to put his finger on it. "There—up ahead. There's someone in the tomb!"

A backpack rested against the lintel of the entrance to the twin tombs. Danilo made us stop and stand still. Paul and I waited as he went to the entrance alone. "Danilo," I whispered, "be careful. They might hurt you again. Remember those thorns."

He didn't bother to answer. He walked to the door, looked carefully inside, then motioned for us to come. He said one word. "Lazarus."

Inside, Perske was hard at work. He had lifted Akhenaten's mummy out of its sarcophagus and was hacking it to pieces with a machete. With Paul and me behind him, Danilo stepped boldly inside. "Stop!"

Perske looked up at him. He was clearly startled. But the look of a savage animal crossed his face, and he hacked all the more viciously. Then he struck a match and held it to the remains.

"I told you to stop, Lazarus!" Danilo advanced on him, but he wasn't quick enough to keep Perske from setting the pharaoh's remains afire. A column of red flame rose up and licked the stone roof of the chamber. Smoke billowed.

The two of them stood facing each other. Danilo seemed poised to spring, like a jungle cat; Perske reared up like a reptile, like a cobra.

"My father." Despite his obvious rage, Danilo's voice was deeply sad. "It is my fault. I was foolish enough to let you follow me here."

"You and your 'Blood Prophet.'" Perske, or rather Lazarus, laughed and turned to me. "You should have died months ago. I set Mahawi to lure you here. You would have found me waiting. How did you know? When did you know? When I heard you had killed him, I must confess it was the first pang of guilt I've felt in two thousand years."

Part of me wanted to tell him I wasn't the one who killed Mahawi, but something made me keep quiet about it. Instead I asked him, "You didn't feel sorry when Kurt died?"

He laughed at me. The smoke was becoming thicker and thicker. "I'd like to know how you managed to leave Pittsburgh between those two storms. If my man El-Lahas had not called me and told me you were in New York…"

"Call it the providence of Set." I smirked a thim.

"I have never understood," Danilo still sounded terribly sad, "your rage against me, you and your master's."

Perske shrugged. "Your very existence proved the lie we told everyone about ourselves."

"That is all? You have persecuted me and my followers all these millennia for that?"

"There was power to be had. There was wealth." He shrugged. "How do you think anyone maintains power if not through lies and manipulation? Is it possible you are still so naïve, Danilo?"

"Hypocrite!" Danilo shouted the word so loudly, the very stone seemed to quake."

The two immortals, the man of truth and the man of lies and darkness, faced each other across the smoldering remains of the pharaoh. I had no idea what to expect. Each of them was tense, coiled, ready to fight. I told myself, Danilo is a man of eighteen, Perske is middle-aged. If it comes to a physical contest between them, there is nothing to worry about. But I knew there was a great deal about them that I still didn't understand. The lies of Lazarus had been only too effective.

Slowly, almost at the bottom of his breath, Perske said, "You and your boys are going to die now, Danilo, once and for all." He pointed at the entrance behind us.

The jackals were there.

They had entered the tomb silently. Now that we knew they were there, they bared their teeth and snarled. Paul put a hand on my shoulder and squeezed tightly, so tightly it hurt; there was no need for him to tell me he was terrified. Danilo and I were immortal, at least so I thought; Paul was not. I maneuvered myself between him and the jackals.

Danilo and Perske—Lazarus—circled one another like wary wrestlers. The jackals snarled and bared their teeth.

"You should have died in the Temple of Set." Perske was much more calm than seemed natural. "You would have. The thorns would have pierced deeper and deeper, the last of your precious blood would have flowed, disease would have entered the wounds, and then…" He smiled a very broad smile. "But this boy intervened. When my children tear you to pieces, see if you can regenerate."

I looked back at the jackals. They were advancing, slowly, cautiously, as if they weren't quite certain what to expect from us.

There was one thing I could think of. I slid my hand slowly into my pack, groped, found what I wanted. There was some of Adam's blood left in the bottle. Not much; I hoped it would be enough to do what…what I hoped it would do.

Cautiously, I stepped forward. "Lazar, please don't do this. Not to Danilo."

"Young love." He laughed at me. "How touching."

I kept my body language as passive as I could and took another step toward him. "Please. Take me instead. Let Danilo live." Another step.

From the corner of my eye I could see that Danilo was puzzled what I was doing. With a hand behind my back, I gestured to him to stay away.

Then I said softly, almost a whisper. "Please, Lazar, I'll do anything you ask." I lowered my voice even more; I made it insinuating. "Anything."

He froze. I think he realized I must be up to something. I had to act.

I pulled the stopper from the bottle and threw the blood straight into his face, into his eyes.

He cried out and covered his face with his hands. His flesh began to steam; smoke spiraled upward from the spots the blood had touched and mixed with the smoke from Akhenaten's charred remains. Perske screamed, and the sound echoed deafeningly in the stone chamber.

But it did what I hoped. The smell of Adam's blood drove the jackals to a frenzy. I pushed Danilo and Paul to one side, against a wall, and the ravening animals rushed past us and fell on Perske.

Within seconds they tore him to shreds. Their fangs tore off flesh; their paws dug into him; one of them sank its teeth into his eyes. Blood sprayed the chamber. He fought desperately, but there were a dozen of them, and he didn't have a chance. As they had done with Mohammed, they pulled him down and began to eat parts of him while he was still alive. His screams turned to low, agonized groans.

Danilo took Paul and me by our hands and pulled us toward the door. "Now. While they're still at him. It won't be long before they realize there is other prey at hand. If he isn't enough to satisfy them…"

Outside, there was still sun. And heat, stifling desert heat. But after the horrors of the tomb, it seemed wonderful, even refreshing. Smoke poured from the entrance behind us, reeking of seared flesh. As we began to descend the cliff, we could still hear Perske, or Lazarus, as he whimpered his way to death.

Danilo handled the *Cleopatra*. There was a slight northerly breeze on the river, as there had not been on the plain of Amarna. It was enough to cool us, and enough to fill the boat's sail.

I realized we were traveling south. "But Danilo, shouldn't we head back to Cairo?"

"In time. There is someplace we must go first."

I trusted him; there was no need for discussion.

Paul sat at the prow, staring upriver. He had hardly said a word since the tomb. I moved forward and put a hand on his arm. "Are you okay?"

"I didn't know. I didn't understand. I thought I knew what you and Danilo were all about, but I had no idea about all this…all this…"

There was still so much about Danilo I didn't know myself. "You're one of us, now. We're family, Danilo and I, and now you are one of us."

He turned and looked directly into my eyes. "Yes. I want that."

I kissed him lightly on the cheek and went back to my seat at the center of the boat. "Where are we heading, Danilo?"

"To a sacred place. The most sacred of all."

I thought I knew where he must mean; I had learned enough about Egyptian myths.

Not far along the river was a small village, not more than a dozen mudbrick huts. We saw a man driving an ox, which was turning a water wheel. The wheel raised water from the Nile to irrigate his fields. It was ancient, timeless; there are reliefs of farmers doing the same thing, in the same way, in the oldest tombs in Egypt.

He agreed to give us food and water. Danilo blessed him. The man seemed puzzled by it, but he let it happen. Then Danilo raised the sail and we continued our southward voyage.

It wasn't far. We went exactly where I expected: Abydos.

There was a great temple there, marvelously well preserved. It had been built by Seti I. Danilo smiled at me; he knew exactly what I was thinking, so there was no need for me to say it: Sir Cedric Hardwicke in *The Ten Commandments*. There were times I wished I hadn't spent so much of my youth watching old movies.

A paved road passed in front of the temple grounds, which were surrounded by a stone wall. Three busloads of tourists milled about, weighed down with cameras and bottled water, waiting for their tour guide to take them inside. Vendors sold them trinkets and faux antiquities, candy bars and bottles of soda.

Paul was disoriented, and Danilo explained to him where we were. "Abydos is the place where Set killed his brother Osiris. And where Osiris's wife Isis brought her husband back to life. The temple commemorates that."

"It happened here?"

"No."

"Then—?"

"The ancients knew it was in this vicinity. The temple site is a good approximation. But the actual place is there." He pointed beyond the temple, out to the desert. "We must go there."

Just downriver from the temple is a village, also called Abydos. The people there make their livings off the tourists. There was a small café where we ate. Then Danilo found a man who owned camels. We rented three and set off.

I had ridden camels before, on my previous trips to the country. Danilo rode like he was born to it. But poor Paul... Riding a camel can be disconcerting, till you get used to it. Unlike horses, they don't have a regular gait; they're so well adapted for desert life that each step they take is particularly adapted to the land underfoot. With no rhythm, it is impossible to relax; the rider has to stay as alert as his mount. I had the impression Paul would never get used to it.

It was late afternoon, and the sun was low above the western horizon. Everything was bathed in its orange-red light. The sky in the east was already darkening to a grayish purple, and a bright star shone there. No—it was a planet. Mars. Or, to give it its even more ancient name, Set.

Behind Abydos is a line of low cliffs. The camels managed to climb them without much trouble; the paths were well-worn enough. Then ahead of us the broad expanse of the great Eastern Desert opened up. In the far distance rose a line of black, jagged mountains; with no land features between us and them to give perspective, it was impossible to tell how far they were. But I knew that the pharaohs had had silver mines there, and copper, and even a bit of gold. I asked Danilo if we were going there.

"No. No that far. You will see."

The sun set and, exactly opposite it, a huge full moon rose; the landscape went from crimson to pale white. An enormous spider, black and ten inches across, scuttled across our path, startling my camel, but I managed to rein it in. Overhead, a flock of bats flew past.

Danilo talked. He told Paul more of his family history and a bit about his long, lonely life. "For two thousand years men like Lazarus have done all they could to bury our heritage and wipe out our divine bloodline. Some of them even claimed to be divine in their own right." He was offhand. "What can you expect from a belief system devised by carpenters, fishermen and tax collectors?"

I did not have to ask who he meant. Lazarus had only been his disciple.

"But surely he vanished two thousand years ago, Danilo." Paul was having trouble digesting it all. But he had seen enough not to be too skeptical. "I mean, he may not have ascended into 'heaven'—he gave the word an ironic tone—but surely he disappeared." He hesitated. "Didn't he?"

"The Roman historian Suetonius wrote that he was alive in Rome during the reign of the emperor Claudius. And Ignatius of Antioch, one of the men smilingly called 'fathers of the church,' wrote in his *Epistle to the Smyrnaeans,* that he was still alive—physically alive, alive 'in the body' as he put it—in the year 100. After that..." He smiled. "Well, if you believe the stories the saints told about how they had seen him..."

Ahead of us I saw a small oasis. Several dozen palm trees, some flowering shrubs, some desert grass. I thought it must be where we were heading, and I pointed there. "Danilo?"

He nodded.

The moon had climbed higher now. We dismounted and tied our camels to one of the trees, and they began happily to eat dates from the smaller palms. Danilo stretched; his new, young body was stiff. There were, improbably, evening primrose bushes; their flowers showed ghostly scarlet in the moonlight. Among the shrubs I could just make out the ruins of a small temple, apparently a very old one. Some large stones were scattered about in the open spaces, sandstone, I thought.

"Danilo?" Something was odd. It took me a moment to put my finger on it.

"Yes?"

"Where is the water? This is an oasis, but there is no water here. What keeps the trees alive?"

He smiled that smug smile he always wore when he enjoyed being one-up on me. I was sitting on one of the sandstone blocks. He gestured to it. "Go ahead, strike it."

I had seen him do it, earlier, at Amarna. "I can't. I don't know how."

"You have the knowledge, Jamie. The wisdom is in your blood."

I got down on one knee and felt the stone. It was rough, cool, hard. I looked up at him and he nodded reassuringly. So I made a fist and struck the block, hard, at its very center.

And water flowed. A little spring bubbled forth; its water formed a pool from which a tiny stream trickled. A dozen yards away, it disappeared into the sand.

I looked to Danilo. "This is the place, then?"

"The oldest place in the world, yes. And the holiest."

Paul pushed his way through the brush to the temple, and I got up and followed him. The stones were badly weathered; the inscriptions on them were almost gone. They were in the most archaic form of the Egyptian language, so rudimentary they barely qualified as hieroglyphs but only crude pictographs.

But the inscriptions were beside the point. It was the image carved into the stone that told the story. It was a rough portrait of two men in passionate embrace: the Kissing Kings. This portrait was even older than the ancient one I had found two years earlier.

"Danilo, you said this place was where Set killed his brother Osiris."

He joined us and said softly, "Yes, and so it was. And where Isis brought Osiris back from the dead, here in the spring, from which flow the waters of life." He took my hand, then Paul's. "It is also the place where Set and Horus made love. The place where our bloodline first began its long flow through the millennia."

He turned to Paul and kissed him. "Are you certain you want the gift you may receive here?"

I could see half a dozen conflicting emotions cross Paul's face. He looked at me, and I nodded at him, slowly, deliberately.

"Yes, Danilo, I want what you can give me."

"No." He smiled gently. "It is not my gift, Paul. It is there already, in your blood. All I can do is assist you in learning the power it holds."

Something was wrong. The light was turning strange. I looked around, puzzled, then realized what was happening overhead. The moon was turning dark; half of it was already blood red. An eclipse.

The three of us kissed. We embraced one another as tightly as we could. Passion flowed from one of us to the other. Paul lost himself in it, as I had done once.

We undressed one another. We made love. The passion was deeper, even, than what I had known. Overhead the moon shone bright red.

When we were finished, we lay tangled in one another's arms. Sand clung to our bodies, but none of us seemed to notice or care. When we had recovered a bit of energy, Danilo extended a hand to me. "Jamie," he said to me, "the knife."

I got it from my pack and handed it to him.

Paul looked up, anxious with expectation.

Danilo held the knife high in the air and plunged it into his own chest. Then he cut my chest open. Paul got quickly to his knees and drank, from both of us. I took the knife from Danilo, cut Paul, and the two of us tasted his blood, in turn.

We made love again, and it was wilder, more passionate than before.

The moon darkened to the color of brick, then slowly began to lighten again.

Danilo looked up at it. "We do not have much more time." He held his knife high over his head, then pushed it directly into Paul's heart. Paul collapsed onto the earth, clutching at his chest.

Gingerly we carried his crumpled body to the spring and immersed it. Danilo intoned the same prayers he had used once in his father's tomb. And Paul stirred. He rose from the spring tall and powerful. White moonlight made his body glisten.

For the third time we made love. And when we finished, Danilo whispered to Paul, "You are truly one of us now."

A desert breeze blew up. It was getting uncomfortably cool. We got dressed, and Danilo built a little fire for us. Our camels were quite asleep.

We huddled by the fire and talked far into that mystic night. Paul kept telling us how wonderful it was, for the first time in his life, to have a real family to love and accept him. After a time we heard a peculiar metallic sound coming from someplace in the undergrowth. Paul and I both looked to Danilo. "The cobras are singing," he told us. "It is their season. Otherwise they would not be active in the night."

In time we slept and kept each other warm.

CHAPTER 15

We spent two more weeks in Egypt, seeing everything of interest in the country. I had seen a great deal of it before, of course, but it was all quite new to Paul, and he seemed to find all of it exciting. A lot of it was closed to tourists, but of course with Danilo as guide, we went pretty much where we wanted to. For Paul, he showed us where the old opera house had been, the one where Verdi had premiered *Aida*. He even showed us the secret, hidden chamber under the Great Pyramid, the one the archeologists insist so vehemently isn't there.

We made love every night, in various combinations. I think Paul felt like a third wheel on the relationship between Danilo and me. But I assured him he was a part of us, now, as we were part of him. Danilo added that there would, inevitably, be more of us. "Jamie is the Blood Prophet, and his call will be irresistible to the ones with the true blood in them."

I insisted that it must have been Adam, not me, who had been the prophet. "I've never felt like a prophet, Danilo, not for a single moment."

Danilo only responded, in a way typical of him, that things were never that simple. "To be a prophet is not a matter of feeling, Jamie, it is a matter of being."

Paul fell in love with Egypt quite as much as I had done. I think we could gladly have stayed there forever, but of course that wasn't possible. We had been gone from school more than long enough. Danilo told us, quite accurately, that we no longer needed to have degrees to achieve what we desired. But we wanted those badges of legitimacy, if only because we had worked so hard for them.

And so it was time to return to Pittsburgh. After the Nile and the Sahara, it would seem like an alien landscape.

Our last night in the country, Danilo disappeared into the tomb of his brother Tutankhamen, as he had on on our first trip. When I asked him what he planned to do there, he merely told me I'd understand in time. That night Paul and I made love on the bank of the Nile under a waning Egyptian moon.

Danilo was still weak from the ordeal he'd been through. I don't think I realized how weak till we were on the plane heading home. He slept nearly all the way, and slept so deeply we had trouble waking him. We had three adjacent seats, and Paul and I put him between us, so we could keep an eye on him.

He had terrible nightmares. At moments, his body would stiffen, his arms and legs start flailing, his mouth fall open, and he would make the most terrible groaning, crying sounds. Several times the young flight attendant on duty in first-class asked if there was anything he could do. We thanked him and told him it would pass, that our friend had just lost his father in a particularly awful way. Nice young man; he expressed concern and fussed over us with special attention. Paul and I expressed knowing glances.

Once, Danilo woke from one of his dreams, looked around in panic and caught tight hold of my arm. His face was filled with pure terror. I began to suspect that Lazarus had done more to him than we knew about. But then, they had encountered one another before; I knew next to nothing about Danilo's life between the time he left his throne in Egypt and the time we met, certainly not the specifics. It was time to learn. I made up my mind that once we were home and he seemed to be over the ordeal, I'd find a way to get him to open up. I wanted to know. After all, his history was my history, too, now.

There was no direct Cairo-to-Pittsburgh flight, so we laid over in New York. It was late afternoon when we checked into the Chelsea Hotel again; this time we took a suite, three bedrooms and a bath. The desk clerk knew me, and he recognized Danilo's name. He looked at him suspiciously, as if he wasn't quite certain this could be the same man. "Professor Semenkaru. It's been far too long since we've seen you. I hope you're well."

"As well as can be expected." That neutral pleasantry was enough.

Paul was beginning to age already. He saw himself in a mirror and turned glum. "I didn't think it would happen so quickly."

I examined his face. There were deep lines there, especially around his eyes. He would have to feed, and soon. We had dinner at an Italian place in Hell's Kitchen I especially liked, then Danilo went back to the hotel and I took Paul to a sex club I knew.

It was one of those "mixed" places, straight and bent. There was the usual layout, a bar, private rooms, common areas for group experimentation. Paul was uneasy, as much because he'd never been naked in front of a woman before as because he would soon be thriving again, on the blood of someone he'd sacrifice.

"Why here, Jamie? Couldn't we go someplace where there are just men?"

"You'll find more hypocrites hiding here."

We took a place in a corner of the largest open room and began to make love. Most of the others ignored us; copulation was hardly uncommon there. But one man watched us, obviously interested. We kissed more and more passionately, and I watched him from the corner of my eye as he inched closer and closer. He was wearing a wedding ring, a wide, shiny, easy-to-spot one.

After a few minutes of watching, he finally came up to us and put his hands on our backsides. He was slightly overweight, and he looked unhappy. "You guys are hot," he said, as if it would come as news that he thought so.

"Thanks." I smiled. "So are you."

Paul almost laughed in my face.

"I have a room." He said it as if it was the foxiest thing in the world.

Two minutes later we were there. I pointed to the ring on his finger. "You married your boyfriend?"

He seemed to find it insulting. "Christ, no. I'm straight."

"Oh."

Paul had told me he wanted to use his teeth; it was an old fantasy of his, apparently. He did, and I watched. And it was a turn-on; I understood why he had been so excited when he watched me.

When he was finished, we kissed long and hard, left the room, locked the door behind us, got dressed and headed back to the hotel.

Paul looked sixteen, and I told him so. It seemed to please him.

"I'm not sure how I feel, being the old man in this family."

When we got back to our suite, Danilo was asleep, dreaming another awful dream. They would pass. I told myself so. What on earth had Perske done to him, more than what we already knew about?

Paul moved into the house in Shadyside with us. It seemed right to all three of us. Danilo said that the house had always seemed too large for just him himself, and even for me and him together. Paul moved into the guest bedroom, the one where Adam had slept. We were a family, or at least the beginnings of one; certainly I knew more love with Danilo and Paul than I ever had before.

Paul, it turned out, was an avid gardener. As the weather warmed, our front and back yards were alive with daffodils, tulips, hyacinths, roses... It was quite wonderful, really, and I told him so. Of course, I couldn't resist making a smart-ass joke in the process; I quipped about a host of golden daffodils. Like Danilo, Paul did his best to ignore me when I went into that mode.

And as if to make the house even more of a home, Bubastis was pregnant. Our neighbor had bred her with his male cat while we were gone. By his estimate, she would deliver her kittens around Easter. I smiled when he told me. "The feast of the Resurrection. It suits us."

He didn't know what I meant, of course, and he didn't ask. The fact that I was happy seemed enough for him.

The music department was in a bit of disarray. Their resident composer had vanished, with no trace of him left behind. The police speculated that he had been killed by the same old campus killer, who had become a convenient scapegoat anytime anyone had trouble. As on any large campus, there were muggings, robberies, even rapes, and the elusive psycho took the blame for all of them.

In the way of these things, word went out to police departments in the surrounding tri-state area, and all sorts of crime investigations, including unsolved murders, got reopened. And the "West Penn Psycho" got blamed for as many of them as could be done plausibly, too.

It never occurred to anyone—least of all the police—that Perske himself had been the villain. It was certainly he who killed my sometime boyfriends Todd and Bryan, and probably a lot of others as well.

One crime in particular: We learned that just after we left for Egypt, Joe Maggio had been found, slaughtered. Cut into her forehead were the words "Damned Dyke." The police were baffled. All of their imaginary psycho's victims had been male; now a young woman had been killed in the same way. The killer's "psychological profile" was quickly revised—he was now bisexual instead of straightforwardly, conveniently gay.

Joe had helped me find Danilo, in her mystical way. I owed her. The news that she had died that way—it left me a bit numb. When the campus gay group organized a memorial service for her, I offered to play the music. It seemed only natural that I played the Chopin Funeral March.

Paul and I both had trouble at the department. We had been gone much longer than expected. And for once, I wasn't able to wrap Roland around my finger. "You're both on probation. Another of these weird absences, and you'll lose the semester." He meant it, and I suppose I don't blame him; he had put himself on the line for me more times than he probably should have.

Paul made up for lost time quickly. He rehearsed twelve hours a day and played the leads in two baroque operas that spring, including *Poppea* again and then Angelica in Handel's *Orlando*. There was some uneasiness about it among the faculty; the Alliance for Christian Morals had made some public noise about men playing female roles. The university, somewhat uneasily, countered by pointing out that that was they way the roles were written, the way they were intended to be performed. It wasn't quite true, but it served to mute the protests.

Danilo and I attended both, and it seemed to us, and to nearly everyone else, that Paul's singing had grown much more mature and rich. He would graduate on time.

As for me, I applied myself to the job of finishing my symphony. The themes had all jelled in my mind while we were in Egypt, and most of the development. Now, it was only a matter of getting the notes down on paper.

When we had the time, I returned to my Egyptological studies—

more history, more hieroglyphs—and Paul went back to his passion for history. He learned more and more about every one of our ancestors he could. The knowledge seemed to fire him.

He told me about Balboa, the Spanish explorer who had "discovered" the Pacific Ocean. "When he realized that it was common among the Native Americans for men to love men, he was horrified. He rounded up as many 'sodomites' as he could and had them torn to pieces by dogs."

Thus did the virus that had infected the old world spread to the new.

"The only thing surprising about our family, Jamie," Paul told me one night, "it that it's taken Danilo so long to find us."

"And us to find him, for that matter." I knew exactly what he meant. Our bloodline was so old and so holy. How could it not have surfaced before?

It had, he discovered. In Renaissance Italy, in seventeenth-century France, in Germany after the Great War… We asked Danilo if he had been in those places.

"Failures. The others were too strong for us then. I was nearly torn to pieces myself, more than once. I fled to what is smilingly called the Third World. In Japan, in China, in a dozen other places, we had flourished, until the others appeared and began to spread their venom of shame and timidity. There has never been a system of belief so evil."

Danilo had worked on a memoir, I knew. But it was in hieroglyphics. I wasn't good enough to read it; Paul was hopeless. Paul made Danilo promise to recount the story of his life, so he could write it down and it would never be forgotten.

"You will need a great deal of ink, Paul. Make it black." A mordant grin crept across his face. "Though there will be times when blood red will seem even ore appropriate."

There were three concerts on campus that spring. All of them were picketed by Heinrich and his followers from the Alliance for Christian Morals. Roland was under a great deal of pressure, but the two of us had support from a substantial part of the faculty for what we wanted to do.

First came a solo recital. I played at the keyboard, accompanying Paul as he sang arias by Mouret, the soprano line from Lully's *Miserere* and finally a pair of songs by Schubert. Then I played several solo pieces, of which my favorite was the Barber sonata. In our introductory remarks to the audience, we made certain to point out the, er, chosen lifestyles of the composers.

At Easter, there was a performance of the *Messiah,* using the campus orchestra and chorus and four selected soloists. The voice faculty had been so impressed by Paul's newfound depth, they asked him to sing the soprano part, an unheard-of thing. Roland seemed uncomfortable with the idea, but the rest of the faculty overruled him. At the end of the performance, Paul received an standing ovation. He acknowledged it with a little speech in which he pointed out the irony that this, the most famous celebration of the life of the Christian messiah, had been written by a sexually active lover of other men.

Danilo and I attended, of course, and we were both quite pleased to hear Paul's happy comments.

Roland saw me in the audience with Danilo. Officially, Danilo was still missing; we decided his long absence would be too awkward to explain. And he told me that the only reason he'd come to the university in the first place was his instinct—like Perske's—that the Blood Prophet was there. His appearance had changed sufficiently that no one had become suspicious.

Until Roland. I could tell from the look on his face that he suspected something. After the oratorio, he cornered me and asked about the young man I had sat with. "He looks like your old boyfriend, the Egyptology professor."

I smiled. "That's my type."

"The resemblance is perfectly startling. Once I noticed it, I couldn't shake the feeling that he's—"

"Danilo is gone, Roland. You know that."

"The resemblance is too close. He's younger, of course, but..." He narrowed his eyes. "Jamie, I want you to tell me what you're involved in."

"Involved in? I'm involved in making music."

"You know what I mean."

"I want to give the world new music, Roland, music it hasn't heard for millennia."

My evasions only made him more suspicious; it showed in his face. But there wasn't much he could do, really.

Then came the final concert of the semester, a program of premiers of student compositions. There were four items on the program; mine was to come last. It was being recorded for broadcast on public radio.

There was a string trio, followed by a faux-medieval vocal piece by one of Perske's students, then a rather Stravinskian piano sonata. They were all…well, student compositions. Formal, interesting technically, not much fun to listen to.

Then came my *Symphony No. 1, Hadrian.* I had titled it that, confident I'd be writing more. I was pleased to see that the campus gay alliance had come as a group. They were wearing black armbands, mourning for Joe. Outside, the Alliance for Christian Morals were demonstrating still again. Rust, as they say, never sleeps.

From the opening bars, the audience seemed to be with me; I had generated a lot of goodwill on campus with my pianism. I used muted strings to convey a sense of Hadrian's lonely youth. Brass heralded his rise to the imperium. And when he met Antinous, for the first time the full orchestra played a theme of triumphant and glorious love.

The final movement was the one everyone was anticipating. The untimely death of Antinous by drowning in the Nile, and his subsequent deification. The themes I used were simple, the development almost as much so. But the music caught the audience. I had never heard a concert hall full of people so completely silent, not even an occasional cough.

The strings mourned when Antinous died. Hadrian's grief engulfed the audience.

Then came the deification of the dead boy. Orchestral fanfares filled the hall, string glissandi underscored them, and the symphony ended on that note of exuberant joy. I had deliberately ended it in an abrupt way. After all, I knew the old show business saying: always leave them wanting more.

Besides, I didn't know the end of the story myself.

The audience rose to its feet, cheering and shouting. I was called back to the stage for one bow after another. They had loved my music, and it meant so much to me. At the far end of the sixth row, near the wall, I saw a young man. Shabby clothes, disheveled hair, looking hungry. A street kid, just like—not, that thought was a bit too painful for me. When he realized I had seen him, he blushed and left the hall quickly. But he had served to remind me that there was one important piece of business left unfinished.

At the party backstage, Roland confronted me again. "Your boyfriend is looking older now."

I smiled and shrugged. "Life is hard, Roland."

"Jamie, please tell me what you're mixed up in." Pointedly he added, "You and Paul."

I played dumb again and he left, frustrated. But he was clearly suspicious; I knew he wouldn't leave things where they were. The trustees were pressuring the department, at leas tin part because of lobbying by Heinrich's group. And of all people outside our family, Roland was the one who knew me best. I was afraid he could make trouble. I didn't want him hurt, and I certainly didn't want him silenced—he had been almost a father to me at times. But I would have to talk to Danilo about him.

The students from the gay group came backstage to congratulate me. And they seemed to cluster around Danilo and Paul. There was definitely some cruising going on. I didn't know whether to be jealous.

In late spring I returned to Spartanburg. The surrounding mountains were green with burgeoning life; the town itself was as barren as I remembered.

I had tried a dozen times or more to learn where Adam was buried, telephone calls, emails… No one knew a thing, not that they would admit. One clerk in the county records office told me bluntly that they didn't want "that kind of publicity—we'd have undesirables all over us."

Finally I decided I had to try in person. I stayed at that same hotel, and the same desk clerk still worked there; he seemed not to remember me; maybe he didn't think his job was worth that kind of effort. As I registered, he idly worked a crossword puzzle in a magazine. I tried smiling at him, but he barely looked at me.

To see the place, you'd never have known that it had been in the world's eye only months before. It was the image of dying towns everywhere, cracked streets, buildings in need of a cleaning, desultory unsmiling people. Some kids played ball in the little square at the center of town, but even they didn't seem to be having much fun.

First I tried the police, and it was a waste of time. Why would they want to help this effeminate Yankee?

At the county clerk's office, things were not much better. "We don't know anything about that."

"Well, if you remember anything, could you please contact me at my hotel?"

"We won't."

That was that, period. I thought about simply compelling someone to tell me what I wanted to know, but there were too many people around.

But a man at a desk in one corner of the office noticed me. He waved slightly. I had enough tact not to acknowledge it. He was a few years older than me, dark hair, pale skin. At dinnertime he showed up at my hotel.

"You were here last winter."

"I was. I'm Jamie Dunn."

"Andrew Macklin."

We shook hands; then he fished a slip of paper out of his shirt pocket and handed it to me. "This is what you want to know."

It was a plot number at the county cemetery.

"He's in the section where they bury paupers and indigents. Mostly black." Somewhat self-consciously he added, "No one wanted to pay for his burial."

"Where did they put his parents and the minister?"

"They were interred in one of the church cemeteries. You should have seen it. It was quite a ceremony."

"You went, Andrew?"

"I have a taste for the sick and the grotesque."

I offered to buy him dinner, but he said he had to get home. "I'm taking care of my mother. She has cancer."

"Oh. I'm sorry."

"Thanks. You're not the first to ask where we buried him. A couple of national organizations wanted to erect a little monument over him. There's no way the city would allow that."

"No. Of course not."

"You won't…you won't do anything like that, will you?"

I told him I wouldn't. "I'm here for private reasons, not public ones."

"You knew him?"

I nodded. "In a way no one else could have."

This puzzled him; I could see it. How could someone from Pennsylvania have…? But he was too polite to ask.

"Some of us are trying to change things here, Jamie. Quietly. We can't…" Whatever he was going to say was too painful to finish. But I understood. Andrew was such a sad young man; it came through so clearly. "You won't tell anyone I gave you that?"

"No, of course not." I thanked him and he left.

Early in the evening I went to the municipal graveyard. There was a map at the entrance; I found the plot where Adam was buried.

The place was as barren as everything else. There was no grass, only dirt. A breeze scattered it in the air. When it got strong, I had to cover my mouth with my handkerchief. A few of the graves had flowers; most did not.

Adam's plot was unmarked. A patch of dirt, nothing more; no way anyone could tell who was there or how he had died. I got down on my knees and whispered a prayer to Set.

Adam had given me so much, without ever knowing it. I had to give him something of myself.

Danilo's golden knife gave me no pain as I cut into my wrist. My blood flowed onto Adam's gravesite. The dry earth soaked it up at once.

I leaned down and kissed the earth, uttered a word of thanks to the dead boy, waited for my blood to stop flowing and the wound to heal, and then returned to my hotel.

I did not sleep soundly that night. A fear haunted me that I had not done enough for him. But what else I might have done, I could not think.

But at the first gray light of dawn I knew I had to go and see him again. My flight home was at eleven o'clock; I had time for one more visit.

In the dawning light I walked. The streets were empty, and there was a stiff wind. Streetlights were on in the half-light.

When I got to the cemetery, the gate was locked. I looked around to make certain no one could see, and then climbed the fence.

The sun just barely notched the horizon when I reached his grave.

Where I had spilled my blood, along the length of Adam's burial plot, there were violets growing.

AUTHOR'S NOTE

In *The Blood of Kings,* I described a pair of interconnected Egyptian tombs. They were based on two real tombs at Saqqara that belonged to belonged to men named Niankhkhnum and Khnumhotep. Their names were joined together in all the inscriptions—"Niankhkhnumhotep"—as if they were proclaiming to the world that they were one. And they are depicted together throughout both tombs, in loving embrace—in the stance usually reserved, in formal Egyptian art, for husbands and wives.

Well, if any of you were concerned that they might have been lovers—horrors! homos in Egypt!—you can rest easy. Obviously, no such thing could be possible. A scholar has recently claimed that the two men must have been, in fact, not a gay couple at all but…Siamese twins! The basis of this thrilling deduction is the observation that the two figures look alike. To which I can't resist pointing out that *all* the figures in Egyptian tomb art look alike. There were strict artistic canons defining the ways men and women were to be portrayed, and artists never varied from them, period.

These hysterical attempts by mainstream scholars to try and bluff any suggestion of queerness out of the historical record keep getting more desperate, and more laughable. It's only a matter of time before someone claims that all the evidently gay figures in history must actually have been space aliens. (And then someone will "prove" that outer space was really Sodom.) Enough is enough.

As for Claude Vivier, his life and death were pretty much as I relate them. It's always tempting, but sadly pointless of course, to wonder what more wonderful music he might have produced had he not been killed.

And as for *Lonely Child,* it is very much the composition I describe in the story. You have to dig pretty deep to find out, though; as is usual with anything queer and substantial in America, it's kept carefully buried. The liner notes for what is probably the best available recording of it, for example, concentrate solely on technical matters and don't drop the least hint what it's all about.

Like Jamie, I find Vivier's music thrilling. And like him, I am quite enraptured by the long, rich traditions of queer art, politics, philosophy...all the many things we have contributed to civilization. It is high time we begin to demand recognition for it all, and to reclaim our heritage, even if there do turn out to be a few space aliens and Siamese twins in the mix.